Emergency Instructions

Book One of the Go Love Quartet

Michael Gills

RAW DOG SCREAMING PRESS

Published by Raw Dog Screaming Press
Bowie, MD

First Edition

Cover: Photo used under the Creative Commons Liscense 2.0
https://creativecommons.org/licenses/by/2.0/
Taken by T-Town Photobooth on Flickr.com

Printed in the United States of America

ISBN: 978-1-935738-95-4
Library of Congress Control Number: 2017936785

www.RawDogScreaming.com

Other Books by Michael Gills

The House Across From The Deaf School: Stories

White Indians

The Death of Bonnie and Clyde and Other Stories

Go Love: A Novel

Why I Lie: Stories

Acknowledgements

This novel owes heartblood to Brandon Bertelsen, Anna Drysdale, Diona Giannopoulos, Laurel Myler, Jackson Myrick, Zander Nash, Suzy Sammann, Natalie Spendlove and Trevor Stott–fine writers all. I'd like to thank my editor and publisher, Jennifer Barnes and Raw Dog Screaming Press. Gratitude to the editors and publications where some of these chapters originally appeared, including *Boulevard*, *The Texas Review* and *The Oxford American*.

for Marion Weldon Treadwell and Edith Funkhouser Treadwell
and, always, for Jill and Lyra

Part I

Part I

1

Illinois Bayou, Arkansas. June, 1999

Above the diggings, buzzards fly eights into the updraft thermals. Seen from air, the green expanse is no more comprehendible. East from the continental divide, the Arkansas flows down from Colorado across the breadth of Kansas before diving south through Oklahoma's Cherokee country into Fort Smith. The river's fat by then, a thousand miles of grit in its veins. It rolls under the foot of the upthrust Ozarks, along the Trail of Tears and the wagon wheel ruts made by the ancestral migration west—kith and kin who'd turned their backs on Carrion Crow Mountain and the deep woods where now thumped gas wells, their pipe mouths flaming into the azalea-fragrant air. Arkansas, its vast green heart untamed by the plowblade, a fearful secret blackened by burnings, the frontier that remains frontier. Truly, from the air, it was no less so, from river silt to calico bluff, the green timber oceans and volcanic mountains named in the old tongue—Ouachita— wherein burned a continent's lone diamonds and the blood from fingers that dug there in vain. Seen from air, the gravedigger believes, the green expanse is no more comprehendible. Truly, from the air, it could be no less so.

Simms, the chimney sweep, holds the Walker dogs by their leashes, and the lawmen, newspaper boy, Preacher Roy Dale Shoates, and six pot-bellied buzzards on the wing all watch Edgar T. Paris's shovel on this gushful of spring day. The newspaper boy has a radio turned on—a wacky college station, no good for Paris's rhythm.

"Turn 'at thang off," Edgar says, but nobody's listening.

This close to the bridge there's still trash, pitched out from logging trucks come screaming down Three Knob Mountain. Beer cans and cracker sleeves thrown down by the stump-fingered Tyson workers. There blows a Slim Jim wrapper, tourist road food—they pass by here all the day long, double-chinned sedan drivers up from Little Rock. Out for the scenic Highway 7 drive—they cruise control up into the hills and hang louies at Booger Holler where they buy their kids sets of bucky-bubba-teeth and go goggle-eyed over one of the Casteen girls working the register in a slinky halter and cutoffs split up to her hip sockets.

Edgar sets the shovelpoint, jumps a vertical foot. A hundred-and-forty soaking wet, he's not a big man, but blessed with that country wiriness that lends intelf to the spade. Both feet come down on the lug so the shovel slices blade deep into the soft earth. The Walker dogs have laid off now, on their bellies in the blackberry briar, gnawing rib bones the cops picked up at Dewayne's Bar-B-Q & Grill over to Dover. A blue jay and its mate make a ruckus. Pissed off fox squirrels bark from every tree.

"You hit it yet?"

Edgar says, "Uh huh. I don't like that got-dam noise."

On the creek, a smallmouth hits fly hatch that drifts down from low branches where wrist-thick cottonmouth lay.

This dirt's been dug before, a scrap of red ribbon says. Mister shovel knows— he'll tell all soon. Then that boy'll turn the noise down.

Titsworth's heifers bawl, chew green grass. The big bull stands alone under a shade tree with a look like he's figured out the long and short of it all. Old man Billingsley's donkeys all have clown nose hard-ons boinging at their bellies. What he'd give for a Quik-spinner right about now, hoss a Hopkins out into the current—the silver line whistling before all hell breaks loose.

A helmeted kayaker dipsy-doodles by, curly red hair down on his neck and shoulders. Been huffing hooter back on the sand bar, most likely, scared shitless by all these cops. Just a whiff of carrion in the air, humidity rising. Blackberry bloom on its last hurrah. Powder blue witchdoctors ride each other, their tails hooked.

Arkansas summer. I do just be goddamned go to hell if it ain't going to be a good day anyway, a red letter day. Edgar digs steady in the soft Illinois Bayou dirt, piece of cake. Fuck this. Directly he'll make a run up Long Pool way, maybe. Track down that peckerwood preacher's boy, make'm unlock the icebox, retrieve some of them frosty Butt-wisers he sells on the sly to the punk kids who get snockered and cook crystal meth. Kick any leaf pile and it's bait city, red and blue wigglers all full of piss and vinegar like little cobras. Find a bream-bed pocked on the bayou floor, and go to town, haul in a hundred bluegill. Shit-fire, why not just run Doctor Peck Titsworth's trotlines, make a real fish fry out of it.

One cop pisses over by the dogs, and a newspaper boy's got his pants down, walked right through a chigger bed. Larry Simms, the chimney sweep whose loony cousin Gene was the cause of all this mess, is assuring the whole lot of them that this is the place. This is it, where ole Geno brought him when he confessed.

"Right down 'air Eddie boy. Yessir, Jesus. She's down 'air."

Nobody's brought water. Put the shovel in one of those lardassed cops' hands and they'd have ten barrels of icewater running out here.

Of a sudden, shovelblade hits bone—jolts right up through the homemade filling in Edgar's back molar.

"Here." Paris sticks his tongue against rough-topped tooth, says *here*.

The news boy buckles his belt and Sheriff Autry puts his dick back in his drawers. Preacher Shoates ambles over from his tree stump nap. Alderman Waylow's here in the mayor's place—alligator tears rolling down his face, fat lips aquiver. The mama and daddy, Rusty and Rhonda Love, had got down on their knees and begged to be here. This second they're under house arrest back at DeWayne's, where the Arkansas Democrat crew sits sucking fountain cokes, ordering hushpuppies, watching *One Life To Live* and playing "Great Speckled Bird" over and over on the jukebox, like Roy Acuff's the cure to all ails.

Paris is careful now. With the first whiff he sweats, feels his way around the thing's length with the sharpshooter shovel. If the dirt could talk, Edgar'd just walk on off right now—six bucks an hour or six hundred. He shaves the four feet around it, gets down on his belly and takes the loamy earth out handful by handful. It gets up his nose, the stench he's known at fish docks and railroad tracks and broken refrigerators. This dirt's cold. Flecks of sun sparkle in each handful. Already, he's got the face uncovered enough to see a green eye, the tiny pores and fine hairs on the nose bridge. Knee-deep now, his face is near it. Edgar Paris uncovers the jaw, enough for the dirt to trickle out of her mouth. Another handful reveals the collar—sunflower pajamas. Santy'd flown his reindeer down a week early so as to deliver them before she rode the bus home with the Simms girl, and the hell that awaited behind that compound gate. Lord God. Above him, dark faces.

Edgar imagines the world westward, across Oklahoma's oil wells, Texas, New Mexico, California, where he'd heard that whale watchers snap pictures of humpbacks breaching and squealing and blowing their spouts in blue water. Time for ever body to pack their shit—get on the hell out of Dodge. What else? Because this second, right now, this world's about to witness him—Edgar T. Paris—drag a little blonde-haired girl out of a hole, see the dirt dribble out of her mouth and how the gold sun shines on her sunflower pajamas.

2

In a white Lincoln with fucked up power seats, Renee Summerfaye Clausson Harvell sits crammed into Joey's mama's pre-set position. Green Arkansas is dense on either roadside. Little Lara is asleep in the passenger carseat, her neck bent at an angle that looks painful. Two days ago she lived in Utah. They'd spent their last weekend hiking Alta Mountain to Cecret Lake, where a blonde bevy of coeds lay out on a snowbank in string bikinis. Nights were chilly and the air was light and good to breathe. In Utah, forget about ticks or fleas or nuclear reactors or *pork-O-ramas* or signs that said REPENT or DON'T MAKE ME COME DOWN THERE or YOU GOT A FRIEND WHO BLED FOR YOU like Renee sees this second near the city limits of a town named Oppelo. Oppelo, for Christ's sake. What was an Oppelo? The Town Car cruises, Renee's knees bent up cello-style around the leather-wrapped steering wheel that reeks of Josephine's gardenia hand lotion and White Shoulders perfume, Marlboro Light smoke and that country smell of honeysuckle mixed with roadkill.

Little Lara, their two-year-old, was born in Salt Lake, in a nun-filled maternity ward on a full moon night when women howled. Renee was teacher of the year for her district. She was a member of a health club. Her and Joey'd given up red meat and pork last Easter and stuck with it. They took ski lessons, camped the red-rock wilderness, purified water and stuffed blue sage into pockets where Anasazi flint chips rattled. Little Lara'd hunted her first Easter eggs along the strewn boulders of the San Rafael river. Utah.

Renee says *Utah*, the word for a place you leave.

In Atkins—pickle capital of the world—a red-tusked pig is painted on a bluff: WELCOME TO RAZORBACK COUNTRY, it says, WE'RE ALL HOGS HERE. The pig grimaces, bares tusks, grunts "Whoo pig sooie," whatever on earth that might mean. An elderly man in a straw hat drives a tractor on the roadside right beside her, waving a big, dirty hand that misses its middle finger, smiling and nodding and waving. Anything more will be overkill, just too goddamn much.

Renee waves back, smiles, has to pee.

A strand of little Lara's pretty hair blows back over her forehead. The air's on high. It's a hundred and two degrees outside, ninety-percent humidity, a three star heat alert that's bad enough to kill your dog, the bubble-butted weather woman drawled last night on Joey's mama's TV. What she'd give for a Margarita and a piece of sandy beach. Renee shakes out one of Josephine's cigarettes, a long Marlboro; she's not a smoker, doesn't like smokers, gives money to the Lung Association. But this state makes her crave two at a time, shotgun inhale and blow double rings. Arkansas—where people really do jack tireless trucks up on concrete blocks in their front yards, tie mangy pit bulls to either bumper and sight in their thirty aught sixes from lawn chairs on front porches, where they shoot out side mirrors, aim low for the chrome. "I have to go tee-tee," Joey's mama'd said. *Tee-tee?*

Little Lara—Joey's face with her eyes. Sleepy little girl. Two mornings ago, on the way out of her house, Renee couldn't bear to look back, to see the threshold they'd carried their baby across during a light January snow after a forty hour labor, when Joey'd made big butcher paper signs. WELCOME HOME MOMMY AND LARA. WE LOVE YOU—the largest said in neat red letters. A handprint and their dog Moon's paw print dripped down one corner. Renee'd ripped during labor and the pain meds had her looped, but she remembered that homecoming and it hurt like hell to leave. Little Lara, this has been tough on her, too. Who knew what behavioral disorders she'd get. Stuttering runs in Joey's family, as does rheumatoid arthritis and mental illness, if Josephine is any indicator. Already, six months of potty training's gone out the door. She's smelled Lara's diaper for thirty miles now, and it doesn't go with scented hand lotion, not at all.

Toward Russellville, where Joey'll soon be Assistant Professor of History with a specialty in southern conflicts involving Mormons at a college in a cow pasture, Arkansas Nuclear One looms up over Carrion Crow Mountain, the white steam cloud mushrooming where planes fly. Renee breathes in through the unlit cigarette and pictures Josephine, how she'd looked at Adams Field airport, come to pick them up and lend the car.

"Welcome home, sugar," she'd said, and Renee believed that she meant it. Josephine had cried a little, and hugged them tight beside the broken down baggage conveyor. "I love y'all with all my heart. You've made me so happy, honey." Her chin quivered—she meant what she said. Renee'd never been able to decide whether to love or despise her.

Josephine was like that. So was Joey and all the Stepwells, mean as pissed-off water moccasins one minute, breakdown tender the next, lay down their life for you—no predicting which at any given time.

She said, "Sweeties, you're home now." Josephine had led them through the automatic doors marked *Terminal*, to the asphalt parking where waited pure and unspeakable heat.

A sign on Scenic Highway 7 says *SEE BOOGER HOLLER, Population 7 and one dog*. The road led up into the hills, past quilt and craft shops and a Sufi commune in Ozone, on into Newton County where the bootleggers and shiners had given way to cannabis growers with their booby traps and plastic explosives who, in turn, had made way for the Meth-cookers who set up along the Buffalo and would shoot you in a second, Joey claimed, their booby-trapped Elk carcasses stuffed with explosives. On through to Boone County with its logging trucks barrel-assing the curves, into quaint Harrison, where Joey's Fancher Party had originated before getting butchered by Utah Mormons dressed as Indians, and signs claimed a ten mile stretch of highway was kept clean and immaculate by the international order of the KKK, whose world wide headquarters was just off Main Street.

"Mommy, see!"

Three donkeys stand blank faced in knee-deep grass, shimmering heat mirage rising off the hot ground. "Mommy, see!"

A grackle pecks the middle one's back, and through the rolled down window comes breathtaking heat, the smell of roadkill snakes. "Hey jackass," Renee screams. "Hee-haw. Hee-haw, hee-haw."

"Hee-haw, hee-haw," little Lara squeals.

The dumb beasts don't flick an ear.

"Want to touch. Mommy, want to touch." Little Lara twists, reaching for donkeys that make way to goats, and yards filled with white laying hens scratching dirt.

"We're almost home. You ready to be home?"

"*No*," Lara screams. "*Touch now.*"

They pass a canoe rental center, two yellow kayaks shining under a display sign that announces rates and guided tours on the Buffalo River, where *Deliverance* was filmed with real natives playing the hillbilly parts. A float trip—time on the river, that's what they need, maybe that would make this home sweet home. Across Illinois Bayou, the Ozarks are in clear sight now, big and green and convincing under the blue sky. It's not Utah, not at all. But this land has an edge to it, a wild feel, outlaw country. In her outlaw days, they'd called her Bonnie, and any old boy she'd take dancing, Clyde. Renee likes that, *outlaw country.*

On a bridge near Dover, two husky policemen point and shuffle, working traffic around a flashing ambulance—the sort of thing that makes Joey spit over his right shoulder, his mojo against bad ju-ju, that silly, silly man just now driving toward them across who knows where with the vacuum cleaner stuck out the Pathfinder's rear window. A sheet-covered gurney's getting pushed up a gravel road that leads under the bridge viaduct. One man carries a radio, and another holds the leashes to a bunch of red dogs that look beat and skinny. A bent man takes pictures, the camera flashes an odd yellow under the big oak's shade.

Little Lara is transfixed by the dogs whose faces are comedian dead-pan, poker faces.

The gurney bumps up to the roadside, whatever covered up thing jigging a little under the sheet, distinguishable in the harsh light. The red-faced men sweat and swat flies, a small body surrounded by men who weep and gag and hold palms out as if to stop a memory that hangs around staring and thinking invisible thoughts into the heat-cursed air.

The double doors of the Pope County Ambulance open from the inside out and three sets of white-white hands make ready to snag one end as the silver gurney's legs collapse. In that way, the thing beneath the sheet disappears.

In periphery: a man with a shovel, the whiff of runover snakes, how the mute lights puff.

Curr dogs lay in wait at the curve where Renee turns onto gravel—Barton Road, her road now, the road name she'll write on envelopes to her mother. They chase Mama Harvell's car, teeth clattering in the tire wells. She blows a kiss into the rearview at Lara's cupie doll face, her and Joey and everyone else she's ever loved, right there, blinking back. "Home," Renee says, and turns into the gravel drive, a hundred yards from the buff-brick ranch-style built into a gentle slope.

A red heeler greets them near a gaping chest freezer that blocks the left side of the three car garage. A brush pile fire burns out in the side pasture, surrounded by shaggy haired kids. Cicadas are noisy in the hickories.

What happens next comes from high dream. Renee opens mama Josephine's door. That second, just when the stench from the chest freezer assaults her outright, the calico dog snarls, trots to the mouth of the garage and squares on them. Before she can even unwedge her knees from the steering wheel. The dog lifts a hind leg, looks her in the eye, pees in little spurts.

Renee dry-heaves. "*Get*. You get," she screams at it.

The heeler bares teeth, skulks over to the freezer which it leaps atop, looks back at her and barks, meanness in its little squint eyes.

Drive away and keep on driving, Renee thinks. Get in the car, fill up and hit the interstate toward anywhere but here. Instead, she undoes her daughter's carseat, pays the freezer a wide berth and makes toward the front door. What else?

All day long, the air conditioner kicking on and off and on again, a stubborn whiff of the departed in the wall-to-wall carpets, Renee cleans baseboards, windows, vents, teases hair from shower drains. She deduces the source of the odor. The previous owners simply yanked their chest freezer outside, where it has sat full of slab pork and beef or who knows what in hell for ten days now under the Arkansas sun. Each hour, the smell intensifies, gains more personality, seeps through the brick house's pores.

Her daughter toddles the floors along with her in the strange rooms where strange people have lived and loved. In the afternoon before they go find a hotel, the house steam-cleaned and ready for furniture that Joey's daddy, O.W., is driving across the big heart of Texas, they are entertained by red-headed hummingbirds—wild in the unbelievable heat—dive-bombing empty feeders outside the picture windows. They hear the cicadas start and stop, smell the creosote smell of the big fireplace. The house is huge and empty. Renee holds a hand over her daughter's mouth and nose while they get in the car. The odor of rotting meat follows them into Josey's Town Car, seething through the air-conditioner vents when the motor starts. The tall hickories make shadows across the two-acre lawn, alive with cicada ruckus. And atop the terrible freezer, the skinny dog raises, then lowers its head, eyes flashing, as if Renee and Lara are long vanquished enemies come back to fight anew.

"Yucko," little Lara says. She's laughing—what a game. "Mommy stinko."

The R'Ville Holiday Inn has a waterless pool.

"Swim-swim,"Lara says.

Renee's forgotten to bring wine. To do so now means getting back in the cramped-ass car, hitting the interstate and driving an hour back to Blackwell, a town with no structures save two competing cathedral-sized liquor stores, one in a cow pasture on the freeway's north side and a mirror image in the cow pasture on the south side. The only discernable difference was that the south side flew three flapping stars and bars flags, while the north side only had one. With the Blue laws, Arkansas was about half dry, and the other half was very wet. Joey's talked her through it, how there's more drunks than a stick can be shook at because everybody wants to taste what they can't have. Liquor, the forbidden dark of barrooms with their piss-stinking toilet troughs—drive a Baptist crazy for want.

"The pool's broken, sweety. No swim-swim."

Her daughter is genuinely hurt, the last two days strange beyond belief. "No," she screams, her face screwed up in a red burst. "*No, no, no.*"

"Fuck this," Renee says.

"Fuck this," little Lara says.

"No. Fuck this," Renee says.

"No fuck this," little Lara says.

Renee dresses her daughter in the Winnie-the-Pooh one piece, and yanks on her own black suit. She fills two bathroom tumblers with tap water and says fuck this many times into the lighted mirror, in which she sees little Lara staring at her, dumbstruck. She curls lips back from teeth, lets the hard K's rattle off the roof of her mouth.

At the empty pool, they lay in lawnchairs, take the sun, sip water and chomp ice all through happy hour. Alarmed strangers, men with square-necked preacher haircuts and their big-haired women, raise brows and hurry to their Mercury Cougars, bewildered by the obscenities flung from the woman and babe at the pool. "Honey, sweet Jesus, you hear what I heard?"

"Yep."

"Dear God."

And behind them, steady through their slammed shut doors—*fuck this, fuck this, fuck this, fuck this.*

In bed that night, Renee hears the dogfood plant. Somewhere out there there's a rumbling that seems alive. It's too cold in the room after the sun. She imagines Joey in a sleeping bag, looking up at the crescent moon, tonight's conjunction which he argued was a great good sign. He was like that, a sign maker and believer. Today's day two. Joey's father had flown into Salt Lake to drive the truck for them, so their last night in Utah was spent scrubbing floors and eating Chinese out of paper sacks. The table phone keeps on not ringing and the ditzy weather woman sounds like Ellie May would if she did phone sex in cloud words: pre-cip, a ridge of high pressure forcing the Ohio Valley, a thourough soaking.

Joey has a scar above his right eye. He misses two molars; markers they'd discussed should she ever be asked to identify him.

On a desk in the cool, cool room, is an evacuation manual with complete instructions in case of nuclear catastrophe. It's a light blue Kinko's job titled

EMERGENCY INSTRUCTIONS: Effective January 1, 1999. A jolly sketch of the power plant alleges cars and trees and little men, a pair of whom pass a football. In the reservoir, bass boats make *V's*, split the atom heated water—somebody's hauled in a lunker, a largemouth—blue eyes neon in the Arkansas afternoon light that leaks into the perfumed room where little Lara screams at the top of her lungs. Renee thumbs to the section that directs her to Hector High School Gymnasium—Home of the Warlocks—where they'll each get a blanket and be safe from the worst of the contamination. *Do not, for any reason, bring your pets. DO NOT, DO NOT, DO NOT attempt to rescue your animal friends,* the manual cautions, *Leave food out and two bowlfuls of water—Bowzer and Kitty will be fine.*

Another section is titled "Radiological Information for Farmers and Gardeners." More pert drawings display how a nuclear plant works, replete with cooling tower, turbine building, and administration facilities. After "What is an Emergency?" comes "How Will I be Notified?" which, in turn, is followed by "What About My Telephone?"

Renee falls asleep on "What Should I Do?"

3

Behind Joey Harvell's back, Highway 80 hauls ass west. It retreats down Parley's Canyon through the Salt Lake valley toward Nevada's shining casinos with their yardfuls of the newly busted, toward Reno and Pyramid Lake and Sacramento, up to the Golden Gate Bridge under which flows the forever cold Pacific where they'd sailed one Christmas Eve on a tour boat when little Lara was about to turn one and the world seemed new with hope. Tractor trailer brakes singe the mountain air. East—the way home, Joey drives east. On the mountainside, a shooting range is inhabited by a lone shooter, the mute pistol-fire bouncing his hand sky-earth, sky-earth. Southward rises the San Rafael Swell, a moonscape where Anasazi ruins weather under the blast-furnace sunlight from Bluff to the Valley of the Gods, Canyon de Chelly, Navajo holy land.

Parley's Canyon, named for the Mormon who'd once charged an arm and a leg to get through before he got himself killed by a jealous husband in Texarkana, where Renee and little Lara, his good wife and daughter, are about now steam cleaning strangers' hair out of a carpet in the big empty house. Moon, the family's half-lab is baffled by all this—has sensed serious shit for the three weeks while they've packed. Renee's Fica leans cattywamp over a bucketful of cleanser, odd sponges, whatnot and a good Boston KS pencil sharpener Joey unscrewed at the last minute from little Lara's doorframe. Sunflowers bloom toward Mountain Dell Reservoir where the white mountain tops shine down into the water and dazzle upward, reflect the blue sky just like the hokey oil paintings inside Park City windowfronts.

His vacuum cleaner leaks dust. Stuck helter-skelter out his truck window, passenger side, the machine occupies the space where his wife would be riding with little Lara in the carseat, some primavera May morning when they cruised over toward Dutch John to hook the toothy browns, rainbows, cutthroats and drink good whiskey while it got dark and coyotes yelped off the eastern banks of the Uintas.

Utah. Joey says it, lets the word come out his mouth, then feels stupid and melodramatic, hallmarks of his people. But fuck it, the word *does* have a sad ring. Say it.

Joey hangs a U at the Summit exit, circles back under the overpass and heads toward where he's just come from. The dog's up on all fours in the rearview, having conniptions, peeing on Joey's spare clothes over this reversal. She yelps and pisses and chews his clean shirt collar. Other vehicles rocket past, carwrecks about to happen. What on earth could the hurry be? All morning the thought's plagued him. A split second, that's all it takes, crash your head through a windshield. What would it be like to never see his Renee and Lara again. To have spoken last words? For them to have to imagine his last moments? Gathering speed, Joey joins the mad rush down, keeps it between the lines, heads West.

The neighbor lady, who for five years they've simply called "the lady," knocks on the front door with a Book of Mormon she's signed for Joey and his family.

"I was afraid I missed you. Give me a hug."

Inside the book, after the inscription, the writing says *God loves you and your pretty family. Love, Dorothy English.*

Her green eyes are watery. Joey's watched her lay down full on the ground in her backyard for hours at a time, combing weeds from ivy with her fingers. Before her pain-in-the-ass husband Rex died, Joey and Renee'd carried over bucketfuls of tomatoes and crookneck squash—the old man's favorite.

"You're sweet. I smell like a hog."

"Yes, that's true. I already miss you all. We've had our time I guess."

"You've been a fine neighbor."

"Not entirely."

Joey says, "Entirely," and hugs the old lady.

Frail, her back cracks. "I'm from Illinois, you know. That's where my people are from. They came here for God. I had my youngest child when I was forty-four. God is good. Remember that. And remember me."

She wipes her eyes and shuffles down the stairs, across Joey's clean mowed grass and FOR SALE. PRICE LOWERED sign, across University Street to the house she'll die in on a November afternoon, where a rainbow sprinkler arcs and the air is cool and sweet. Somebody's strumming a guitar—all these college hippies. Down the street, dogs romp in flower beds. Joey unlocks the front door, walks the empty house one more time. He takes his time, pauses over a scar in his daughter's baseboard, an abandoned painting of white daffodils in the washroom, the room where his freshwater and surf rods were hung up from floor joists, the spot of carpet where little Lara first walked to him on the day after Halloween when he had a black eye and Renee'd disappeared to Red Butte.

In the empty kitchen, the sink faucet drips into the basin where Lara'd had her first bath, and Joey thinks of that part of her that washed down the drain into Utah earth. Silly, melodramatic, and true—Joey laughs hard out loud. Water drips out of the unplugged refrigerator's top freezer. A thin bead—when it hits the floor, Joey remembers why he's come back. The smell is quite frank already when he opens the door. Inside the dark Frigidaire, Joey finds the night before last's German potato salad—uncovered. Along with this, he hauls three sacksful of his last-night-in-Utah's Chinese out to the dumpster, locks up and rechecks the mail. The crooked Century 21 sign advertises—*A home for the 21st Century* along with their ditzy realtor's name and phone numbers.

Waiting to turn into the traffic, a diet Coke ticking in its drink holder, Moondog has settled. In his head, their realtor, Jennie Jones, how it would've been for her—unlocking the property door, "Please, you go first," she'd say, "Notice the hardwood. Check out the airy parlor." Her hips would sway and she'd summon that sweet-dream, *wouldn't you like to find out* look. The would-be home buyers would saunter right on in to the shiny maple parlor, the realtor's words arriving with olfactory shock of ten-day rotten Moo Goo Gai Pan.

Joey pictures it—the hasty retreat, a scene ripe with comic possibilities.

Behind him, just behind the trimmed pussy willow, the lady's face hovers behind sparkling glass, waving a white-knuckled hand.

God loves you and your pretty family. God is good.

Outside Cheyenne, Kurt Gowdy State Park still has snow on its backside, ankle-deep and shining in the good afternoon sun. Joey eases up to the gatehouse; Moon's awake and breathing hard, knows they're about to set camp, gather firewood in side canyons where deer flash white tails and rabbits bolt. Inside, a stocky girl in forest greens and a Mountie-looking hat smiles big, and it's the best smile he's seen all day.

"Howdy," she says. "You got a vacuum cleaner stuck out your window. Here for the night?"

Joey says, "Yeah," and hands her a ten dollar bill. The low sun's on the lake; here's where they'd camped on the way back from Arkansas, after they'd bought the farm, him and Renee and their little girl. A nice night, no wind, they'd cooked chicken burritos and had a fire and bourbon and frost in the morning.

She returns a receipt with today's date magic markered on it. "Hang this on your rearview. Leash that dog. And honey—can you keep your vacuum cleaner shut down? Just for tonight? Please?" She's laughing now, brows raised, a little scar semi-circled on her cheek bone. Maybe she's a little silly from a day in the gatehouse, or maybe she's drinking or high on skunk-weed. They sniff blue sage out here, Joey's sure. And that's okay, Kurt Gowdy looks empty, a lonely place to sit in a shack.

"No problemo," Joey says. "I'll keep her shut off."

She tips the Mountie hat, and licks chapped lips. "Why hon, enjoy your time then. No fire outside the rings."

As the Pathfinder bucks down the rutted road, Joey sights Venus, already constant beyond the lake. On the mirror, ink from the host's receipt bleeds through the backside.

This is still mountain country, the Continental Divide where the land's back is about to break and water ceases its westward flow and begins the slow rut toward Mississippi. This ridge where the world falls away east, mountain to plain to flatland delta and the gulf. It's brisk, Moon's silent by the fire. A conjunction—Venus, the crescent moon and Regulus—frames a triangle in the southeast. When dark comes the sky is crazy.

They share food. He leashes her, unpacks the truck, then lays the rear seats down and unrolls his bag. Joey pushes the button on his keychain that locks the door and zips himself in.

In Arkansas, Harvells lay cinder blocks around their dead, rake in white gravel that forever needs tending. The custom necessitates the ability to use tools. Form, saw joint, drag screed over footing—you're shit out of luck if you're a Harvell and can't do that. Work is prayer.

In the dream, Joey Harvell hammers a block with the butt end of a trowel, forces the left edge plumb against the straightline and scrapes the side joint, the metallic *shring* singing out over the cemetery to the woods. Masonry grit has got into his eyes, but the course holds true. Where the mud conjoins with the granite stone—he's proud of that, how he'd known to paintbrush the seam-crack with a fine-bristled Purdy, an old finisher's trick. His footing's cured tight in the heat, his lines hold, and the mud is good, mixed with five gallon bucketfuls drawn from the pond down below the barbed-wire fence, where white-face loll belly-deep under August sun, the mud is pure gold. This short wall, eight inches to the top around Jimmy's grave, it would be here through hell and high water.

Joe goes back, hits the joints again, paintbrushes seams. Another edge gets the backside of his trowel hand, but that's okay, a little blood makes sense. He splashes half a coffee can onto the board, hatchets the stiffened mud and thins it down. Ten feet over, James Lon's wheelbarrow sits on Joe's spot, three plots north of Jimmy, next to whom will lay Daddy, then Mama, who Joe'd be beside. Renee. Little Lara one day. He'd once watched his own granddaddy, well-bourboned on an afternoon in May, piss the spot where he'd one day lay, then dance a jig—hammering out pipe-fire on his trouser covered prosthesis.

Further up, his sister, Traceleen, and her people—out here under the bare blue sky near Solgahatchia, Arkansas, Indian names that your mouth had to do some work to get through. And Jimmy? How Mama'd had his state champion football picture encased under glass and implanted on the stone, so that this second, the sun thank God lowering to the east, his brother looks at him and smiles the crooked smile that he's seen on his daughter's face.

Joey paint brushes the joint's length, a leg cramp just starting in one calf. The straightlines and stone grit, the physical work of all this, watching his maternal grandfather lay down the big stones around Papa Treadwell's mound, who, in turn, had done the same for his father—the sons of four generations buried at the blocked-in feet of their fathers. Family lineage, the 1850 migration from Henry County, Tennessee, the names time has erased, out here in what was once Stepwell land, the Trail of Tears passing right over Solgahatchia. But Jimmy? Six-feet tall and summer brown with sawdust in his hair? It was all fucked up, for this to happen like this, him nineteen, break anyone with a heart's heart.

He drops the hand trowel, joiner, and brush into one of the compound buckets, knocks the mudboard off in yesterday's pile and sets to wiping the dark stone clean.

Here Lies Our Precious Son
STEVEN JAMES HARVELL
August 24, 1966-May 9, 1986
Romans 8:38-39

Joey unfurls his sleeping bag and lays down with them for the night. It's August, hot, and the sky puts on a show—alive with bullfrog and cricket and cicada and far-away whippoorwill, the three notes sung and heard and sung again, lightning bugs stinging the horizon. Some day, his people all flown off to other places and him in between, neither here nor there. And the lake shines reflecting the dizzy eyes of horses resurrected from the day's heat, down on their knees drinking the spring water. His daughter, little Lara's eyes like her mother's, the color of good dirt shining in rows on plow day after the vernal equinox: *Arkansas, Utah, love.* The good sleep after good work, the dreamless sleep.

4

The Holiday Inn Breakfast Buffet offers steaming vatfuls of buttered cheese grits, sausage gravy, country ham, backslab bacon, patty and link sausage, home-style rise biscuits, eggs three ways, fried green tomatoes, muscadines, blackberries, buttermilk and whole cream, piles of onion-spiked hashbrowns, silver dollar pancakes, fresh tomato juice and chicory coffee—these country people knew their shit when it came to breakfast, Renee would give them that. She'd loaded up, why not? Only little Lara was picky that morning, refused the silver dollar pancakes and eggs three ways, wanted peanut butter toast, instead. As pig-headed as her daddy. It was a big room with a long row of poolside windows—Nuclear One steaming off in the distance beyond ArkaTech.

Their waitress is a tall girl, coal black hair and lean with country blue eyes and a little scar on her cheek. Not as young as she seemed at a distance, she carries a pitcher of ice water in each hand. Renee motions her to their table. "Peanut butter toast, is that possible?" The morning music, low over speakers, is jazz for Christ's sake—the world looking up.

Lara smiles. "Please?"

"Surely. We can do that," she says. "What's your name little cutey?"

"Say your name, honey."

Little Lara covers her face. "*No, no, no.*"

The name tag on her chest says *Your Server, Rhonda.* "Peanut butter toast. To drink?"

Ice clinks in her glass pitcher—a good sound in the bright light. "Bourbon," Renee says. "A triple. Straight up."

"Amen. Make that two in our dreams. Pope County's bone dry 'cept for private. You ain't *from* here."

"Thank you so much for knowing that." Her voice, Rhonda's, has Joey's ring about it, and Renee'd always loved that.

"You're welcome." Rhonda says. "How 'bout coffee, chicory or regular?"

"Regular."

"A chocolate milk for her, I bet. Be right back."

Renee watches her, dipping to fill water glasses, something sad in her eyes. A little bit of hippy about her, maybe, the smell of vanilla on her skin. Ray Ray—a groomsman from her and Joey's wacky wedding party, once lived just north in a communal Sufi compound named Ozone, until he got kicked out for general drunkenness, a failure to comply with sex policies. Rumor was he was back— living up in Newton County with the Wiccans.

It's late, brunch time really, and Joey'd be rolling in soon, driving up the gravel drive to the home he'd insisted they buy, a romantic idea he'd always had about owning a farm at the foot of the Ozark mountains, ponies and chicken coops, cows—the place was perfect for all that. Fourteen miles from Russellville, the Barton place had been a steal, really. Ten acres, a barn, wooded and cleared pasture with a bubbling brook cutting the far border under towering hickories where woodpeckers hammered—it was a pretty place. The house was goliath— five bedrooms and three baths, with a cathedral ceilinged great room and wall-length fireplace—they got it for 90. Who could believe that? Ninety. Inside of two hours, he'd be here, Joey.

Rhonda serves out the drinks.

"Where y'all from."

"Utah. But we're not *from* there. Joey, my husband, he's from here. I'm from Washington. D.C. Everywhere, really."

"He from Russellville?"

"Lonoke."

"Lonoke. That's close. What's his last name, honey?"

"Harvell. Joey Harvell."

"Why I know Harvells. Ricky and Rita and Bruce. He related to any a them? They all from Morrillton down the road. Know any of them?"

Renee sips the hot coffee, feels her husband's approach, can read his mind, how he believes he's returning like a king in golden mail or some such baloney. "I couldn't tell you. There's an Aunt Naveen somewhere."

"They're wild, the Harvells. I've known a few of them. No Naveens. You one hell of a long way from Utah, now."

Little Lara smears peanut butter, gobbles the toast down and sucks milk from a sippy cup.

"How about you? Are you from here?" Renee scoops egg yolk into the grits, pushes them into the hashbrowns.

The woman tilts her head one way and then the other. She sighs outright, swipes at her right eye. "Here. I grown up down the road. Me and my old man. Born and raised."

"What's he do."

"Rusty makes concrete mermaids. Yours."

Renee points toward Tech. "He's going to be in History, right over there. On the other side of that cow pasture. That's why we're here."

"So you're staying?"

In Renee's plate, sausage gravy has started to congeal.

"You have children?"

Rhonda's face reddened. She lays down the check, holds up a finger. "One little girl," she says and walks away, across the room, disappears through the double doors that swing into the kitchen.

Mother and daughter wait in the front room of the empty house, the air kicking on and off, on and off. They've bought the farm. Taken possession. Soon their surname name will be writ on the catywhomp mailbox wherein will fall birthday cards, bills, summons to court, suspensions and newspapers describing the life and times of where they live now. Outside, the freezer meat rots to kingdom come, maggots in there probably, many days gone under the god-awful Arkansas sun, guarded by the red heeler who snarls and yip yaps. The Elliotts' derelict son is burning brush piles in the pasture not a hundred yards away, aided by a circle of beer-drinking hillbilly kids. Blue smoke plumes up over coordinates 35 22.28 north, 09300.75 west, Arkansas River Valley country, where the land lifts toward the Ozarks.

Today is Sunday—Renee's third in the natural state. Hummingbirds dive-bomb each other around the empty feeders hung outside every picture window.

Tuned to a gospel station, she sits here zonked, watching dust fly when the odd vehicle crunches by. The morning seems to hover in-between places, but they've planned an afternoon outing, a drive and swim at a place called Long Pool, an old Indian camp where Josephine used to bathe on summer days as a girl—which must have been a thousand years ago to look at her. Lupus is Latin for wolf, and that's what Josie looks like, somebody a wolf's chewed on.

Months from now, Dr. Georgina Dunlap—the two-hundred-pound lesbian and gap-toothed Queen-Dean of LFA (Liberal and Fine Arts) at ArkaTech, who causes subordinate profs of both genders to pee in their shoes, whose fondness for Elvis paraphernalia, hair art, genitalia sculpture, pure bred beagles, and mouth-watering charcoals of French school girls is celebrated along with her trademark safari outfits replete with scabbarded machete with which she'd once castrated a Sudanese warthog—will tell them about the bacteria in picturesque Long Pool up Highway 7, how the clear water sometimes grows stagnate and, if ingested during a swim, will cause a type of yellow diarrhea that permanently stains toilets such as the almost-new Kohler in the faculty lounge. But how on earth is Renee to know this? There is no Georgina to tell her this first week, when, if the rotten meat, heat, blasted cicadas booming from every sorry tree, the *thumpa-thump* out in the woods, isn't enough, Sunday, 18 July, 1999, the morning's news in *The Russellville Courier* confirms the worst—"Little Shiloh Love Dug Up on Illinois Bayou," the headline says, just above another that says, "Decapitated Man Found with Hands Cut off: Mutilators Leave Wallet In Victim's Back Pocket." And this catty-corner to a third piece titled, "Fish Kill Set For Lake Overcup: No Limit Restrictions For Time Being." Added to this is a note on John John Kennedy's plane crash with his pretty blonde wife and her sister for Christ's sake. Senator Ted's on a Navy ship trawling cold waters this second. And, just so she gets the point, one last article points out how Friday's middle school shooting took three lives down in Atlanta—teacher first.

They've moved to Arkansas during the summer of death.

5

On the road before light, eighty-miles-an-hour on cruise control, Joey Harvell drives through Ogallala along the South Platte, where his grandmother Floradee and her people had once lived and breathed. The sun rises in his face—red, then orange going to gold. The river's silver thread parallels the dusty ruts cut west by pioneers who themselves followed the track ancient ones made following buffalo, and before that those who'd walked across the land bridge with their Clovis points to slay the wild camel and giant sloth, in a land patrolled by condors whose wingspans threw shadows the length of eighteen wheelers that blow by in the fast lane. He's filled up, washed bugs off the windshield and checked the oil, as he'd once done while working his old man's gas station with his brother, Jimmy, where there'd been a room with pool tables and a jukebox that played Folsom Prison Blues about an Arkansawyer who'd shot a man in Reno just to watch him die. Windows down, the morning smells like sweetgrass. Antelope materialize on the river plain. He finds a blues station out of North Platte, Lightning Hopkins singing about Mr. Charlie, how his millhouse was burning down, and feels for the world like Odysseus flying home to slay suitors and take a rightful seat at the table of his people.

Mr. Charlie, Mr. Charlie.

In Sutherland he leaves Mountain Time, gains an hour, prairie in every direction, as if he's driven onto the back of a great green turtle: the Lakota thought for home.

He'd been here once with O.W., a long-haul trucker, and remembered the antelope, how you'd look out on over a hundred miles of mesa and see nothing, then one would flick an ear and a hundred would materialize. A freak summer snow had fallen and they'd followed a semi hauling a Tilt-O-Whirl carnival ride across the flat mesa. His first time west, the sun had come out, just like today, and the glare from the mirrors and snow on that day when he was thirteen might have been seen from the moon. That's what he'd believed.

All day and the next he drives like that, his heart welling, thinking neither of food nor water, traveling toward wife and daughter, how Cap must have felt when he approached port and flew the number 1 flag, the code for Renee and Meg and young Rockie that he loved them, that he was coming home. That the USS McCain had completed its orders and now requested permission to come aground. Surely this moment of return is what we live for.

South of Lincoln he hits a riverside state park, feeds Moon, unrolls the bag and sleeps.

How Arkansas lay down before him, hill country, a little hazy, heat rising off Boston Mountain. Joey skips the new Interstate, cruises old Highway 71 through Mountainburg and Cain. Here was highway meant for hauling ass with windows cranked—he'd driven it in big-motored Monte Carlos and Cutlasses, a 280-Z, it was the very stretch where he and Renee had fallen in love one double-rainbow afternoon when the world shifted gears. In a curve's blind spot, a concrete sign says *21 MOTORISTS HAVE DIED HERE—DON'T YOU BE NEXT.* Jimmy'd driven him this way once, back from a spring break they'd spent digging out the sludge retainers at the Remington Arms plant. What a sight that was—Jimmy's rubber suit all smeared, that crooked Stepwell grin on his face.

At Alma, 71 hits Interstate 40. Go west and you hit Fort Smith, *True Grit* country at the edge of the old frontier, the ancestral road his blood kin had walked. Joey eases into the Alma 66 which advertises "Heaven's Radio with Tony Alamo." Gas is cheaper, air's free. Broke, he'd driven off from this place more than once afer a fill up. Poor people pump two dollars at a time, five on pay day, carry lengths of garden hose to siphon from a passerby when they run out, know to keep a piece of bread handy—sure cure for gasoline mouth. He was amazed at how Renee'd just up and click the pump nozzle on full, walk off and let it run. Filling-up lifted Joey Harvell's heart, what great good luck to be able to fill up your goddamn truck to the brim and not have to drive off shitass scared. Good tires were a thing to marvel at, none of the belted radial showing through.

Hell, for that matter, just look at this ride, silver Pathfinder with a rack on top. He was coming home in a goddamn fine ride. The times he'd broken down on this drive, thermostat out or burned up clutch and had to back his way on the roadside to whatever bumfuck gas station where cur dogs lay under the lifts and slow-working men grunted curses at busted knuckles.

In the gas station bathroom, someone had sketched a cross with a stick man on it. Underneath in red letters, *TRUST.* He brushes his teeth, combs his hair. Brainwashed kids still sell roses at the front door for Tony Alamo, Alma's mayor and world famous cult leader, who raises his own wife from the dead every Easter Sunday as a Passion Play fundraiser.

Joey hits I-40, the last fifty miles.

Through Dyer and Mulberry, where he'd once floated the river at flood stage in nothing but a canvas life jacket with crazy Uncle Earl, his mother's brother. Near Ozark, smokehouse pork cooks over hickory—they'll chop it right in front of you, lay on the sauce. Here's where the Pig Trail starts, an ethereal road that disappears into the hills laced with booby trapped meth labs, the banks of the glittering White River with its own storied monster and a Yeti, even, rumored to wander the bottoms. Not fifteen miles south of the interstate, the Arkansas sluices though the river valley, big now with mud in its current from Colorado, Kansas, Oklahoma. Following the river back seemed right—it'd been where he'd been, seen rocky mountain turn to grass. Hunt, Clarksville, Lamar—tornado alley towns with ground-level doors marking the shelters built into every other front yard. "Frady houses," O.W. called them.

In the history of the universe, fourteen billion years and counting, no soul had ever rejoiced with such vigor at seeing a nuclear steam-cloud mushroom into big blue sky. Fifteen minutes later he hangs a left at Exit Two, turns north on 124 toward Carrion Crow Mountain. All morning NPR's gone on and on about John-John Kennedy's plane going down, the search for wreckage or bodies, now interspliced with surreal music from a Conway show called *Heart of Space*. After fifteen hundred road miles, come home for the first time in a dozen years, the heft of the journey hits home. Odysseus had wept at the sight of his dog; the old maid knew him by his scar.

Joey kills the radio for the last few miles, heartbeat fast, generous tears dripping down his face. The sign he's waited for appears just before the turn at Moreland toward Barton Road where his wife and daughter wait not five minutes away. There, standing on a flat rock beside a pond levee and lily pad studded water, a woman is dressed in a wedding gown white as a bank of Utah snow. Her blonde hair dazzles. The wedding train unfurls across knee-deep grass and she's grinning, white teeth shining. In one gloved hand, a spinning rod casts glittering coils over the still water. A photographer's bulb flashes.

This is no dream.

On Barton Road, a pair of roadrunners scutter down the gravel then duck under the barbed wire pasture gate. Joey drives slow, the dust sifting in through the open windows with the good scent of blackberries and hay mowing and MaMa Stepwell's yard smell come to him from twenty years ago. The farm they've bought—ten acres with a barn and tractor stall, a hayloft and garden plot—it's good country. The land spreads out from him—immaculate greens splashed by shadows. The barn loft doors are open. A shaft of light shines through from the west side to the east, his path reiterated. Climbing out, Joey weeps freely.

Right off, Lara shrieks *Daddio!*

A heeler dog Joey's never seen hops off a deep freezer which for some reason sits unplugged in his driveway. The thing hikes and pisses on the front tire of the ticking Nissan, driver's side.

Then the dog gets both rear tires.

Renee appears at the step of the long porch. She has that look. "Hope you didn't expect us to make a sign," she says. "Because we didn't."

Lara runs to him gleefully, Renee behind her. He lifts Lara, holds her to his face. "I love you," he says. "I missed you."

The three embrace.

"It stinks." Joey points at the dog. "Who's he?"

"They left him," Renee says. "Dirty little fucker."

Joey opens the back hatch and out hops Moon. That second the red heeler mounts their black lab, just like that. It mounts, makes little humping motions, before Moon wheels, snapping. The heeler whimpers and runs, leaps back atop the fetid freezer. Three seconds tops—that's all it takes.

"What's the smell?"

"Guess."

"What's the smell?"

His voice is the voice of a man who's just driven fifteen hundred miles to have his dog humped by a blue-eyed stray, outside a house that reeks to high heaven. Renee leads him into their home where the air-conditioner has it under control, air you can deal with.

"Oh, that. They left their freezer." She removes two plastic glasses from a bag in the styro cooler where a cut lime leaks, pours vodka deep into both, tops them off with a splash of tonic. "Unplugged. Full of meat."

"Meat?"

"Meat rotting," Renee says.

The Kennedy's were found in dark, cold water; they'd recover bodies for decent burials. Things would make sense. Later, a little happy, they'd held hands, took a turn at a two-step across the wide deck. They'd hear for the first time another sound from the deep, dark woods beyond the gravel road. Beyond land the Bartons had long ago right-of-wayed to Arkansas-Louisiana Gas Company, a half-mile inside the gravel where a four-wheeler trail disappears into overgrowth, way off in the hollow where the woods drop into who-knows-what, a low *thump-a, thump-a, thump-a.* Sitting on unpacked lawn chairs under the tree-blot sky, they hear it intertwine with the whine of tree locusts, how they start and stop, molting into alien things.

The air kicks on and off. Renee breathes beside him. He's brought them here—his family. This is where they live now. Lara's room is across the hall, where the Elliott's daughter had come of age, where she'd dressed for the wedding that was held outside under trees, his trees.

All night long in the new-strange house, on the unpacked, home-scented queen, the sounds issue from the deep dark wood.

As if the place has a pulse.

6

On top of grave digging, Paris pockets fifty-a-month caretaking the Tri-County Coon Club, where men from Pope, Conway, and Yell Counties respectively play hooky from work, wives, floozies, and the rigors of sobriety. In particular, Tri-County is safe harbor where kith and kin reenact blood sport rituals whilst celebrating the ancestry that binds them to the dead, living, and those brethren yet to breathe the good air of Arkansas. Tri-County: wherein boys learn to move among men. Here they are protected by the oath sworn against the old murderous enemy, the blasphemous snake whose decendents have grown rich and gloat from behind the Rocky Mountains where they've forgotten how to fear. Who lay out their victims' bones in the BYU museum like dumbass dinosaurs, the skulls arranged by size so that the single bullet holes near the cranium's apex repeat darkly down tables in Utah. The disinterred bones, even, of husbands and wives, brothers and sisters and babies who journeyed westward from these parts toward what they did not know, but hoped for. Toward Utah Territory and Mountain Meadows, treachery and slaughter and death they struggled. Tri-County Coon Club, founded through writ and charter in 1857 by Marion Poteet, sole survivor of the terror perpetrated by the hands of Mormons at a place called New Harmony, where, in cold blood, the unholy alliance murdered Captains John T. Baker and Alexander Fancher en route from Boone County, Arkansas to California, their sweet-voiced children cut-throated by the vile whore whose name can only be mentioned here under penalty of the strap. Tri-County, under the foundation of which, buried upright beneath the ancient fire pit, the bones of Grandfather Poteet his own self, drawn Bowie knife in hand, whose prophesies and revelations, writ on the tanned hide of an unborn calf, tell of how a great one will one day rise and walk forth from these very doors to unleash a reckoning upon the serpent's head such as has never been see before by human eyes.

Paris's old lady—a Mars Hill looker—has left him for college, like enrolling at ArkaTech made her shit not stink. Long-legged Tina, one of the Casteen girls whose fame went way past this neck of the woods, wore good skin and shiny hair. Good riddance. More than once Edgar'd had teeth broken on her behalf. Her brothers were just as bad, and her old man, and the rest of the long-legged sisters and cousins and whatnot—lookit, the whole bunch of Casteens was shithouse. Wasn't no pansy-ass book-learned poetry writing in the world could change that. Edgar's had it with that, packing broken molars with home-melted lead. These days, he sleeps on top of a bunk bed with Edgar T. Paris written on its head in big red letters, against the wall in the Honorable Departed Sheriff Marlan Hawkins Great Room. Spring and summer he tends Coon's vegetable garden, keeps the flies swatted and the rats down, mows grass and digs out the shitter when need-be. Fall and winter, between hunts, all night affairs he'd just as soon avoid, Paris never lacks for company—Moreland fire boys, DeWayne's people come over from Dover, Sinyards and Mayfields and Roaches and Stepwells and Thackers, Funkhausers and Titsworths and Gilleses, Preacher Roy Dale Shoates and Beryl, Meryl, and Jeryl Suggs, Alderman Waylow, Sheriff Autry and his pack of lardass-kissers, big-chested Taylor boys, the concrete finishers, with their sweet-mouthed Walker dogs from Carrion Crow Mountain, artsy-fartsy professors from ArkaTech like the one 'sposed to deliver the annual Tri-County Lupercalia Mardi-Gras talk tonight, a Harvell, not bad people though this one's gone and got book-learning and bought old Zimmerman's place in Moreland. There's reactor supervisors, Judge Goodno and Hector warlocks with their long braided beards, stoner re-hab men from Charter Vista, squarehead Baptist deacons who'll drink you dry, the stray Wal-Mart millionaire, Tyson boys smelling of hog offal, a couple imperial wizards down from Harrison, Red Sam from the *Courier,* and Larry Simms, Geno's cousin, the chimney sweep who habitates with a Cherokee bride in a geodesic dome off Longbottom Pool. And now, the poor, sad, whiskey-soaked Rusty Love, grief-struck over his little girl. Sooner or later, everyone darkens Tri-County's door.

A schoolbus full of yard apes who've just been set aloose from retaking third grade at Russellville Middle hoops and hollers by. King snakes crossing the yard of late, swimming down early from Carrion Crow Mountain, they've slept the winter in ancient dens where artesian waters leak cool and sweet. On the concrete porch, Paris studies last year's freezer-burned garden. Big Boys dead on the stakes, unpicked tomatoes bloated. Dead pea runners climb rusted wire. A couple butternuts and a skunk-chewed pumpkin—all history. Spring come soon. Alderman Waylow's wife's pink panties mark a row of runt collards—in praise of her feminine spirit—every last one of which grows out of a gutted flathead, they alone have survived the winter. Good eating diced with onion and slab bacon, red pepper.

Dust flies as Cleafus Wynn's jacked up dodge bucks up the rutted drive on gumbo mudders. Chilly-willy, the frost has his teeth hurting. Behind Wynn, Sheriff Autry, Shoates, Waylow and Simms, the whole sorry lot.

"Evenin' cocksucker." Wynn steps down out the truck in Dingo boots and a pair of cutoff church pants, opens an Igloo cooler duct taped to the tailgate. He's a concrete finisher, hell with a screed and trowel, but about half-whacked like his mama. "Looky here, Uncle Ed."

A shitload of hand-sized bluegill respirate on bloody ice and loose Budweiser cans. Their pink gill-slits open and close. Fat crappie leak roe on top of three nice bass, a chomper blue cat and a couple pollywogs. The blue's head noodles out of a feed sack beside Wynn's bullfloat handles—it'll go eighteen, twenty pound maybe. A fine steaker, she'll feed.

"It'll do, Cleavis."

The others close in and inspect the mess.

Waylow's wearing Bible-black head to toe, and Shoates is wheezing, snootful most likely. Some rain'd be nice, knock down this dust. It'll threaten, but won't come.

"Hit this'n on the way." Larry Simms, the chimney sweep, tail swings a fox squirrel and a grey in amongst the fish—the little rat-faces showing bucky-beaver teeth.

A couple bullfrogs are added, and a brace of doves gets carried to the cleaning station. Out by the pumphouse, the youngest of them strop filet knives and go to dressing, while Edgar heats oil in the big cast-iron over the gas cooker.

Somebody's strung green Mardi-Gras beads around the mermaid's neck out beside the gravel drive, and the red-eyed Beelzebub's got a splat of brilliant blue bird shit run down his spike horns onto his belly. Out of the Shiloh Love Sympathy Fund, they've now collected a llama, or is it a donkey? who can say?, Jesus on the Cross, and naked Thinker squatting with a hand on his chin. And the newest ornament, the avenging angel child wielding her two-bladed sword, a look on her face that'll shrivel your nuts.

The lawn ornament's author, stoned likely, racks off glass packs out by the mailbox, idles on into the drive and parks behind Wynn. Edgar sees him through the tinted glass, sitting in a bucket seat, just sitting there, rolling it over in his head. Worrying it, like Edgar does his sorry teeth some nights when the moonlight pours in and bugs thump the windowpanes.

Easter coming on, which Edgar guesses will be the real deep shit for Rusty and Rhonda this year. Thanksgiving, then Christmas, everybody with a plywood Santy and reindeer leaned up in their yard, the tree, all those twinkling lights and Christmas trees, gifts wrapped up with last year's bows, all the felt stockings with each cursive name writ in sparkly glitter. But Easter's the genuine shits—all that stone rolled from the tomb resurrection malarkey: tulip, jonquil, redbud, and dogwood sprouting idiot-wild in every front yard from here to Calico Rock. Not to mention forsythia, how it yellows the countryside. Nobody talks about the Love girl, not one word.

Oil hisses in the deep fryer, time to cut potatoes.

7

What can you do when you live in a place where people are named Peck Titsworth?

Renee guns the curve where three mobile homes stack up to the roadside, each one more dilapidated than the last. Somebody's crashed on this curve— three tiny crosses are strung with plastic carnations and road scrap. What a place to go. TALKING BIRD FOR SALE one sign says. FLATES FIXED, another reads, the childish letters gnarled like chicken claws. Armless shirts flap on a cord strung between pine trees, under which sits a heavy woman sucking a popsicle beside a boat motor hung off a busted lawn chair amidst ceramic rattlesnakes and pointy-boobed mermaids. A child roots at her feet. Lord God. Nothing makes sense. What on earth was *Peck* short for? How can a junior high principal call himself that and expect you not to get laughing sickness. Renee doesn't get it. Arkansas could jump in a goddamn lake, it makes her want to smoke cigarettes two at a time, cloves, Camels, wide muffler pipes. Everybody and their mother has cancer, is morbidly fat, or both. *Why-oh-why-oh-why* was she here. How long does it take to mail goddamn biopsy results fourteen miles? How long did it take to fall out of love?

Joey's oblivious. The trees are turning, a nip in the air, bourbon and cider weather. He's got money in his back pocket and it's thirty minutes 'til happy hour. He's a fencepost with a seatbelt strapped across its shoulder. Worse.

"After I die, don't you bury me here," Renee says. "You'd think we live in Mexico or Guatemala or some goddamn place."

Joey says, "Here we go."

Foliage blazes above a bevy of yard chickens—lit up yellow and gushing out the busted door of a fall-down barn, stepping glazed-eyed over blown off roof tins. "Burn me. Take my ass home to Maryland."

In the carseat behind them, two-year-old Lara says *peckerhead, peckerhead,*

peckerhead, the odd mantra she's picked up at CHILDHOOD DEVELOPMENT, INC., where the toddlers conduct afternoon *hot, hot* drills, marching through what all they'll do when Arkansas Nuclear One melts down out on Lake Dardanelle. *Boom-poof,* Renee pictures it, how her silhouette will burn into the middle school black board, room number one, a door down from homo Peck Titsworth and his buck-toothed secretary.

"Technically," Joey says, with that professor look he gets with wacky reading glasses half down his nose, "you wouldn't have an ass. Cremated, you'd be assless."

The Nissan jerks hard to the right, bucks over the road curb. "How was your day, sweetie," Renee says into the rearview. "Did you poo poo in the potty?"

"Watch where you're driving."

The Pathfinder rights itself between lines, and she gasses it. "The way these people go into conniptions about embalming. Peck's mother put in her will that her mouth's got to be formed into a smile, so everybody'll know she's happy with Jesus."

"Slow down."

"They'll have to sew hunks of plastic inside her gums to make that kind of smile."

Dusty Billingsley's donkeys have got loose. Two gnaw knee-high grass over at the Roach's bus stop.

"Slow the son of a bitch down or let me out."

Renee nails the brakes, sends the donkeys braying across the highway. A dead dog grimaces in the curbside ditch. "Fine," she says. "I knew you'd start. Go ahead, walk."

She sees him get smaller in the rearview, his mouth moving. Renee can't help it he's lost his license. He should have thought about those eighteen-year-old offenses before he dragged them to the *Natural State.* Anyway, who on earth could rack up three DWI's in one year? You'd have to stay snockered and chase cops twenty-four-hours-a-day. All of 1982—the year they'd started writing letters—he'd been knee-walking for an entire year. Skip bail and don't even go to court? Did the heat and ticks and pork and blue laws fuck up every last one of their brains? Had aliens flown down and interbred with these people? She'd have never licked a stamp had she known.

"I'd never marry *my* pen pal," the Captain had said. "Not without some sort of check. He might be a criminal, Renee."

"He didn't ask you Daddy. He asked me," she'd said. And that was that.

At least Joey'd finished college. At least he'd had the decency to make good on that promise while she spent her life thumbtacking bulletin board turkeys over last spring's leprechauns.

She pulls over and waits.

"Da?" little Lara says. "Where's Daddy?"

The radio plays a sweet hillbilly song about *drinking* and *thinking* and *teardrops a'sinking*, music from roadhouse taverns where rough-faced cowboys swept your body across sawdusted floors.

"He's right here, sweetie. Daddy's coming right here."

Joey climbs back in, buckles his seatbelt—a stone, dark matter, block ice. His temper's cooled, but it's still there—somewhere. Downwind, the dead dog smells like hell.

The three of them roll down 124 toward Moreland, through a cutoff loop where Billingsley's donkeys lope loose and randy, and the white horse glares at them just like always. Dust-covered blackberry briar shines down the gravel road. The Elliott boy from a quarter-mile down the road, has whomped their mailbox again. It leans cock-eyed with the silly little red flag bent half-in-two.

Joey gets out to retrieve the mail, where maybe there's a letter from Pope County Regional that says what happens next.

Through the windshield glass, their eyes meet, just for a second. The stupid woodpecker hammers a tree off in the back pasture, and a hundred yards off, their garage door *click-clacks* open.

"Welcome fucking home," Renee says. "Happy weekend to us."

Joey'd lassoed the Blue Heeler, driven it to the Pottsville pound where they shot a hypodermicful of air into the little thing's neck artery—too cheap, even, for decent drugs. Now, an hour into happy hour, Renee can't get that dog out of her head. They could've kept it. Fed it, taught it to fetch the morning Courier from the moron paper man, named it Bandit or some such and built it a little doghouse with a half-moon sawed above the Visqueen doggy door. It was a sweet dog. It liked biscuits. Damn Joey. Damn him to hell. Where did he get off being such an ass. No wonder his students threatened to blow up his truck in evaluations.

He's up in the barn hayloft with vodka tonic numero three. Twelve-gauge shotgun across his lap, still-hunting the skunk that's whelped under their air-conditioner pad. Afternoons before dinner, the skunk swaggers out into the back pasture where it roots up grubs and whatnot.

She sees him up in the loft. What on earth could anybody be thinking up there, smoking cigarettes and drinking Bartel vodka with a gun? What had the skunk done to deserve such tactics?

Big, fat raindrops thwack the deck boards. Killer's out jogging the road in nylon shorts. He's an engineer at the reactor. A sheet of plywood is nailed to a tree outside his back door. There, the life-sized bodies of a man and flowing-haired woman—holding hands for Christ's sake—are painted in fine, colorful detail. Both heads have been shot through many, many times. Blue sky pours through the vacant craniums.

Renee waves. "Hello fuckhead."

Not five minutes into the rain and the breeze is already ripe with house trash, a neighbor's couch, kerosened tires. These good country people and their tire-burnings. Out here, beyond trash collection, some bury but most burn.

Two days ago Renee'd found a little red light going off in the big dark room and a voice she'd like to choke saying—*Missus Harvell? Missus Harvell? This's Judy down to the lab. We've mailed your lab report. And I set you up an appointment with the surgeon. Call if you-ins need us. Bye, hon.*

Appointment with a surgeon?

She's dying, Renee knows it in her cells, has felt it all along, ever since the blazing humid day they got here.

"Those goddamn fires make me mad. They piss me to the core."

Down from the loft, Joey's given up skunking for today. He's about half happy, a little rain in his beard. "Renee?"

"What?"

"Tell me what you want to hear. I'll drive there right now and find out. You say."

"This fucks up our weekend. Doesn't it?"

"You want me to say yes?"

"Yes."

"Yes. Our weekend's fucked. Fucked to the gills."

A siren banjoes out on the main road where somebody's tire-fire has got too hot. Away somewhere, brush burns up a storm, you can smell it mixed with rubber in the wind. Little Lara comes blasting out the sliding glass, joyful, singing a song whose words bleed together. She straddles her trike and goes off riding into the yard. Night's not far now.

"You remember that dog? Little Bandit?"

"Bandit?"

"The dog you killed?"

"Killed?

"It was a sweet dog. We could have kept it. Why'd you kill the dog, Joey?"

It's dinner time, spaghetti tonight, hot bread, salad and cobbler. Then they'll watch whatever dumbfuck movie Joey rented at Price Chopper, and he'll fall asleep on the floor and make funny noises with his mouth open and the big ranch house will tick and settle and Renee will listen to her phone message in the dark. Lights would all be out by ten, Lara hugging her stuffed Piglet doll under the nightlight's glow. Christ.

"Good god, Renee."

"Good God what?"

"You hated it. Why do you say that. That I killed it?

Overhead, airbase planes from Jacksonville. At night they carve eerie circles overhead—light such as must come off the tails of comets. Lara pedals hard under the hickory trees, happy, shining faceful of her and Joey coupled.

"Joey?"

"What."

A gust whistles up under the deck, up under the slick black rocks where Renee saw a copperhead crawl that first nauseous morning here. The cicadas blasting all night long in the still heat. The fire, the dog, little Lara crawling the big empty floors. The Kennedy plane—John-John and his pretty blonde wife— had disappeared that weekend. And that Sunday, just a couple miles over in Dover, five bodies were dug up along Illinois Bayou. That first Sunday, out in the bitter-weed country, they'd exhumed five bodies and one was a little girl.

"What if I'm malignant?"

Joey wraps foil around a loaf of french bread. He says, "We're believing you're not."

"Why are you so goddamn mean to me?"

Joey stands at his end of the plastic table. It's almost dark, November in Arkansas.

"I'm making a salad."

Their daughter, two-year-old Lara, has managed to get herself into the red and yellow tree swing Joey hung from a high limb on a fresh August day when the big lawn had been mown, and all around was that sweet smell of summer about to end.

Out there, little Lara kicks both feet so the swing sways.

"*Me*," she squeals.

Before Renee ever got mixed up with Joey Harvell's kith and kin, when Arkansas was just a far off keyhole-shaped state with towns named Smackover and a hee-haw accent spoken by Honorable Earl Cleopatra, the Congressman she'd interned for on Capitol Hill, Renee'd danced naked on a beach somewhere between Nice and Monaco and believed herself pre-ordained for greatness. Rocketing toward her was some monumental task—a job for the ages. When it was time, she'd know.

Horseshit.

Renee hand rolls cigarettes in the basement. Forty-some milk jugs filled with well water line the walls, Joey's bozo precaution against the millennium catastrophe set to go down on New Year's Day. Above, dishwater sloshes through the drainpipe, down the long length of house from the kitchen to the side pasture where a septic tank gurgles beneath deep green grass.

A foundation wall divides the finished basement from a crawlspace entered by a withered plywood door that opens to pitch-black dirt and insecticide. The fume-stoned house inspector killed a hognose snake in there and left it lay. Renee pictures the pattern of color on its throat, the white-scaled underbelly, the little tongue lockjawed at the fork.

When big rains come, this room floods. The high-water mark is three feet above the concrete floor—a good six-inches higher than the electrical outlets, Renee sees. *Hazardous Voltage*, their circuit box says, *Will cause severe injury or death*. Outside, rain spackles the fall leaves. Injury and death, right under their beds. Under her daughter's bedroom. Does Joey understand? Electricity and water? Or, while she draws *K* for *Kangaroo* on blackboards for the bewildered, has her husband and the rest of the world gone entirely to the bonko?

Stacked on wood shelves around the foundation walls are mildewed boxfuls of her past life. The most explicit are magic markered with genius fabrications: *1984 Taxes* or *Seventh Grade Knitting* or *Notes on Tapestry*. Inside though, what she'd held onto, Joey'd shit bricks.

Renee splits the tape on a journal box masquerading as *Dactylology*—her Euro-journals from the year she graduated University of Maryland. Her and Cath and had spent one whole summer on Eurorail passes and hostel beds. Granada to Barcelona, then eastward up the sugary Med beaches where boys lit your cigarettes with their bright brown eyes on your bare flesh. She'd write nights by candlelight, her hand slurred by whiskey.

She sweeps the wispy tobacco off journal six, the handwriting raggedy-ass, suffering from ouzo: *August 12, ripped, the gaudy sky, Perseids the boy said, a meteor shower, no bullshit, sand in my mouth, dance naked, Jesus and Mary Chain now started*.

That August night by beach fire and lowtide surf, a little drunk, not bad, the two of them had stripped off road-sour garb and shaken hair down and danced for the world to come. They went at it, one-upped each other, hootchiecooed under this huge night sky with the Perseids zinging into the Mediterranean—how strange to be alive, breathing salt air, the strangest thing.

"Renee," Cath'd said, a breathful of lemon. "Don't see me. I'm not here."

At the edge of the night's fire ring, boys, three or four, hunkered, their eye-whites pink and glittering. They looked like boys. Beyond the waterline, boys watched them dance with gleaming eyes. The fine sand crunched between her teeth. Two barefoot tourist girls with tampons in their backpacks, gleaming shards of light in the breaking sea.

My life's pivot, Renee believed, something big comes my way. And she marked the moment, savored it, carried a baggie of beach sand so she'd never forget. It's there this second—locked in each glassy grain, the girl she was then. It's in every cell of her body. Even the one, no doubt, that the clinic woman had syringed out of her left breast last Tuesday.

Outside, Joey's silhouette at the barbed wire fence, Lara at his side, one big arm around her back. On tiptoe, she eases up behind them, close enough to touch, just barely. They gaze up toward Polaris, the little dipper where green and red lights just now creep.

"I'm not here," she says, gets Joey and Lara in a hug, her face against the fabric on their backs. "Don't see me."

The rain has stopped, low clouds breaking. Her husband exhales.

Above them hovers the still soundless light.

"Mommy? Will you die?"

The cry is sudden—Renee pulls her daughter tight. Joey says, *oh*, the three of them close now, safe in Mommy's arms. This is it, now she knows the worst.

An Air Force plane, surely, the experimental kind they try out over the Ozarks, it glows above them, becomes a fixed point, electric in the spider veins of tree leaf. In Utah there are desert roads through empty towns—all night the light turns yellow, red, green and wind gusts through the blue sage. This is like that, a vacuum, a hole in time.

8

Tuesdays, his day off, the ranch house creaks and settles, has a haunted feel and there's not enough light for Joey's taste, the long hallway with its little nail holes from the senior portraits of the Elliott's derelict kids stippling the too-dark paneling that opens into the great room's vaulted, beam-crossed ceiling, a stone hearth taking the entirety of the far wall, the pit's width enough for four-footers, of which Joey's chainsawed a good many before his unit busted, and this bright shiny November Tuesday a week from Thanksgiving he's expecting Larry Simms, the chimney sweep Dean Shock recommended with three shakes of a raccoon penis.

"He's eccentric," Shock had warned, raising the shriveled dick like a wand.

Country folk believed it was great good luck, coon penis, could summon rain during drought and heal impotence if your pecker was on the outs. "And he's cousins to Geno. For what that's worth." The dean raised bushy brows.

"Geno?"

"Simms," Shock said, "our mass murderer. Go ahead. Taste it. It's on the salty side."

Joey'd been warned—you weren't on the dean's good side until you'd tasted his raccoon's penis.

"No thank you, sir," Joey'd said. "But thanks." Renee was probably right, aliens had surely flown down and mixed seed with Shock's kind. Raccoon penis?

"We have a mass murderer?"

"Did," Shock said.

The coon penis bobbed in his right hand—about eight inches of shriveled dick. How folk could decide that such a thing was lucky—who'd be first at such a guess? Dean Shock wrapped the thing in red cloth, put it on a bed of papers in his desk drawer.

"Geno kept his wives in a compound out on Long Pool Creek. They found him eating Christmas dinner with a roomful of dead family. Standing rib roast—he'd cut everyone a slice."

Shock's voice had a lilt to it, feminine, almost, the wide vowels shining.

"Wives?"

"And a shitload of kids—some with his elder daughter."

"I've heard of it," Joey'd said. In Utah, some prophets married nineteen times.

Shock's desk has a picture of his wife on it, and another of a son in a sports jacket with a white flower on his chest. Beside the photos, a copy of his cookbook—a collection of Arkansas recipes from the Caddo and Quawpa to the present, the most exhaustive on earth. No doubt, a recipe in there for coon, instructions for detaching its member.

Shock said, "Right up your alley. Come back here from Texas." A big U. of A. ring shone on the hand that had held the penis. "But Larry's cool. He'll fix your wagon."

Ever after, even on the day he'd invite Joey to deliver the Mardi Gras lecture on southern conflict with Mormons, the dean kept his distance. Who did Joey think he was—turning down the penis?

Now, the farm's humongous woodpecker—a pileated big as a goose with a fierce red crest—a dinosaur of a bird goes off in a hickory out back. This far in the sticks, wild turkey strut right out of the woods and gobble-gobble across their land, and they've had to paint all the fenceposts purple—*Arkansas* for posted. The land has a feel to it, wild and wooly, unease in the shadows, steam rising at daylight from the soft earth down toward Isbel Creek. Joey keeps a fully loaded thirty aught six next to the Model 11 twelve gauge and .22 long rifle in the corner of his home office, a spare bedroom at the far end of the T-shaped house. There's a couple of pistols and some big-ass Buck knives stashed here and there. More than once he's got out of bed, searched the house with the Model 11's safety clicked off, flicking lights on room to room with a magazine full of number one buck ready to roll. Renee's convinced there exists a camouflaged figure she calls *Hunter Man* who surveils them day and night, says she can feel him out there scoping their windows.

Joey hears Simms crunch gravel before he sees the truck.

Frost shines on the well house. The leaves have started falling so there's more light, golden this time of year. There's a nip in the air, and it feels like when his old man would drag him and Jimbo to the Fordyce deer woods, the Walker dogs baying at first light.

"I been here before," Simms says, a wisp of silver-black hair blowing across his grizzled face. He offers a dirt-spackled hand, eyes blue as the sky at his back. He's tallish, decked out in a top hat and cutoffs. "I remember 'at well-house. Got a lightbulb run up her in case of freeze."

He points across the three acre front yard. Joey didn't know there was a lightbulb run up his well-house. The thought of a mass-murderer's cousin knowing this is unsettling.

"Yeah," Joey says. "This way."

Joey escorts the chimney sweep through the front door, down into the great room that ever smells of woodsmoke that's got into the carpets and curtains that stayed with the house when the Elliotts pulled out.

Simms nods, pulls a salt and pepper beard to his Adam's apple. "Hmmm," he says. "The Zimmerman deluxe."

"What's a Zimmerman?"

Joey follows the man through his kitchen, out the side door and through the open garage where his Rossignol downhill skies hang unused.

Simm's raises the lid on the tool box in the cab of a white Ford F-150, hauls out a clear milk jug full of water. "My well," he says, sloshes the water in the jug. "It's damn fine water. Already had some coffee this morning with color to it."

A shotgun lays in the gun rack, vented rib, a magnum, twelve probably. No road rage in Pope County, everyone driving around with a twelve-gauge behind their back. Joey'd grown up with guns, they didn't bother him.

Around the house's T, they walk to the big cedar deck where Joey's pissed a dead circle off the grass at the far end. The rollers on the sliding door are slow— he needs to soap them.

"Zimmy built this place," Simms says. "And that's the best fire pit in the world. Cousin Geno laid the stone himself. Care if'n I drive 'round to this deck?"

Joey says fine, "Let me know what you need," and the name—Geno—sticks with him. He's heard it before, Shock? Of a sudden, as if he's leapt there, Simms is on the roof, waves at Joey from the six-foot chimney which he stands upon astraddle.

"He's got the wind," Simms says, face to the sky. He flaps arms and dances foot to foot on the chimney lip. "What I need?"

Tracing a circle in the sweet country air, a red tail hawk whistles once, twice, the third time shrill and piercing. Sunlight catches the wingfeathers underside, goes light and dark, light and dark, so Joey will recount the event on three vivid levels.

"Need a lot of things," Simms shouts down from the roof, an extension cord dangling from his rotor-brush, zinging soot from the fireplace liner. "Seventy-fi' dollars. That's all I ast you for."

From ground-level, Joey surveys the property. The barn is a well-made structure with three stalls and a hayloft above, a tack room with an old chest freezer for all grain. The slope falls west to a creek lined with cedar beyond the wooded back pasture. He'd walked the perimeter of the ten-acre lot while Renee toured the house before making an offer. The realtor, who'd finagled it so he represented both buyer and seller, had said "You sure you want to do that?" because of the ticks and chiggers that didn't bother Joey a whit, because he'd grown up outside with a gun or rod or a crawdad stick in his hands, one of his people to the bone. Above, the rotor-brush zings sparks up out of the chimney masoned by a man who'd inpregnated his own daughter, the sound of it like a dentist drill when he was thirteen and Dr. Gorman had called Mama out in the hall and said in a dead cold voice, "You're dooming that boy to dentures, Ma'am." And she'd cried and bought him a blue leisure suit for Easter, a lime green one for Jimmy, the year O.W. came back from rehab in Florida, meek for a while. He worked his way up from sweeping warehouses to mechanic school, and finally he'd bought a gas station near Tipton manufacturing in Lonoke. Joey'd played guitar for a First Baptist Royal Ambassadors for Christ Youth then, and somebody who wished to stay anonymous had paid his way to Monarch Pass Colorado that spring break, so Joey'd snowskied in overalls, burned ass down the mountains and pissed his name into a blazing white snowbank at the headwaters of the Arkansas River. On the way home, the mountains this huge black backdrop the bus seemed to drag along behind, Joey'd snapped a Polaroid of the Rocky Mountains above

Leadville. He swore the blood oath that he'd come back, live in a log cabin and ski every day, the house high drifts cushioning his dreams for a long time. When he got home O.W.'d put him to work pumping gas and changing tires at the combo truck stop gas station. He'd learned to break down tires on the machine, how to patch the inside and plug the outside, the air rachet *rat-tat-tatting* lugnuts on and off, the smell of Go-Jo when he'd wash up in the bin that had once been white, but was now the color of bearing grease, watery rainbows swirling inside. Jimmy'd be right there with him, O.W. off having his sleep time during the heat of the day before riding up on his motorcycle, counting the money they'd taken in the register, sending them off for chicken fried steak and gravy at the truck stop restaurant where they got half price. There'd been a jukebox with the Eagles in it, this sad song about how we give up our hearts to the wind, and he and Jimmy'd shoot pool listening to the washing machines and dryers, chalk up the cues and play nine ball, until the hose went ding-ding, ding, and Jimmy'd walk out and start the windows, while Joey'd check oil, pump the tank full, and keep on not forgetting how he'd sworn the blood oath to get himself out of Lonoke.

Simms is inside now, giving it hell, grinding the iron tubes that bend with the hearth's contour—Joey sees him through the sliding glass, a black top hat bobbing above the flagstones. The day is bright and crisp and the omnipresent thumps issue from the dark wood across the street. The green grass under which the septic tank is buried is spongy. Horse hair flutters in a strand of the barbed wire fence, and paint's peeling off the satellite dish abandoned by the Elliotts. He doesn't know it but he's square on top of the Moreland Gas Field, remnants of an ancient alluvial fan where grew a rainforest. Crocodiles swam this very spot and once swooped down a winged pterdactyl after the sweet-meat mammal that would one day manifest through the genes of Joey and Simms and Titsworth, and mass murdering Geno, even.

He'd ended up dating Dr. Gorman's daughter, the dentist who'd made his mama cry. And he'd think of that afternoon when blood had leaked down his throat, the coppery taste of it, and the cold voice in the hallway, *you're dooming that child to dentures.* He'd think of that when he french-kissed Gorman's cheerleader daughter, Rhonda, how her tongue found its way to the empty socket.

Why all this comes to him while the chimney sweep does his thing, what tongue can tell? There's a nip in the air, chili weather.

When it's done, the two men stand on the back deck and Simms instructs him on using the Zimmerman deluxe, when to turn on the extensive blowers, how low to turn the air intakes, and how to use the chute in the bottom of the hearth, a dump system that sends ash into the pit cousin Geno built below.

"Your cousin?" Joey asks.

Simms nods.

"Stone mason for this house?"

"Yep. Damn fine work."

Joey turns the thought one way then the other. The redtail's back, she circles above, a high whistling above the treetops. What would this place, his small family, look like, seen from such a vantage. Grandmother Dee dreamed of flight, said the power lines were hell. And now Lara, his daughter dreams of flying. His hearth? A killer set their stones?

Simms asks for the money. "And don't worry. I checked that pit. Ain't no bones down there to speak of."

9

On a rough-hewn and much storied table before the fire in Great Coon Hall, spread upon the front and subsequent pages of *The Weekly Warlock: News From the Hector Specter,* the Mardi Gras Lupercalia fish fry steams. Grease has got on a clown-faced woman who sits on the hood of a silver Trans Am, her welcome home parade from Ringling Brothers Barnum and Bailey Southern Edition. Seated at the head, beneath the silver tines of a Boone and Crockett citation Whitetail, Adam's apple bobbing as he clears his throat for the silence before the oath, a little red in the face, Honorable Dean Fancher Shock. To his left, tugging an arm through the sleeve of a High Coon gown, Reverend Roy Dale Shoates who'll offer the prayer between snorts, and beside him, Herkey Waymack—the Dover dentist who sometimes brings a tank of the good stuff to huff during guitar jam after supper. Sherif Autrey and Alderman Waylow belly up to the right, and there, beside Shoates, sits the night's speaker, Joey Harvell, new Asst. Professor to Georgina's beleaguered History Department over to ArkaTech. His specialty—*Southern Conflicts Involving Mormons*, of which there is a great good many, it turns out. His guitar leans in the great Coon den, a D-28 for Jesus' sake.

Rusty Love mopes across from Dr. Harvell, his hair uncut and unwashed, looks like, from the day it happened 'til now. He's got it bad, Paris can tell, maybe been into the bad shit. *Crank*, his peckerwood boy calls it—what the backwood boys are cooking now that drought's made them give up sinsemilla. Across from him, face darkened with chimney dust, Larry Simms. A pine knot bursts in the fireplace. Shock throws it an evil look, goes on. Paris scans the whole lot from the kitchen door, his ear to a batch of hushpuppies going gold in the deep fryer.

"Your right hands," Shock says. His voice always surprises. It's not what you'd expect from six-foot Doverite, a man of position, a dean, rightly feminine sounding, a girl's lilty vowels rolling off his tongue. Shock raises a big speckled hand with a gold ArkaTech ring glittering on the ring finger. All up and down the long table the right hands go up—some heavily calloused and ragged nailed, oil-stained and concrete spattered, some the size of split chickens, hands that had grasped and mastered the use of tools, that'd broken noses and backhanded smartass mouths, whose prints could be found on carburetors and ball joints, jackhammers and slick-blued 44's, the necks of mandolins and bourbon bottles, and others soft-white as underbelly, clean-nailed and lotioned, the cuticles tucked under and sweet-smelling, and the blue-black fists of Dr. Darquah Banchie, whose fingers had pecked out a book proclaiming the Negro Jesus, Negro Abraham and Negro Moses and Negro Virgin Mary—*Africans of the Bible*, he calls it. Paris's own hands are toughened by shovel and hoe handles, one long row, his life.

Shock unfurls the calf hide, reads the words.

Paris lays hand on his heart, swears the oath again, its odd combination of fire and brimstone—like the Bible with cusswords, their own *Lamb's Book of Life* for the here and now. He himself has never met a Mormon, wouldn't know if one walked up and shook his hand, though word is they sport horns, little sharpened tails, marry nineteen wives young as they want and have these big all night parties where they, all of them, get in bed for two weeks at a time, holy Jesus. Paris has heard tell of what happened at New Harmony, Utah Territory to Captain Fancher and Captain Baker, how on September 11, 18 and 57 the sons-a-bitches killed a whole wagon train of Johnson, Pope and Yell County folk. And he knows how this very year marks the 144th year—a holy and biblical number prophesied by High Coon hisself, and how Vengeance with a capital V will soon rain down and the appointed day draweth nigh.

Shock spits out the good part, which the whole table repeats with vigor, Darquah Banshie's booming voice like the African Moses siccing his snakes on Pharoah's candy-ass serpents, about to part the Red Sea and swallow up the sons of Egypt.

"Amen," Reverend Roy Dale Shoates says, hard to slur that word.

Amen, the collective voice says. And it's done.

Paris adds the puppies to the mix, pours iced tea all around, adds a hickory slab to the fire, while taking stock of Harvell's guitar case, black, C.F. Martin embossed in hard plastic. He sits at the end nearest the kitchen. The last of the purple hull peas goes round, no more 'til summer.

"I been to his house 'afore."

To his right, Judge Goodno, the bushhogger, who some call *Nogood*.

"Back pasture's got the soft spots to it."

A plateful of crappie sallies by. Paris forks the top fillet, sops some tartar on his plate and a lemon wedge. Slaw's already got under his homemade filling—*seepage*, Dr. Waymack calls it.

"He thought a hunnert was too high, but I told him how I got upkeep on that Kyboto. All that joltin' and rattlin'. You listening to me, Paris?"

Paris nods, chews. Somebody missed a bone, but that's okay. The white flesh is moist and good—hard to beat deepwater crappie. And Goodno's not all bad, just partly, playing the hillbilly with a bank account like a Wal-Mart millionaire.

"Joltin' and rattlin'. That's what happen when they go off to University. Think they shit don't stink. Piled higher and drier, Ph.D., I always heard."

"Haw," Paris says.

"Haw," says Goodno.

Shock is standing, introducing the Harvell boy whose granddaddy was none other than Marion Weldon Stepwell who folk called Si, a semi-famous guide down to Shangra-La on Ouachita, a one-legged man who'd owned the state record for largemouth for a time, and run a half-dozen duck clubs including QuackShack outside Stuttgart, fowl capital of the world, where Frank Broyles and the starting Razorback D had signed the shower stalls. He'd been an Honorary High Coon, Si Stepwell, and his grandson bears him some resemblance it's been said, the hooked nose and tendency to take a nip. The boy could shoot straight, if you could believe what you heard, and he can play the blue pee out of the Martin D-28, just now leaned fireside. Edgar's eyed it—what he'd give to get his hands on that instrument, slide his fingers up to the high E on the rosewood neck. He's held a Nazareth-made Martin, the sweet spruce top, mother-of-pearl inlay on its frets.

Middle of the table, the bearded boy stands up, nods.

"Doctor Harvell," Shock says, pretty as you please. "Our speaker, as you know, is professor of History over to ArkaTech, where his specialty has to do with *momans*."

A collective hiss rises with the word. Ronnie Love's eyes roll back in his head—his ears go red.

"He's here tonight to speak of the white flag treachery," Dean Shock says. "Kindly give him what he deserves as an Honorary."

Mean as a snake, carrier of the raccoon penis, High Coon, how does Shock he get away with that womany voice?

Doc sits, and it's real quiet like a church, only a church with a fire burning in it before the snakes come out and heads get anointed with oil and the holy ghost shit breaks aloose, when the bleached-blonde preacher's daughter gets down on the tremolo of her hot-pink flying-V so holy ghost spirit amplified through a 100 watt Marshall singes the air. That's how it feels, which strikes Paris queer. Why would it feel that way now? What's up? Tornado season's on them—Paris can sense them spawning, but his radar's clear now. How come?

There's a spattering of applause and Harvell shakes a handful of papers in front of his chest, pushes reading glasses up his nose and takes a breath. Across from the table, Rusty Love hasn't touched a bite, not a snippet, nor sipped his sweet tea. Ain't buttered a puppy. Ain't even squeezed the lemon. Sits there with eyes rolled back, pathetic, all wrapped up in guilt and sorrow with a side of rage. Somebody ought to rip his rompers, put his head straight.

"There exists a long-time enmity," Harvell says, "between Arkansawyers and Mormons."

More of that gospel-laden quiet, like when he was a boy at Lonoke County Fair in the tent with Gorilla woman and the moon shone through the ripped zipper, before she bent the bars and leapt among them.

"I speak to deeds of carnage and strife."

Carnage and strife? From the hilltop Paris envisions a lightning struck tree, outside the long chicken house where arm-thick rattlers writhe a-suck on a mound of rotten eggs from his childhood.

"Of murder and mayhem."

A murmur, something like a murmur, a trembling rises up from the floorboards. Paris feels it through both soles, tastes seepage on his tongue.

"What I'm saying," Harvell says, that preacher's voice with *I know and you don't* wrapped around it, "is that that day at Mountain Meadows is at its base a temple to guile and deceit, betrayal and murder."

Only the murmur's not coming from the floor—the source is a person, one of them at the table about to explode, or implode, Paris gets them mixed.

"Captain Fancher waved a white flag. They head-shot his daughter. Right in front of him. With the white flag waving."

"You don't *mean* it."

Rusty Love—first words out of mouth all night, hell, all month. He's leapt to his feet, flipped his plate plumb over. "You don't *mean* it," he repeats, fire in his meth-red eyes.

Harvell stabs the air across from Rusty Love's face with his right index finger.

"Yes I do," he says. "Poteet saw."

Each syllable is a finger jab.

10

East of Fort Smith, Highway 40 takes Renee through a quarter known as River Valley, flood plain laid down between national forests, the Ozarks to the north and Ouachitas to the south, land with a gentle wave to it, sweetened by ancient floods so soy and milo and rice fields grow fecund for a long season and there's always water to siphon because the river's near with its barges and tugboats honk-honking, and backyard gardens bearing heirloom tomatoes—Arkansas Traveler, Hillbilly, Mortgage Lifter, Cherokee—ripening alongside the purple hull peas Joey goes ape about, okra, butternut and crookneck, hot peppers and cucumber out the kazoo, Hope melons the size of Volkswagens, only not now, November 23rd of her fortieth year, sunny day of the Full Frost Moon, there's not a lousy green bean to be had at Price Chopper save canned or frozen or the ones ground up in jars for babies and toothless people, which there's no shortage of here in the Natural State. En route from Florida this second, her parents could score some beans before crossing the River of No Return, only her dad won't answer his cell while driving and Meg doesn't know how. She'll call from Russellville middle, leave a message for green beans, a whole bushel, slivered almonds and good chocolate. And don't forget liquor—that's important when you cross the River of No Return, bring a barge of liquor, and watch out for the law, because if you've bought say a case of wine, twelve six-dollar bottles in a cardboard box, and the law pulls you over in Pope County, then you're officially bootlegging and they'll impound your car, revoke your license and lock your ass away in a cell full of walk-ons from the set of *Deliverance,* only worse because this is no movie. It was all too much, but *at least* she wasn't dying. *Thank you, God. Thank you, thank you.* The news had sent a tingle down her spine, all the way to her toes and back up to her heart. Renee lets out a breath, downshifts into the last of the curves before town. At least she would not breathe her last here, not in this place, some purpose—a task for the ages—hurtles toward her. She senses it now, just around the bend.

A razorback hog grimaces from the bumper sticker on the blue pickup in front of her, all the live-long-way from Moreland to the turn off by Whattaburger, at one of the town's five red lights. Russellville Middle sits adjacent to Russellville High which, in turn, is just down the road from ArkaTech, an island of college buildings, the signature of which is a shining white cupola growing up out of a cow pasture, beyond which lay Lake Dardenelle swelling from the dammed Arkansas, heated six full degrees by Nuclear One, spouting its omni-present cloud of steam.

"Hot-hot," Lara says from her carseat, a note of concern in her sweet little voice. "Hot-hot."

"Yeah, sugar. Hot-hot won't hurt us." She's speaking into the rearview mirror where her daughter's face shines, the same hazel eyes as her mother's. "I won't let it."

A guy in a blue Chevy passes her and smiles—thinks she's been talking to him, moron.

"Tank you," Lara says.

"Thank you, sweetie."

Joey gets a discount at *Cow Jumps Over The Moon Daycare,* where a sweet black lady always waits for Lara, has a bowl of oatmeal with butter melted in it, and brown sugar with cinnamon sprinkled on top, only today the whole place is surrounded by Russellville cops, lights swirling. One has a megaphone to his mouth, while another diverts traffic.

Renee powers a window down. "What's going on?" she asks a woman whose red-haired daughter is Lara'a playmate from class.

"It's Tubbs," the woman says. Her radio's on a talk station—Renee hears it through the window, vile, mean-spirited, godawful stuff—who in their right mind can start the day out with such invective? "He's taken Mildred hostage again. She's his wife." From the carseat in back, the little red-headed girl squeals at Lara, throws a sippy-cup at the back of her mommy's head, smiles a wicked two-toothed smile. "It'll blow over directly."

A cop with a flat-top cuts them a look and motions her to park, and that's what she does because Renee's learned to do whatever cops out here say—they mean business. He spins on a boot heel and motions to the next car, pistol butt shining.

Five minutes later, the coast is clear and she leaves Lara in the arms of the strange lady of color whose one blue eye seems all-knowing, like it recognizes Renee for what she is on the inside, what's coming her way. Maybe its the cheese grits Joey's sold her on. Russellville Middle has a bright red American flag flapping beside one with a diamond on it. Peck's Lexus is cross-parked under the diamond flag, so nobody can dent it with a car door.

Bagful of graded papers in one hand, and a paper sack lunch in the other, she's tempted to key the door, leave a stripe right down the entirety of the driver's side. He's in there looking, no doubt. What else does a middle school principal have to do but stand at his window and watch his car under the flapping stars and bars before Thanksgiving break.

Today's half-a-day and her kids arrive in various stages of disarray. All morning they trace handprint turkeys onto multi-colored construction paper which gets thumb tacked up to the bulletin board under the block letters Renee's arranged to say WOBBLE WOBBLE GOBBLE GOBBLE. Her third graders absolutely love tracing hand turkeys, only one traces his middle finger, tacks it up on the board and gets sent to Principal Titsworth after the whole bunch of third graders hop up and down flipping each other the bird.

When the bell rings at noon, Renee eats a sandwich in her car. Peck doesn't even see her, driving off that huffy way in his Lexus. Her parents are due in tonight, and she has that feeling she had as a girl when she first saw her Navy captain father's boat gleaming way off port, closer and closer, until appeared the white flag with a big number 1 on it, the symbol between them for *I love you.*

Buying a bottle of wine, say a low end Cabernet, nothing fancy, just happy hour combo pizza night dinner wine, necessitates a drive through Moreland on Highway 164, two lanes for the ten miles over to Oak Grove, where a right turn heads south on Arkansas 105, a two-lane blacktop that crosses Isbel Creek and half-dozen colorful hippy houses and Tri-County Coon Club before climbing toward Carrion Crow Mountain where gutted house trailers have horse heads stuck out the windows and junker Chevys really do sit on concrete blocks just like some seed tick movie, past a hillside of leafless blackjack where lawn ornaments and a For Sale sign glitter in the fall noon sun, on out to Atkins, pickle capital of the world with its own parade featuring Miss Pickle driven around on the hood of a black Trans Am, where Interstate 40 seems like the Autobahn all the way to Blackwell, just over the county line in Conway County, which is wet, where two barn-sized liquor stores have full parking lots any time of day, and the attendants have sawed-offs hidden under the counters, and eye you in mirrors strung in the corner of the wine section. Renee hoists two cases of Chilean red into her cart along with a couple half gallons of Bartel vodka and a case of Tacate. President Black-Brown, from Arka-Tech, is rumored to shop here, as does Reverend Roy Dale Shoates, and Sheriff, everybody ends up here, sooner or later.

"You have a good one now," the clerk says, snapping the Pathfinder backdoor shut on the haul of booze. "Watch out for smokey."

"Smokey?"

"Gumball machine," the clerk says, tracing a halo in the air above his head.

Renee's not surprised by anything, not anymore. Not in the least. Today's a Tuesday. She was born on a Tuesday. Tuesday's child is full of grace. She turns 40 next month. Aliens—the *ET* variety—are night-hovering over her house, probably slipping down the chimney and going through her underwear—their little ET fingers glowing. Her husband has brought them here from Utah where he'd managed the doctorate, despite the scornful Latter Day Saints. This is the place, home now.

How now brown cow had she let this happen?

After they'd met, that flurry of a week at Easter time in Fayetteville, on her last day Joey'd driven her out to the White River, brought a basket of wine and cheese, grapes and cantaloupe and chocolate, and they'd picnicked at a bend where skinny-dippers frolicked, bare-assed college kids from UA in the cold clean water. A king snake had wended out from a rock ledge, dragging a bright skein of almost shed skin, and Joey'd taken it as a sign. She knew nothing about him really, but she'd wanted to believe that he was who she'd been looking for, five years of letter writing, the gaps between the seasons of that odd long-distance conversation, that started and stopped when she'd least expected. He was handsome enough, and funny, and had a wild streak a mile wide, that was sure, but weren't all southerners like that?

Anthony Cleopatra, House Rep for Arkansas's Second District certainly was, how he'd hired her and taken her club-dancing the first week, his Capitol Hill office full of colorful folk, syrupy-voiced eccentrics who pined for barbecue and moonpie. She'd worked the congressional aid gig far as it would go, got to wine and dine with Ronald Wilson Reagan, who Cleopatra claimed was the anti-Christ because the letters of his names counted to 6-6-6, and the beast would be known by its name.

Joey'd shown up at her apartment in Adams Morgan on a night she was out in Georgetown and came home to find him in her living room, her roommate a little shocked on the couch, listening to a Velvet Underground album about halfway through "Sweet Jane" at the instant she walked in. She'd maybe known, or maybe not known he was coming, but there he was—he'd sold his shit—with two typewriters and a backpack, a little high from the guy he'd met on the plane whose girlfriend had picked them up at Dulles with weed and whiskey, driven him straight to her front door. They'd just rented a flat at 12th and N when Joey's brother, Jimmy, died in a one-car crash. When Joey returned from the funeral, she was pregnant. By him. A baby was out of the question. Her child would not be a stand-in for his dead brother. The event does not get spoken of, not ever. She simply does not think about it. How he'd gone berserk, after. How the scar on the back of her head aches when a storm is coming. Whether it was a boy or girl? If it had Lara's eyes? If it knew?

He somehow talked her into moving to Arkansas that first time, and on the way out of D.C., just beyond the beltway, their U-Haul had caught fire. He'd forgot to disengage the parking brake, Joey. Just past Falls Church, they'd watched it burn—*Adventure In Moving* written in big black letters on back, all lit up in flames. A trucker swerved in and leapt from his cab with a fire extinguisher and put the trailer out, and UHaul had hauled out another unit they repacked beside Old Highway 66, the smell of burnt wires and paint on the bed where she was conceived, a faint whiff, even, on the shoe box full of swimming medals and hair clippings and love letters from her life up 'til then.

Later, she'd draw horns and a moustache on Carole King's *Tapestry*, the album of her life up 'til Joey, "Where You Lead, I Will Follow," sandwiched between "You've Got A Friend" and "Will You Still Love Me Tomorrow."

11

The afternoon the Rockersons are to arrive and so initiate Joey's first holiday back in the Natural State, they walk the path into the shady wood across Barton Road where the neighbor's four-wheelers have cut waffle tracks. There's the good smell of fallen leaves and the sunlight has that gold tint to it that will ever remind Joey of opening day deer hunts down in Fordyce—him, O.W., Jimmy—eating beans out of a can, cheap-ass sleeping bags thrown padless on the ground so they'd wake with frost in their hair, tromp off to tree stands to watch the world wake anew, shake itself off and come to life. It was the sort of November afternoon—family arriving soon to eat, drink and be merry in the big farm house, with its great room and table set for ten—when the world felt right, and coming home to Arkansas to gather his people for the feast was a great, good thing to have pulled off, surely. How wily Odysseus must have felt the hours before he strung the bow and slew the suitors and the maids who'd slept with them to retake his house and home and people and birthright. He's made it home, bygod. Joey Harvell has remade himself and is home to claim what's his.

Between Joey and Renee, little Lara. She holds each of their hands and sometimes they swing her way out in front of them, so she squeals as they make their way into the wood, off in front of them the occasional flash of a whitetail, squirrel chatter, and the omnipresent *thumpa-thumpa-thump* from who knows what resonating off blackjack and hickory. In the periphery, a flame-headed woodpecker swoops tree to tree. Back home, Joey's made a stew. There's fresh bread and a garden salad. The larder's loaded with wine and liquor and a cobbler cools on an oven rack. Tonight is full Frost Moon. And the light will shine down on the stones not twenty miles distant, Solgahatchia where his people lay on a hill overlooking a lightning-struck tree.

An old logging trail kept passable by four-wheelers, the path winds into the wood where sound comes from the earth itself. They step into a circle of light, littered with broken beer bottles and grease tubes, scraps of newspaper and a scattered deck of playing cards with naked women on them. A heartbeat thud fills the air, *thump-thump, thump-thump, thump-thump* issues from the tin-draped platform before them. The three of them stand before it. The inner workings are hidden, but on the topmost gleaming sheet, big hand-painted letters spell out AJAX.

"What on earth?" Renee walks to the foot, touches it.

Joey's dumbstruck, as if they've walked up on some forty-foot God in the midst of the woods, speaking the strange and familiar language of Gods. "Gas," Joey says, at the same time he smells it. "It's a gas pump."

Lara's found a rusty mattress frame off in the bushes, jumps up and down on it so the thing squeals. Arrows are stuck in a carved heart on a tree across the dumped on circle, four in all, red-feathered as if they'd been gleaned from the clean air by hand and set into the heart as some sign of what had happened or was going to happen.

"Cool," Renee says.

The pump whishes and thumps, whishes and thumps.

"It's like our own secret fort."

"Want fort-fort," Lara squeals.

Inside the well-housing, knifed-open cans of pork'n'beans lay in a heap, a couple Slim Jim wrappers and a empty Boonesfarm bottle. Unbeknownst to Joey and Renee, the Barton clan had long ago sold all the gas and oil rights down the river, and their farm, this second, sat in the heart of the ancient deposit, gaseous remnant of a time when forty-foot crocodiles swam the swamp-infested bayous and no light reached the ground save in the season of fire, when the long drought came and the earth dried as will happen eon to eon, when the Ozarks and Ouachitas were towering glaciate Himalayas and the ancient rivers ran reverse of today's course, so one day hunks of Ouachita quartzite would shine in Utah mud.

"Someone's been living in there." Joey pulls one of the feathered arrows from the carved heart. "Up to no good," he says and they leave AJAX thump-thumping behind, walk back up the wood trail, light filtering through tree limbs.

A fox squirrel leaps onto the path, and then the fork of a redbud, barking. "Mines. Fort. No," Lara wails.

The Rockersons are near now—Cap and Meg, on the heels of happy hour. Thanksgiving's in two days, a twenty-pound bird thawing in the refrigerator. The thought has thunked his head that they should reconfirm their vows, him and Renee. That he'll ask Cap for Renee's hand in marriage, just like he should have done the first time, and that the old man could play preacher and Meg could serve as her daughter's bridesmaid, little Lara a bedazzled flower girl. Sometimes these ideas weevil through his skull into his head, he is half Stepwell after all, though this one seems solid.

A ways north, dust rises from the 164 turnoff. They hear the gravel crunch of a slow moving vehicle. "They're here." Renee says it so that happiness, downright joy rings in her voice—rare since their arrival.

"*Meemaw and Poppy*," Lara sings, and they step from the wood into light.

That first night, Joey wakes on the leather couch in the huge den, buttressed beams dark against the cathedral ceiling, and the whole room lit up by the fierce pale light of the Full Frost Moon which pours in through every window, magnified by a power of ten through the double sliding doors where Renee has hung heavy curtains so deer hunter man can't look straight in on them at supper time. Stones hewn from the back pasture form a glittering hearth along the entirety of the west wall. It is as if Joey has woken up in someone else's house which, God knows, has happened oft enough, especially back in the day, not that he's a teetotaler now, far from it, but he was different then, before he met this woman—who he'd proposed to this very night.

Thirteen years earlier, she'd stomped into his life like a freight train from the heart. He'd dropped out of college then and was living at the end of his rope, eyeing the scoped thirty aught six that leaned beside the bedroom window, out of which you could see the Arkansas Ozarks, a wide swath of new-green climbing to Old Main where a mile of sidewalk was imprinted with the names and degrees of graduates from across the ages. The shuttle *Challenger* had blown up that January on national television, so pretty space-teacher Christa McAuliffe had exploded in front of her homeroom fifth graders on a T.V. somewhere in Virginia. The evil of this last thing was just too much. This was Fayetteville springtime, Easter Sunday, the air drunk with flowery love.

"Are you *him?*" she asked, after three feisty knocks on my screen door, a shimmering jonquil tucked behind an ear.

Renee had gazed across the living room into the bathroom where, shirtless, and in jean shorts, Joey was just then scrubbing the toilet. They looked at each for a moment, her framed by blue sky and him on the floor in Comet dust.

"No," Joey'd said. "I'm not.

"You." She laughed.

He'd heard the voice three or four times over the last four years, late-night phone calls between college towns when she'd be liquor-breathed and he could hear her smoking.

"You're early."

"You're late," she said.

Joey shut the bathroom door, heard her voice in the living room just as he turned on the hot, ran a piece of floss through his front teeth and washed his hair.

"Happy Easter," he yelled. And then, "He is risen," though that immediatly felt stupid, who knew what to say?

When he finished, there she was on the couch, reading a signed copy of *In the Land of Dreamy Dreams*, with its cover painting by the wife of a Fayetteville poet who'd shot himself in the head and had *his* tombstone inscribed *Piss In My Face, Just Don't Tell Me It's Raining*.

"You never wrote me that you did toilets, Joker. I like that."

Renee'd toured France the year before. He'd gotten a postcard with a picture of a topless woman on a pink-sand beach. "Men keep offering to light my cigarettes," she'd written on the flip-side.

"You have a suitcase?"

"We should do something. Ceremonial. Or something?"

"This is my house."

"Are you a lunatic?" She looked straight through him, the first time he ever saw her eyes and her face together, how they caught the light. "Daddy said I should've had you checked."

She looked him in the eye.

"No. I'm not," Joey'd said, only a half lie, maybe.

"Good."

She led him to a brand new Pontiac convertible, her rental, parked on Hill Street, just up from the Purina plant where men were always monkeying around with the loud speaker, calling out each other's wives' names, feigning the sounds of intercourse.

"I got lost in Missouri," she said. "And I had to pee so bad. Missiouri will always be having to pee real bad."

"Missouri? You mean Oklahoma."

The screen door banged behind them and he showed her to the bedroom with its queen-sized cherry wood bed his Mama'd sent up from Lonoke.

"It's all the same," she said, "these keyhole shaped states."

"I'm taking the spare," he'd said. "You know where the bathroom is."

She'd looked clean through him again, who'd come a thousand miles to him that day. "This is where it starts," she said. "Goodnight, Joe Harvell."

The night before she left, they'd sat on a blanket spread over the grassy slope in his backyard. It was dark and clear, the sort of late spring evening in Fayetteville when the night sky shimmied out into space and he'd felt drunk with love. The air was cool and fragrant with spring flowers and the odor that wafted up from the Purina dog food plant down past Brenda's Bigger Burger on Highway 71. She smelled like oranges. Once she'd written about driving her grandmother's ashes to the old home place in Philippi, West Virginia. How they'd rented a Lincoln Continental and filled it with flowers and dressed for funeral, only the countryside was so beautiful, and joy had somehow worked its way in despite Grandma's ashes.

Cool to the touch, the thirty aught six lay unloaded, the three-to-nine scope's lens shining. "Look through this," he said. "It's Jupiter. You can see the four moons."

She sat there, quiet as stone, the starlight on her face. He could hear her breath. It was a heavy gun, a gift from Si that smelled of gun oil and tobacco. Last

November, down at Camp Fordyce, he'd neck-shot a spike buck, then followed the blood trail.

"I should leave. This second."

"It's unloaded."

"No such thing."

Awkwardly, she'd lifted the deer rifle, set the scope's rubber gasket against her right eye. The steel butt found her shoulder and her hand closed around the stock. Her index finger curled into the trigger guard. Starlight poured into the white of her eye. She braced the thing against a knee, the barrel wavering.

"I see," she whispered. Her *s* hissed against the false front tooth—she'd knocked the real one out as a girl skating on pond ice. "Galileo's moons. Me as a stick-figure. Here's me smoking while I run ten miles. You're a pimply-faced nerd, Joe. Aren't you."

"Our first letter. You see that?"

She clicked the safety off—just like that, a sound you remember.

"Here's one of your poems, "Night Dreams in Logic Class."

He said, "Put the safety back on."

When she pulled the trigger, the empty chamber slammed shut, a metallic clang echoing down Hill Street. He'd unloaded the gun on a cold night, buried the shells in a backyard hole, the taste of its cold steel slicking teeth and tongue.

"You're crazy."

She said, "Missouri."

Next morning, she was gone. The Pontiac convertible with leather smelling seats was gone. He'd walked from room to room visualizing what had happened. On her pillow, a crisp $50 shined up at him. Written in frail blue across U.S. Grant's face—*Meet me for the Cherry Blossom Festival. Can you?*

Spring light filtered through his window onto the floor where a forgotten sock lay. A dent in the corner marked where the gun had leaned, where the steel sight had dug in. Lint flitted through the shafts of light, went crazy with a blown breath. It got real quiet.

The whole thing, from their first writings until then, was a test, the fork in his road. The fifty between Joey's fingers was real, the blue words *meant* something, the question demanded an answer.

And there was something else: just before sunrise, as he felt her living heart beat against his, the songbirds erupted—goldfinches and warblers and common sparrows, a great bewildering wall of sound had fluted over them. "*Holy-moly,*" Renee'd said, and the high notes trilled through his house and heart.

Love wins. And if you can believe *this*, you can believe anything.

Only not tonight. After the stew and boozy road stories, after little Lara had been gushed over and the dishes were done and shining in the drainer, after the tour of the trophy house and the Rockerson's clothes were hung up in the guest room closet, with all that needed saying between them broached or avoided, Joey asked Cap for his daughter's hand in marriage.

"Guess you need to ask her first," Cap said. He'd captained three destroyers, was up for admiral on his last tour.

Meg looked down at him from a chair at the dining table.

"What if she says no this time?" she asked.

12

Edgar T. Paris witnesses history from three chairs away—close enough to have scoured upon his senses for all time—the snap of teeth, bone breaking, the pitiful cry and blood fountain that follows. Harvell drops his papers, looks from one end of the table to the other, then back at Love. Since his little girl got dug up in her sunflower pj's out on Illinois Bayou, Ronnie's been a mess. Word is he's turned from snorting to smoking that shit the shiners have switched to making. The wife's called Sheriff Autry out a time or two, sporting shiners and fat lips, spitting blood.

Dr. Harvell surveys the table, one end to the other, as if he waits on someone to intervene on his behalf. "He talking to me?"

The fire hisses and pops. The fish is getting cold.

"What I mean to say is that the incident at Mountain Meadows, our folk were murdered, stripped, thrown in a hole."

"You don't *mean* it," Ronnie Love says.

Edgar sees light glittering in the glass eyes of the mounted deer, carnival red, and he remembers once when he was in a semi-rig with his daddy and they'd witnessed a Tilt O'Whirl being hauled on a flatbed trailer at hot tail end of August, the vermillion glare, how it shone fiercely through space and time.

"What do you mean I don't *mean* it?"

A wood knot bursts in the fireplace, and Edgar worries that Harvell's leaned his D-28 too close, that a stray coal will burn through the hard shell case of that handmade instrument from Nazareth, Pennsylvania and that it will incinerate the Indian rosewood before he can ever lay the throat into his palm, make fingers into the sweet low E that so suits his singing voice.

It happens fast.

When he remembers what comes next, that's how it starts.

The wood knot.

He thinks about the guitar, the rosewood neck, the sweet-E hammered to a *7*.

Harvell jabs the crooked index finger he'd once broken in a slammed men's room stall door while cribbing notes for a history test in Old Main up to the University, so that his was an identifiable appendage with an x-ray trail, he jabs that finger into Ronnie Love's face. At Ronnie, who's got this Hell's Angels—Pale Rider-on-crank face, about to open the seventh seal, spill loose the scorpions and poison toads.

"*You don't mean it.*"

"You talking to me?" Harvell says it, jabs the finger in Love's face.

Love's answer is more sound than word, a noise everyone present will remember as important, though none will ever reproduce it, nor wish to in this world.

In one fluid motion that surprises everyone at the table for the rest of their lives, in a move that will be retold until the Tri-County Coon Club becomes synonymous with the act that follows, and the phrase "he *Loved* him" comes to be understood as a metaphor for the very act that transpires before their eyes, just after Joey Harvell jabs his semi-famous finger, the man opposite him explodes to his feet, flips a full platter of untouched crappie fillet, hushpuppies and slaw. Harvell looks through professor glasses and points his finger into the face of Love gone ballistic. Ronnie, who's leapt onto the table, brings his face near, shows teeth.

Harvell points the index finger of his right hand, the tip tobacco-stained just inside the nail. Paris remembers that, the half-moon stain.

"I'm sorry about Shiloh. I'm sorry you lost your daughter."

And that instant, in front of the High Coon and all the brethren come to partake of the holy rites of the Lupercalia Mardi Gras fish fry supper with motivational speaker and guitar music to follow, Ronnie Love opens his mouth wide so teeth and the dark inside shows, snaps viciously at Joey Harvell's index finger.

The bite is clean through the top knuckle.

Love *swallows,* leaps off the table, out the front door, and runs, the dogs would later prove, down into the Isbel Creek Bottoms, where he would hide, sustained by nothing but branch water, and the crooked finger of flesh inside his gullet.

Professor stands there pointing the missing finger—a piss-straight spurt of blood with each heartbeat. He's got the surprised look, yells pitifully. "*Give it back.*"

The whole lot of them sit there.

So near spring, the red-head house finches whistling up a storm. The skunk hour, some call this. Jaws drop.

Reverend Roy Dale Shoates continues chewing, the consumption of human flesh and blood nothing new under his sun for christian folk.

Sheriff Autrey sits pale-faced, Harvell's blood fountain spurting.

Shock breaks the dumbstruck silence with words that chill Edgar to the bone, a curse in the old tongue he has not heard since a boy, when his time came, and he'd flinched at the knife's curved blade.

13

Thanksgiving morning, when it's all about to go down, Poppy's brought his flesh and blood granddaughter a hand-painted hobby horse just like the one he once made Renee, their first project together after his six months at sea, her and Rocky and Mom stuck on base in Charleston with all the other ding-bat wives and derelict brats, a million-zillion miles apart.

Why on earth did she have to think that up now?

The pony's unveiled in the den early, while Joey stuffs the twenty-two pound Butterball with cornbread dressing and Renee sets to deviling eggs. Meg's on the leather couch in front of El Rustico, the den cabinet that holds the T.V. and stereo, and about a hundred LP's from the day— vinyl Adam Ant through Ziggy Stardust, one whole shelf for the piano jazz they've inherited from Mom who'd been a piano teacher, a West Virginia grad who'd once been president of a secret sorority. Joey'd found the original charter book one weekend home, pointed out the handwrit line inside lamenting the fact that she'd never-ever-never have a beauty queen daughter who'd marry a dentist and live in a coastal condo with a veranda and a slip at the marina. Why had Joey told her that? Him and his bloody penchant for history—some skeletons are best left to lay.

Sleepy Lara sits on hobby horse, a chubby hand on each handle with the bridle on her lap. The Macy's Thanksgiving Day Parade has kicked off clear as a bell, the dingy announcer *oohing* over the Pillsbury Dough Boy afloat with Central Park in the background. Thank God they've bit the bullet for the Dish Network, out here in Bumfuck the only thing they get using the antenna is Channel 2, the Arkansas Educational channel, which is surely to Jesus an oxymoron. Put that in your pipe and smoke it. She has a vision of Peck Titsworth—that smug look he gets when he observes her classroom, pretending not to notice her, looking at his fingernails, all caught up in himself. An ArkaTech grad, he'd played bassoon in the marching band, wore his green and gold costume on dress up Friday before Halloween.

Joey's people, Josephine and O.W., Mom Dee, Uncle Hoyt, Traceleen and her boy, they're all teetotalers, are set to start arriving by noon. Mom and Poppy are already lobbying for mimosas, only they've forgot the champagne and it's too early for vodka tonic. Russellville's Price Chopper is bone dry—fifty parched miles between here and Blackwell—maybe they need a still?

"Beer maybe, bloody bulls?" Joey squeezes half a lemon over the big bird, grinds black pepper and crumbles handfuls of sage from far away Utah, where strangers have cut a doggie door in the back entrance of what used to be their home. "The French do something with red wine and eggs." He covers the turkey pan with foil, seals edges.

"Joey," Renee says. "Get real."

He's trimmed his beard—the little moustache hairs.

"7:30 now on the nose. Twenty minutes a pound." Joey counts on his fingers, says the numbers with his lips just like one of her Pope County third graders. "That's 3 o'clock, straight up." He snaps the foil-tented bird into the oven, pre-heated to 450°, immediately dials the temp down to 325°, on the low side it seems to Renee.

"You sure, Joe?"

Renee's elbow deep in a second batch of dressing, the whole fight over cornbread or oyster that takes place every live long year thusly avoided, and they're both good, really, just different. "*Joy of Cooking* says twenty-five minutes a pound. For a stuffed bird."

"Trust me," Joey says, reading glasses up on the bridge of his nose.

His blue-blue eyes twinkle. He asked her to renew their vows—just last night, about half snockered.

"Seven-and-a-half hours. We'll unfoil her the last hour so she'll brown."

Trust him? What other options are there in this life where people name their sons Peck and drape snakes from tree limbs to bring rain and paint all the fenceposts purple for *POSTED* since nobody nor their mother can read. *Trust him?*

"Sure thing," Renee says. She slides good smelling oyster dressing into an oiled pan, covers it with foil. "Here," she says, pops a raw one into Joey's mouth, horseradish and a slosh of Tabasco.

"You never *answered* me."

Certain moments are like windows she can climb through to the blue-eyed boy she fell in love with all those years ago in Fayetteville where the names of graduates from across the ages are written on concrete sidewalks from Old Main to Razorback Stadium.

"Yes," she said. "*I will.*"

The twenty-fifth of November, Thanksgiving 1999—cusp of the millennium, holy day of glut and football and the endless reinactment of Squanto's monumental error of aiding and abetting those who one fine day would wipe his ass off the map—unfurls golden and rife with the edge of in-laws arriving and arrived at the big house with its wooded five-acre front yard and corrugated tin roof shining on the old-fashioned barn beyond the grand deck like the backdrop for a photograph from Southern Living, the aroma of turkey roasting with the dressing fragrant now, brown-sugared sweet potato just coming on, the first of the early afternoon beers cracked by the time the Harvell's white Lincoln turns into the long drive, crunching gravel before halting under a leafless hickory where the engine ticks when O.W. kills it.

Seeing them through the criss-crossed window in the front prayer room, where the Elliotts had set up a pulpit with a red-lettered bible opened to the *Beatitudes: Blessed are they that mourn: for they shall be comforted,* Renee's felt them coming for twenty minutes now. Like a tuning fork, something in her thrums at a set pitch when Joey's mother is near, though O.W. draws a blank, dark matter, nothing at all. When Jimmy was killed in the one-car crash, Joey'd flown home to the chaos, then returned to her in the family's blue Cougar a week after the service, weeping at the drop of a hat, wild with liquor. She intuits the loss of the living son, a brother. The passenger door opens and there struggles Josephine Stepwell, grin cracked wide on her pale white face.

"Happy Thanksgiving sweety," she says, one foot in, one foot out.

Renee takes an arm, breathes in the scent of White Shoulders and cigarettes, and a faint whiff of the way Joey's skin smells when a rain hits it. "Happy Thanksgiving, Ms. Harvell. You too, O.W." Joey's sister and her boy crawl out of the back seat and stretch, smiling.

On the front porch, Lara squeals, jumps up and down. *"MaMa! MaMa!"* she yells.

And just then Grandmother Dee turns into the hundred yard drive, a white Corolla followed by an SUV—her brother, Uncle Hoyt who used to be a Green Beret, with his wife Willy, short for Wilhelmina. The sun shines down on the whole lot of them now under the hickory trees, and Renee can see her mother Meg's face in the same square of window where she stood just a moment ago— the sweet, sad look of regret ever on her face, a tear in her eye, maybe. Her brother, Rocky is home in Melbourne Beach, no doubt him and Bet sloshed by now, surfing the high tide breakers only two blocks from his front door with oil still hot from turkey frying for his redneck FIT engineer buddies.

All those family Thanksgivings on the farm in Plainfield, Uncle Charley doing the hokey-pokey on the squeaky floor in the front room of her ancestral home. The one year Grandmother Anna dropped the blue turkey platter, the very one that sits this second on their dining table, the white chipped spot glowing. Time has got weird on her, as if these Ozarks have somehow bent space and time. That's how she feels, bent.

Ten minutes and they've got the whole crew inside, offering sweet tea and setting out deviled eggs, pickled okra and a whole slew of nuts. It's hot in the house. Renee opens the sliding doors in the great room so the light and air pour in from the huge deck that overlooks the barn where Trace's boy is just now chasing squirrels. This is what family feels like, time to breathe, break out the booze and be merry, something she's not entirely aware of having missed until this second, aswirl in the house she's made for them. The Harvells and Mom Dee, Uncle Hoyt and Willy, they've brought pies—pies and pies and more pies.

While Joey gives the men the outside tour, Renee walks the girls down the dark-paneled hallway, past the spare bedroom her parents occupy to the master bedroom, with its twin Victorian sinks and mirror where she'd found a photo of a chubby woman in a red teddy giving the photographer a Baptist version of the come-hither look, little tassels hanging over her belly, during their walk-through. Joey's twelve gauge leans in the closet. Its being there makes her feel no better, no precaution against hunter man she imagines at every periphery. The times Joey's been away for a few nights have been nerve-racking sessions of closing curtains and still feeling exposed. Lara's in the lead, about to bust her seams. "See my room," she squeals.

"This is our bedroom," Renee says. Light pours in the windows. "You can see the side pasture out one window and the barn out the other." Here's where she feels most vulnerable, watched, a hunter man out there has her in the crosshairs of his scope.

Grandmother Dee beams and Willy runs a finger over a tan dresser. Josephine sits on the queen bed, turns brown eyes toward the barn window. "Can you give us a minute," she says, and sighs. Jesus, southern women really *do* sigh.

They look at each other, Dee and Willy and Traceleen, Josephine on the bed with tears in her eyes. "Well. Can you show us your bedroom, sweetie."

"Yes, Mom-Dee," Lara squeals, takes her great-grandmother by the hand, leads them to the big paneled room adjacent.

"Hon?"

"Ms. Harvell?"

"You asked me once. Is there anything you should know about my son. Joey."

Renee remembers the exact moment in Greensboro, North Carolina, all Joey's Fayetteville friends up for the Christmas wedding, one of them had brought a boxful of clear moonshine, "coffee lace" he'd called it, and Cath's boyfriend drank a half-full rocks glass that put him on his ass in bed dog-sick for three days, while Ray Ray, Joey's demented dwarf friend made-out fourteen different ways with Cath, her nympho maid of honor.

"Our wedding day. Before the ceremony?"

"Yeah, hon."

"I remember," Renee says. She remembers and remembers, the rehearsal dinner, Joey with hiccups, naked Cath riding Ray Ray in the laundry room.

Light just now strikes the barn, so it shines out beyond the green grass of the septic. The doorless loft has the same light pouring through, so a box of lit up blue sky appears, and that spliced with winged tree limbs.

Renee sits beside her. "Okay," she says.

Josephine reaches both arms to her. "Come here, hon."

Cigarettes and White Shoulders, the smell of roads and of herself, how they have mingled with the ones who lived here before and will come after. "Hey," Renee says.

In the doorway, her mother.

"Sorry," Meg says.

"No, it's okay Mom."

"I was just telling her," Josephine says, "we're so proud to have y'all in our family."

Meg buttons a blue sweater, and smiles. "Everything smells so good," she says. They get up from the bed. "He's a bewildered boy," Josephine says.

"Bewildered?"

"Always has been."

Renee flips through the dictionary of her mind, *puzzled*, she thinks, *tangled, confused.* She can think of not one good thing that hooks up with the word *bewildered.*

"This room has such good light," Meg says.

"That's the truth," says Josephine.

Freud has this theory about first born boys. Renee'd had to learn it during student teaching in Alexandria—her first job, only it was physically handicapped then, so she'd had to take this one little boy, racked by muscular dystrophy, to pee, unzip his pants and insert the catheter, and coax him to relax. So the theory goes, the one she'd had to study and write a term paper on says that if a boy-child knows himself to be his mother's undisputed darling, he'll maintain for his whole life a sense of triumph, confidence that he'll succeed in all things of this earth, and all evidence suggested actual success followed such boy children as men.

"You have your own bath?" Willy's walked in, and the rest.

Renee steps in, motions the rest to follow. "There's room for two in the shower, " she smiles.

It's true—the Elliotts had splurged on the deluxe duo with its two pulsating and movable heads. If this thing could talk, *good god.*

"Tell me honey," Grandmother Dee says behind her. "Has Jesus taken that lump away from your chest?"

Jesus? How words spring from nowhere. She turns her face to Josephine's mother, her green eyes like shined ivy. Eighty years old, she'd been the first one of them Renee'd met, her first Arkansas night in the ninth floor Himalaya House, overlooking Little Rock with its dark river winding south.

"Honey?"

"I hope so, Mom-Dee."

"I believe," Dee says, smiles wide, reaches a hand into the shower, so that the fingers behind the filmy wall made shadow. From a family with eight children, two shared the second sight, could see and warn against future danger, if you believed. "That's the trick in this life, sweetie. To believe."

Dee's blouse matches her eyes, just as bright as the first time she ever saw them, when the lady had prayed out loud right in front of everybody.

"Okay. Dee. I'll believe."

An alarm's going off somewhere far away, across the river of the too-big house, and the bathroom seems cramped, the wrong place to be, an entirely inappropriate room to hear the *beep, beep, beep* of the kitchen smoke detector.

Dee says, "It's all happened before, honey. That sound. This light. What we do next. It's all part of the same story."

14

The turkey takes forever.

Three, four, seven times now Joey's skewered it under the thigh, only to have blood leak out, seven-and-a-half hours and not even close to clear. Noon toddy-time has stretched to early happy hour which has shifted to regular happy hour which now morphs into hippity happity hour, which Joey's people are not good with, not good at all. For all his life he's never had a drink in front of his people without hiding it in a screw-top coffee mug or a slurpee cup or some other equally lame guise. Now, visible drinking has commenced. Almost 4, the Rockersons are drinking with holiday gusto. Things are being said. The hors d'oeuvres platter has been utterly trashed—the oyster stuffed mushrooms and Renee's spinach balls, the Gouda and crackers, Josephine's Velveeta cheese block—all of it's a mess. Uncle Hoyt, Mama Dee's younger brother, doesn't miss the chance to badmouth Si Stepwell, Joey's maternal grandfather who, before he'd run off with Floradee, had been a high school basketball star in the Dixie League where Hoyt was part-time referee. He was military, Hoyt, had been a Green Beret and famously killed an informant in Laos, so this whole tribe of Laotian Buddhists had made him their physical representation of God incarnate and followed him clean across the ocean to reside in Yell County where now can be found the best Pad Thai noodle in Arkansas. He runs security for 5-star hotels owned by the Cardena brothers down in Cabo San Lucas. Joey keeps a business card in his wallet: a black glock pistol and his name, Hoyt Funk—that's it, his name above a big-ass pistol and a phone number.

The whole lot of them sit at the dinner table, Hoyt hard and heavy on Si, dead eighteen years now, Joey's maternal grandfather who Hoyt'd hated with a white-hot hate.

The dining room adjoins the kitchen and it's hot, 3:57 now, turkey time. And the drinking's full speed ahead, so Cap and Meg are happy on V and Ts, and Joey's knocked back a child's portion of Old Crow, masked in a coffee mug that doesn't fool Dee or Josephine for a second. O.W.'s at the head of the table, munching peanuts from a glass bowl and Josephine's beside Hoyt as he launches into this new story. Renee's approaching the bottom of the first Cabernet and little Lara's conked out, the air rasping over swollen tonsils, on the couch. Outside, the light's doing back flips, is pure gold, with the pileated woodpecker hammering out his afternoon rhythm. The last of the sun-lit hickory leaves whirl to the ground, so the trunks and limbs are bare and dark.

"Your grandpappy," Hoyt says, and he gets this sideways grin on his face. "Joey? You heard about Si's holy boat?"

They could throw the fucker on the grill, blacken it good, goddamn turkey. "I guess not, Uncle. I don't know that one."

"Dinner'll be ready any second," Dee says at his elbow, intuiting. "It smells divine."

Across the slick, white linoleum-floored kitchen, the potato filled pressure cooker *cha-cha-chas* on the stove, and Rocky's left out the half-gallon of vodka, a Smirnoff bottle right there on the bar counter for everyone to see, a hefty knock of it gone already. Renee's skillet of good-peppered gravy steams, a full cup of sherry in the bechamel sauced pearl onions. A tray of brown and serve rolls awaits browning. Dee's potful of French sliced green beans and slivered almonds lay half-grazed on a plate. Meg's made pickled beets and Poppy's baked a whiskey-laced bread pudding—his specialty.

And still, no turkey.

Joey's people are Baptist, though they hadn't always been that way. O.W.'d been a drunk of the highest order, had broken a cop's nose the second time Josephine had papers served on him. On the day he accepted Christ, the whole church wept and sang out *praise God* and *amen* and *thine be the glory*, so you'd have thought the devil's own lieutenant had surrendered.

"Well, he got to drinking. You know, Joey boy. Your grandpappy liked a nip."

Hoyt has a chair at home big as a king's throne, though for a killer, he's not a large man, 5'6", maybe a hundred-fifty. Beside the king's throne sits this kid-sized chair, a real teensy little thing where Willy sits, only she's huge, a six-foot German woman who'll go 220 if she weighs a pound. After a visit to Hoyt's, Joey and Renee'd got fall down laughing sickness in the front yard, the two of them set up in front of the room like that.

"So's he's snootful on Lake Dardenelle. That green flat-bottom. Fires up his Merc and cuts it under a yo-yo branch, about to run his trotline." Hoyt measures the table. Everyone's listening, except Rock and Meg who gaze across the great room at the T.V. where the Cottonbowl plays out, the Longhorns stomping the shit out of Mississippi State.

"Turn up the oven, Joe." O.W. says it, face like stone.

Hoyt says, "Only a moccasin fell off the tree limb, coils there hissing. Strikes his wood leg a few times." Hoyt hisses, makes his fingers into split fangs, thumps them on the table a few times.

"I'll get the potatoes. Check the bird, Joey?" Renee's giving him the uh-huh look.

Lara comes squealing, a pair of squirrels looking at them through the double sliding door. "Got a little girl in the boat. 'Bout your age sweetie."

Lara crawls up in Hoyt's lap. How could she know better?

Josephine frowns.

Joey sets the tin foil pan on the stove top and again skewers a thin blade up under the thigh—a pink rivulet winding down into the cornbread stuffing where the bird sits.

"That's enough, Hoyt." Dee says it. "Can I help with those rolls?"

O.W. sniffs something's up, regards them with a stone eye. On the way back to the table, Joey pours three fingers of straight vodka into his coffee mug, tinks in an ice cube and a squeeze from the plastic lime.

"And a sixteen gauge shotgun, too. You know he had a sixteen?"

Josephine shakes her head. She hates it when he drinks outright, without even trying to hide it. Meg hoots at the T.V.—Texas has thrown the bomb. *Cha, cha, cha* goes the pressure cooker.

"I killed a deer with that gun, Hoyt. My first."

"Well," Hoyt says.

"Well what?"

"He shot the snake right through the boat floor. Out in the middle of the cove. And you know what, Joe?"

"*Father God,*" Dee says. "*I call you this second . Help us. Give us peace.*"

Dee praying out loud gets Cap's and Meg's attention. They're Episcopal—whiscopal, Renee says, and whiscopals don't spontaneously pray.

"Hoyt. That gun's in my office right now," Joey lies. "You want to see?"

Renee beats the potatoes in a silver bowl, you can hear the mixer tines tinging. The Smirnoff burns going down and it's hot in the house, the fire burning down in the huge fireplace at the far off end of the great room, upon which sit their photos—this family, that Joey has brought together—this first holiday.

"Someone light the candles," Renee says. "Get down from there, Lara."

Dougie, Traceleen's boy sings out, "Hello Mr. Turkey."

"The motor wouldn't start. He sank right there in the middle of the cove. Remember swimming that cove, Josephine. When you was five?"

"Wobble, wobble, wobble."

"*Joey.*" Renee's taken the bird from the oven, stands shrouded in steam. "*Carve it.*"

"Gobble, gobble, gobble," Dougie goes.

Joey's sharpened knives three times, they're good to go, a whole rack of them—mincers and chefs, an eight inch butcher. Hoyt's baited hook hangs between them, and both men know it. Joey's been likened to Si ever since he can remember, the old man's hooked nose and temper. The two men look at each other and it's the sort of moment, at least for Harvells and Stepwells and their kith and kin, when family members step out into the front yard and beat each other with sticks and worse. O.W.'d almost killed his brother, Chester, once, walked right out from the dinner table and busted each other's skulls on the driveway, the sound of it, an awful thing. Uncle Earl had thrown a fork at his wife's face, and Little Leo had got up from banana pudding and poured gasoline on a naugahyde La-Z-boy, set it afire so they had to drag it out back where it smoldered all Christmas day by the barn. Throw liquor into the mix and you've got yourself a show with Joey's people.

But not today.

"That's a good one, Hoyt." Joey puts an arm on his shoulder and the two men shake. "He never told me that."

Hoyt nods, shakes. "I guess not."

Hands are washed and each of them hustle plates to the table. Joey carries Renee's antique turkey platter, the plated Butterball goldened and robust and sweet smelling, surrounded on one side by cornbread stuffing with the Rockerson's customary oyster dressing on the other. The family holds hands to pray, Cap at one end, Joey at the other. Deer, two does, grace the backyard where a garden once grew.

The eleven of them stand holding hands at the long Malaysian mahogony table Joey bought for this very moment when he'd reunite his people, and take his place as its head. Rock offers the prayer—words for the homeless and the destitute and the mentally ill, for the ones not present who remain in their hearts. Josephine sobs, Jimmy powerfully present in his absence. Joey and Renee meet eyes. Hers are hazel, just like Meg's and now Lara's. Beautiful, really, flecks of fall and plowed earth shining. He's made it home, linked his people. As Dee Amens Captain Rockerson's Amen, with his whole heart, Joey Harvell gives thanks— not so wide a river between belief and disbelief. Even Si'd listened to a holy roller radio station in the backyard during happy hour when they'd hulled purple hulls, and the old man drank bourbon and branch, sometimes clapping his big fisherman's hands together and singing the rapturous words far beyond tune.

Joey takes his place before the family turkey platter. "I want to thank each of you for being here," he says, a gleaming carving knife in each hand. "Especially you, Mama. I've missed you."

"Cheers," Josephine says, a tear in one eye. Water and wine glasses clink, and Joey sets to carving. He makes the horizontal cut below the breast on the side nearest him, carves eighth-inch slices pretty as you please. Serving bowls pass hand to hand, Dee's green beans and creamed onions and real cranberry sauce, followed by cornbread and oyster dressings, buttered rolls and a bowlful of steamed Brussels. Waves of mashed potatoes are sloshed with Renee's good peppered gravy, so that only a few—dark meat eaters, O.W. and Poppy—see the bright red blood leak from an undone thigh.

Joey doesn't miss a stroke. He masks Poppy's raw serving with oyster dressing, serves slices of white meat onto the fine Czechoslovakian china that once belonged to Meg's mother, ladles out the good gravy.

"Here, here," Hoyt says, lifts his water glass.

"Here, here," Captain Rockerson says, lifts his.

"Thank you for all we have to be thankful for," Hoyt says.

"For family."

Josephine lifts a shining long-stemmed glass wherein well-water has miraculously transformed to wine. "For love," she says.

And they eat, rest, then eat again 'til all have had their fill.

After they've made soup with the carcass and fixings, stacked away the fine china and silver and bright blue platter with the chip on one handle, when they've vacuumed and mopped and taken the middle section off the Malaysian mahogany table on the underside of which Joey's written *Happy 40 Sweety—Love You With All Of My Heart,* when the last of the pies have been cellophaned, the compost carried out to the pasture bin, and the liquor stowed far far away, when the day lay out in front of them and there's neither hunger nor football nor a houseful of company to distract them, Joey drives the Rockersons over Carrion Crow Mountain and down onto the Trail of Tears, land his people had owned before the Depression, to the Adams Family Cemetery with its arched gate and gold letters and glittering carved stones overlooking a lightning struck tree. Here, kith and kin from across the generations are head-to-foot with fathers all the way back to the ancestral tromp down from Henry County, Tennessee before the war between the states.

Today, a November rain's brought tree limbs down all over the hill, especially on Jimmy's spot high on the north side. His brother's stone is silver, the color of a jet wing, with his senior picture embossed above the name, the letters of which still conspire to shock in the split second they take to form the word. He parks under the huge oak he'd first taken refuge under at Papa Stepwell's funeral when he was three, opens the door and breathes the rain-cleaned air. Off in North Carolina, a grave plot seller had once surprised him in a maple tree, sawing a limb off in bright October, just walked right up, said, "Feller? Where you going to be buried?"

"*What?*" Joe'd said.

"Buried. Where you and your missus going to be buried."

He'd missed a lick, so one sawtooth nicked his thumb, made it half down the ladder before the salesman could retreat. "You get your ass out of my yard."

"That's a fine stereo in 'at front room. Ought to lock your door."

For a while after the peckerhead ran off, Joey thought on it—where he'd be buried, what earth would have him. Would Renee rest beside him? The cemetery was a good place, it had a good feel, peaceful, and brown-eyed Susan bloomed in the summer, blackberry and honeysuckle and cows grazed near a stock pond a quarter-mile downhill. This was Solgahatchia, not far from the creek where his great-grandmother had married Papa Stepwell under a tree with the water swishing behind them. His grandfather Si was buried down hill, Uncles Leo and Willard, and there, MaMa Ella Stepwell who, at eighty, had been a girl at heart, a friend who sat at the kid's table with Joey and the cousins for Christmas dinner, who'd lay on her back in the green grass at night and point out stars and planets in the galaxy's ribs, make up whoppers about when she was a girl with a talking chicken. This second Renee wears the gold wedding band she passed down. A caretaker visited twice a month. He might never know his blood-father's people off in Arizona, but this was enough. It was enough.

Little Lara climbs out of her carseat and hits the ground running. Renee meets his eyes for a moment—this is holy ground, they've never fought here, though it's outside of her realm, all these dead people she's never met, Jimmy especially, who'd been killed the month they met.

"Up here," Joey says.

The wall around Jimmy's plot is plumbed and shining, but weeds have taken the pea gravel and limbs have blown down from the big oak.

"It's beautiful," Meg says. The first words from her to him all day.

"This is Jimmy, my brother."

"Hi, Jimmy."

Cap's spent the morning in the guest bath having a shit-fit. Now he's across the grounds, keeping to himself, reading inscriptions. Renee has gone another direction and little Lara's romped off toward a pile of faded ribbons and worn out silk flowers near the barbed wire fence where they throw brush. "Back in Phillipi, we have a place like this. Not as nice," Meg says.

"Your mother's there?"

Joey's gathered an armful of limbs, fistfuls of weed. Way off, walking up from the stock pond in the far pasture, a shirtless man has a fishing rod thrown over a shoulder. A new road below the cemetery spiderwebs toward a trailer, two trailers Joey sees now.

"Yeah," Meg says. "Marcie."

Joey carries the armload of brush to the fence, throws it over onto the pile where keepers of the tombs have thrown the scrap from their loved ones' graves for a hundred and fifty years. Jimmy'd stuttered, six-feet tall, he could sing the alphabet backwards.

"*Hey*," the shirtless man screams. "*Hey.*" He's thrown down his rod, broken into a trot, the whites of his eyes flashing, a little rat dog yapping at his feet.

Joey feels Meg behind him.

Skin and bones, he huffs up to the barbed wire. Breath wheezes in his lungs. He clears his throat, spits the wad over his shoulder. "You'ins get yo trash off my propty."

Joey's dumbfounded.

He feels the Rockersons behind him, sudden shame. How they should have seen this place plays against how they'll remember.

"Who the hell are you?"

Through barbed wire, the man's ribs show. "Who the hell are *you*?"

"This is *my* cemetery."

A time had been in his life when he'd do violence to this man. In college, Joey'd been arrested for unloading a thirty aught six deer gun into the sky above an offending neighbor's trailer. His mama's brother, Earl would pull a pistol from his boot this second, head shoot the son of a bitch straight away, cut his head off and piss on it or worse, let the dogs chew out the tongue. O.W. too, likely, who knew what dark alley he'd pursue. Grandpa Si'd knocked a policeman through

a plate glass window. Hell, even the women would have no truck with *this*—
Joey's own Mama'd laid more than one man open with a fingernail, and MaMa
Stepwell'd once cooked Papa's stash of condoms up in the Sunday meatloaf. All
of them look on now, the Rockersons, Renee, his own daughter, his brother from
the silver casket and the whole lot of his blood kin from the grave.

"Go on now. You'n 'at lady pick it up. My side ain't your dump." The skinny
dog's having a conniption, pissing all over itself.

"All right," Joey says. "Can do."

When he crawls through, one barb catches his back. A hundred times he's
felt this same bite, sometimes in hurried trespass or theft or lusty visits to Carly
Jane, the naked dance teacher who'd wrap herself in a horse blanket, sit astraddle
a bale of straw in the cedar barn waiting and the moon would cast stripes on the
loft ladder where eyes of horses shone from buckled straw. Breath rattles in his
chest. His shirt rips—the banjo whir wire makes. A high E.

Behind him, Renee yells, *"Don't."*

Part II

15

Celestial Universe, a church before it was a gas station before it was a telescope shop, is cram-packed, everybody carrying a piece of the shiny-new telescope they've cursed for the last twenty-four hours. It's day after Christmas, sunny and clear, six days from when the world's supposed to end with the new millennium. Larry Simms, the chimney sweep whose cousin was the mass murderer, squats in the corner with a medium refractor. Over there stands Preacher Shoates, beside him a raven-haired slut with a tee shirt that says *satin worship*. Three pale fingers of midriff show above her navel. Don McLean's "Starry, Starry Night," drones out from the one speaker strung up on an unhinged door. The room stinks. It reeks of people who've glutted for many days in a row and now have bad gas which they're not shy about passing. Anybody with any sense would open ten windows and the garage door.

Renee's is a six-inch reflector, a small cannon on a Dobsonian mount. What Galileo used, only smaller, to see the moons of Jupiter, how they orbited the gaseous fifth planet and therefore not earth and therefore earth wasn't the center of the solar system, much less all things, and God is a lie and Preacher Roy Dale Shoates is full of horseshit, and every last soul in all Pope County is descended from a root-eating she-ape. Renee permits the sad-eyed beast to grunt its way into her head. Bare-titted and whisker-chinned, she tweezes head lice off the skulls of young whose seed will one day drop laser guided smart-bombs, paint cathedral ceilings, make love to her sweating body on a far-away beach named Lookout, and come here, end of the world Pope County, and set up shop at a po-dunk college without air.

Little Lara walks straight in, sits on a cardboard box marked STARHOPPER, *do not open.*

"How do you do, little girl. Happy hollerdays." Preacher Shoates winks. His satin worshiping floozy, seventeen—tops, bares teeth stained with bloody lipstick, crinkles her nose and makes swallow noises in her throat.

Lara says, "Witch. A witch."

Shoates licks his lips. He says, "Well ain't dat tha truth," and turns his attentions to the girl whose fingernails curl around a four inch light bucket with a cracked mirror.

Outside, neither sun nor cloud—wet, humid air, the dogfood factory has kicked up a notch.

Joey's home feeling sorry for himself. His back went out on Christmas Eve while he sawed down a cedar in the back pasture thicket. He-man, he moaned his way home and threw it on the back deck. "Stupid bastard," he said through clenched teeth, so their daughter, little Lara, thinks that's what all manner of things are rightfully called. "Stupid bastard," she said while they decorated. "Stupid bastard," she shrieked at mixed-race Hopscotch Heather, what Santa left. Poppy Rockerson's train whistled under a lighted trellis, *stupid bastard,* little Lara said. All Christmas Day long, while glazed-eyed Joey overcooked pork shoulders and rhubarb pie and they drank mimosas, tended the fire, switched to vodka tonics before pretending to be entertained by television football and an endless playing of *Elvis Sings Christmas,* it was *stupid bastard* this, *stupid bastard* that. By happy hour, Renee tended to agree—stupid bastards one and all.

The Christmas telescope was Renee's idea, something for her husband Joey to do at night besides drink himself silly and call up old high school buddies to brag how he's now assistant history professor at ArkaTech in Russellville, the one town in the natural state with a nuclear reactor—Arkansas One—out there waiting to melt down on Lake Dardanelle.

She opens her mouth, little Lara, sings off the cardboard box, "Witch, witch, witch."

A big-bellied boy in corduroys says, "Five little monkeys jumpin' on a bed. One fall off and bunked his head."

"How cute," the white boy's mama says. She's tall, gap-toothed; Renee's seen her mouth twenty times this month—in Wal-Mart or the pork display at Price

Chopper, once at Blackwell Liquor, and a dozen times on the faces of children who sit bewildered in her classroom where every broken-backed dictionary says *fuck you*. It's nothing here for blood relatives to marry and produce offspring just like the pharaohs of old, no bastardizing these lines. Everybody looks like somebody else—in Whattaburger and The Emporium, from Butts's Video and Worm to Dover Grocery, traits got added and subtracted and added again.

"Santa come to see you good little girl. I can tell. Lawd," she says, shuffling up beside Renee, moving the Christmas trash scope from one sweat stained armpit to the other. "Don't tey grow up fast?"

"Yeah," Renee says. "That's what I've always heard." And some ought to be tied inside burlap bags and thrown off the river bridge, she thinks, the words bringing color to her face.

"Boys come sniffin' her out soon, I bet." The woman's wearing pink long johns under cutoff jean shorts. A hickey blooms on her skinny neck.

What on earth could such a person want with a telescope, even the piece of junk she's been fool enough to spend good money on. Renee says, "I guess so."

"My own girl's run off to Georgia."

Little Lara's got her tongue stuck out at Preacher Shoates, who doesn't notice, though the little slut flip flops her weight from one knob knee to the other.

"I'm sorry."

The white woman snorts, "Not me. Them boys all going on like dogs in the bushes."

Over in the corner, the astronomer's assistant is sanding a wood chunk— *swish, swash, swoosh*. He's either a little boy or a little man, you can't tell, but he's going to town. Down the street, the dogfood mill groans, and that means the chicken processors are back at it, and Tyson's hog operation too.

"It's some of'em never grow up," the woman says, making a shy smile, rolling green eyes back to the yellow whites.

Renee squares shoulders, wishes the woman quiet. The room's smell has personality. If it could talk, it'd no doubt sound just like the white trash lady beside her.

Her long lashes flutter. "It's some dogs you *like* though."

Renee focuses her energy on a gaudy piece of wall. The she-ape grunts her way in again, only this time the thing's dark upturned eyes ask a question, need desperately—it seems—to know the answer.

"Watch here, honey babe." The woman spins toward her son. "Bark like a dog, Sinbad." The little fat boy yip-yaps. Little Lara squeals.

Across the room, the red-faced clerk is having a muted argument with Betty Strickland, a husky pink woman who shakes a broken tripod every three or four seconds in lieu of voice. The two go at it quietly while the rest wait turns.

Display posters of the glorious universe are duct-taped to every conceivable empty space—they shine from the ceiling, they're stuck on every free inch of wall and dangle from the oil-stained racks of the old garage gas station, stuck up in the high lift position, a little crooked like a dinosaur skeleton about to fall down. Boxes in various stages of getting opened lie helter-skelter on the floor, amongst bulky telescopes and star-tracking units with chicken scrawled prices written on last year's Christmas tags. A big picture window is sealed from the outside with rolls of white butcher paper, upon which is written N-A-M-E-D-A-Y in red painted letters. Seen bass-ackwards from where Renee stands, the dirty paper says "Y-A D-E M-A-N," what Arkansas boys say when somebody drives up with a dead deer roped to their car hood or gets caught in the skating rink bathroom *en felatio* with a beaver-toothed Tech cheerleader. "*Ya de man, boy, ya de man.*"

"It ain't my fault," the clerk finally says out loud, his voice high and reedy. "I got overhead. *Overhead*," he says loudly, throws both hands up so you can see numbers written all over his palms.

Miss Strickland raises the tripod up over his head like a deformed cross, whacks this way and that. "It's broke," she says. "See here?" She shakes the bent instrument at an unkempt child that Renee's seen before, maybe in the special-ed yearbook, or a field trip to the reactor. "He bawled last night, the moon up and purdy like that. You fix this," she says, *whacka-whacka-whack.* "Or you'll talk to Peck. He knows where *you-ins* live."

"Next."

"He knows where *you-ins* sleep."

Preacher Shoates insinuates a spontaneous prayer.

"Next."

The astronomer's assistant hops up from sanding, makes faces at the kids, pitches a fistful of sawdust gleaming in the air. "Reckon you come this away, lady" he tells Betty Strickland, who follows him without complaint through the unhinged door which, Renee realizes, connects to somewhere else, if only crookedly. The little man hops back inside, goes back to sanding. Outside, beyond the butcher paper, Renee sees the big woman and her little boy, their blurry images moving away, the broken tripod whomping air.

A field hippy elbows his way up to the plywood counter, potted Poinsettia in one hand, a Mylar solar filter in the other. The whole mess starts again.

"My Shelly raised a black shepherd named Satan. We had to put it down 'cause it bit the postman's butt." The woman sighs. "Bled and bled." Outside, clouds roll in from the south, rain on the way. "You got a dog?"

Renee wonders how she fits in—how she came to be here of all places on Earth, today, surrounded by folk willing to stand with their eyes to the sky in yards where hogs eat their own afterbirth and people are named Peck and preacher's mistresses wore satin worship shirts. How-oh-how had she managed to end up here? The country wasn't so bad for children, not bad at all if the crystal meth makers would quit beheading informants and pitching body parts into any old bayou they came across. On the border of the Ozark National Forest, near Newton county where stills brewed apple flavored shine. It was an okay place, much preferable to D.C. where her and Joey'd once lived above prostitutes and transvestites and everybody and their mother walked around with four fingers in the air, the sign for crack. Better by far than self-righteous Utah, where you couldn't even light a cigarette in public without being scorned. They have a nice house with two barns and a chicken coop and a Ford Model 6-T tractor, a creek in the back pasture, deer, wild turkey, and a neighbor who shoots the painted silhouette of his ex-wife and her lover over and over with a thirty aught six. A bowlful of blue sky pours through the blown-out heads. Were there not worse hells in which to daily rise? Now, Joey says the millennium's about to fuck everything up, so what does it matter? The holidays make Renee this way. Maybe she should join a church and pray like Preacher Shoates to a Jesus who has it in him to forgive all.

"I ast you, you got a dog?"

"One."

Little Lara's up, pokes at the Horsehead Nebulae bursting across an eight-foot piece of sheetrock wall. A couple of other kids wince up at the ceiling where a map of the celestial universe sags from corners hammered with eight-penny nails. Pegasus and naked Hercules swirl colorfully, like funnies in the Danville Littlejohn, into goat-headed Capricorn, who looks about to butt Sagittarius right into the scorpion's venomous tail. Renee's been promised galaxies with this telescope—DEEP SPACE EXPLORER it's named.

"One you said?"

"One."

"Ought's his name?"

"It's a she."

"Ought's her name?"

"Moon."

"Moon what?

Across the room, the red-faced assistant squats sanding his wood, a little monkey man with eyes like skim-ice on Illinois bayou where a little girl in sunflower pajamas got dug up last summer with her mouth full of dirt.

"You want'a win 'at horsey poster for your little sis? Say?" The clerk's on her out of nowhere. "What can I do you for?" he says straight into her face.

"*Do me for?*"

He's shaved his moustache Hitler-style, to scare people he's swindled most likely. The heater's on full throttle in the corner, an accordion oil unit that smells like french fries.

"T'day's name day, ma'am. You tell me what's on at poster, it's yours. Just like 'at."

Lara plops down on another half-opened cardboard box at her mother's feet. The place is a wreck, really, way below health codes, surely, not a doubt.

"Ask'er 'bout her moon-dog."

This close she can smell his hair oil, see the chipped corners of his front teeth, hear phlegm wheeze in his lungs.

"You forgot my eyepieces," Renee says. "I'm here for the remainder of my ticket."

"The remainder of what ticket?"

"You owe me the 10 and 25 millimeter eyepieces." Renee shoves her receipt under his nose. The terrible music finally shuts off. Shoates praises god.

"This here lady says you got a moondog. That the name you're saying? Moondog? Told you, it's name day."

On all fours, the little man eyes Lara from the corner where sawdust hovers.

"The eyepieces come with the telescope. See. You forgot them when I cleared my layaway."

"Tell me the name of that there."

His points to the huge poster where a quadruple star glows brilliantly at the core of an ancient novae. Like the midget, his bottle green eyes lock on Lara, silent at her mother's feet. Renee hears her daughter breathing, air rasping through the gap between her swollen tonsils.

"My finderscope's screwed up too. I'll need that kind you have that uses a red dot."

The astronomer's eyes are entirely vacant, nobody home. The monkey man moves forward on all fours toward them—his eyes aglitter, no look in particular on his face.

"Name anything you see and I'll give it to you."

"I bet her moondog's a bush rattler."

"Say it's Orion Nebula. Tell me its below the belt. How about them apples?"

Renee says, "Don't talk to me that way."

"She shaves that moondog. She tolt me that."

"Shut up," Renee says. "Will you please shut your mouth, please?"

The place is quiet—preacher Shoates and the satin slut and the white-trash woman with her blooming hickey, top-hatted Simms, and the people she hadn't noticed but now sees—everyone in the room that once hosted marryings and buryings then oil changes and fingers cut off inside hoist rings, where voices have been offered up to the Lord of Hosts, fan belts, radiators, black holes and kiloparsecs interweaving in their pasts, presents and futures. Everyone is looking beseechingly at Renee and little Lara, eyes wide, as if they are the center of some alternative universe about to explode outward and somehow nick their worlds in the process.

The clerk says, "Your little girl."

Renee says, "Keep her out of this."

"Your girl, ma'am."

Renee says, "I *mean* it."

The celestial clerk looks her straight in the face. "Your daughter," he says, measuring each syllable, "has a razorblade in her hand. Be still."

Renee looks down. The backward half-glance hurts. Her neck arteries radiate. From her core outward, she thrums. It's true. At her feet, Little Lara's got hold of a box cutting blade. She weaves the razor through the air in front of her face.

"Lara," Renee whispers.

The preacher holds his tongue, the satin slut's gone white. Nobody says a word.

"Stupid bastard," little Lara says. "Mines."

She stands to her true height and looks at her mother. The blade tilts on its axis, held at arm's length, the prismatic universe carouseling in its mirror finish.

"Mines," she says again, the voice ringing with confidence.

The girl takes two dance steps toward the room's center. "Stupid bastard," she says through teeth, whirling on them. "*Mines.*"

Skirting Carrion Crow Mountain to the west and Hogeye Ridge to the east, mother and daughter drive 105 north from Atkins, uphill through the poor-poor shacks and shanty-churches where Joey once lived with a houseful of Cherokees named Mayfield. In the rearview, back on Lake Dardanelle, Nuclear One looms, the white cloud mushrooming up where steam turns the red tower lights gauzy pink. Daughter Lara entertains herself with the burlap bagful of telescope shop goodies. Here, for their holiday viewing pleasure, a Telrad Illuminated Finderscope, solar and lunar filters, a dozen colored eyepieces, erecting prisms, dew caps, orthoscopic, Plössl, Erfle, wild-field and Panoptic eyepieces, a planosphere and star charts for the next two hundred years, a bundle of hastily ripped down posters, a book—*Nightwatch: A Practical Guide to Viewing the Universe*—with a couple kinky girly cutouts pasted inside the back flap, a welder's mask and a pint bottle of Old Charter Bourbon, unopened—a stargazer's motherload.

Little Lara looks at Mommy through a red moon lens. It's past nap time, she nods forward, her hazel eyes squint then open wide, full of light. The dangers of day. Razorblades in the hands of babes—what in the name of a thousand gods was the world thinking?

On the right side of the road, a horsehead bobs from the door of a fire-gutted trailer, beside which leans a cedar board shack where a woman sits on a five-gallon bucket with her eyes shut. She's shaking her head, yes, no, yes, no. No, uh huh. "Look at that lady, Lario. What's she thinking about?"

Behind the moonshade, little Lara's eye is piggy pink.

Up a ways, three shoeless children chase a litter of puppies through junked cars that line up one after another, windows busted out so dogs and kids scutter over frayed seats, knocking heads on rearviews and fall-down ceiling fabric. Hoods yaw open. A stick house, a hogan, blinks beneath strands of red Christmas lights, tons of them, and three fat boys in suits stand around a rusted Toyota, stuffing their mouths with jumbo biscuits. A funeral, Renee understands, a funeral's going on inside, cars lining the potholed drive, in the yard, pulled through the pasture gate. Inside, somebody's earthly body had lain on a tabletop for three days now, flower shop carnations laced with baby's breath masking the truth of it all. An important message resides inside on top of that dinner table, but Renee drives on, passes derelict houses, colorless in winter save the glorious plots of septic tank clover.

The child in the backseat looks out the window, slipping in and out of sleep on a hill country back road, no idea where she's going or where she's been. The trouble back at Celestial Universe was over as quick as it started, the astronomer and his midget assistant apologizing up one side and down the other. Now, Carrion Crow Mountain rears to the west where the land rises to meet its shadow.

Uphill, past a gospel revival sign saying TRUST THE ONE WHO BLEEDS FOR YOU, a yardful of lawn ornaments glitter in the pleasant light. Out here, the land is sweetened by its proximity to sky, knuckling toward the Ozark Mountains with their little towns named Ozone and Sufi-City, Buck Snort, Horseshoe Bend, Fifty-Six, Black Oak.

Renee takes a hard right up the empty drive. A trailer with trash on the front porch sits uneven beside two satellite dishes, one of which has been backed into and leans cock-eyed silly. A concrete mixer hulks beside a sandpile where shines a waterhose's one dark eye.

I believe the worst is over, Renee thinks, the world's intervened on her behalf today, no one's disfigured, all's well. She pulls the e-brake, climbs down out of the truck, clicks the key button so the door locks, and wanders out into the grassy hillside to look for an anniversary gift. What'll go with the scope and nighttime? What'll make Joey happy? What'll make him make sense?

The choices multiply right in front of her eyes: diamondback rattlers—coiled for the strike, heavy breasted mermaids and mermen, perky-boobed nymphs, a lusty Adonis, Jesus on the cross, throngs of bearded Beelzebubs, goat-footed satyrs, centaurs, elves, dwarves, humpback camels, three wise men, tomb angels, infants nursing albino tits, rabbits, lizards, Kokapelli, Geronimo, a gaudy rendition of Mt. Rushmore, John the Baptist's head on a platter, Goofy and Pooh-bear and Christopher Robin, several fowl species headed up by decoy mallards, thinkers in various attitudes of thought, a skirt blown up Marilyn Monroe's thighs, a bullfrog family, many lovely longhaired Madonnas as tender as flesh and blood dancing with no shoes, and more tomb angels, whispering into the stone ears of souls about to raise from the dead.

Renee is stunned, she hasn't eaten since last night. What she'd give for an apple to chew on. There's whiskey in the truck. She squats by a bearded Beelzebub whose goat-slit eyes gaze up into her own. *Everthing here's yours, honey. All of it. Go ahead. Pick sump'in.* Renee surveys the stone world. A shot of whiskey'd be nice about now. The world is sweet. This's the holidays. *And it ain't no point in trying to please 'at Joey. Ain't nothin' ever made him happy. Ain't nothin' ever will.* On Satan's other side, one of the long-haired Madonnas seems off-balance, her bare feet about to tangle. *But you'll try. You'll try and try. And you got your daughter to think about. Deal with it. Could have been a awful day for you, huh?* Renee shuts her eyes. She feels sunlight on her eyelids. She hears wailing down the hollow where the funeral unwinds. Her hand fits perfectly in the cold space between Lucifer's horns, like that space was made for her alone. She imagines what it would be like to sleep here, to lay among the smooth faces of stone lambs and lions, here in the clearing beneath the wide sky where stars spin through the galaxy's white ribs, a gift on any hoarfrost night. *All us god's children come from shitass apes, you know. Honeybabe, I gid you all this'n more. Go on and take it.*

Renee gets up and breathes.

Woodsmoke's in the air, the smell of it pungent and comforting, takes her back to Girl Scouts when her mom was den mother, and they'd roasted marshmallows skewered with clotheshangers in the backyard. Her hands settle on a ceramic fish—a big Chinese carp with ribbed gills and shining white scales. Joey has a thing for fish—he's a real fish man. The truck tick-tocks as she passes, her sleeping daughter's neck cocked at a painful angle.

A T.V. talks through the trailer door. Renee knocks three times for luck. Out in the country, anyone was likely to show up at your door, and a shotgun leans in every corner.

"Hep you?" A woman, twenties—thirties? says. Renee recognizes her straight away, the waitress from the hotel buffet. They look at each other through the door crack. Both the waitress's eyes are raccoon black, two shiners and the nose swollen blue going to sunset purple. She's wearing pink socks with flour drifted on them.

"Hi," Renee says.

It's a talk show, the kind where people have staged fights in front of a studio audience that hoots and hollers for one side or the other. "You just picked that fish I said nobody'd want. That what you come for?"

"Tomorrow's my anniversary."

"Which?"

"Eleven."

"Eleven is heaven."

Renee smells bread baking, nice in the chilly air.

"You want to come in?"

Renee points. "My daughter's asleep."

"Okay."

"Thank you." The two women look each other up and down for a second. "My husband likes fish. Joe's a fish-guy."

"My man makes them things and sets 'em out there. He's on a coon hunt, supposed to be. Just an excuse to get drunked up and burn things."

Renee takes a breath, she's hungry and the smell of bread cooking makes her stomach roll. "Are you okay?"

The woman touches the corners of her eyes with index fingers. Down the humped road where the funeral party's going on, children have run out to play in the yard, yellow-haired kids make a joyful noise.

"That's Grandma Staggs's brood down there. They been holding watch on her these two weeks and she ups and goes home on Christmas Day. You believe that?"

"I'm sorry."

"It's everbody got to go home sometime. What's your girl's name again?"

"Lara."

"That's sweet. I lost my little girl. We're trying for another. If I can keep Rusty outta the coon woods long enough."

Renee unfolds paper money from the purse where the Old Charter bottle clinks against her keys. It's afternoon, in Arkansas, ten miles from home.

The black-eyed woman reaches a flour coated hand out, touches Renee's wrist. "Keep it, honey," she says. "Ain't nobody else wants that fish."

"No, really," Renee says. Poor people'll give you their last breath if you let them. "You take this. Let me pay you."

The woman shakes her face. Behind her, catching light on the far wall, a gold framed photograph shows a husky man holding a little girl up in the air. Lawn ornaments glitter in the background. The two faces smile wide at each other—a joyful moment.

"Uh-huh. You'ins have a happy anniversary. Eleven-heaven." She says "Bye-bye," and lets the rickety door shut.

"Take care a that little one."

The fish is heavy—it tugs Renee down the three steps and the slope to the truck. She stuffs a ten dollar bill in the roadside mailbox. Between the gap in the dirty blue drapes, Renee feels the black-ringed eyes. Downhill, the mourners have poured into the yard. They carry paper plates, have untucked shirttails and let hair down, are pitching horseshoes in pairs, the metal posts ringing.

On the highway, past fall-down houses and burned out trailers and grassless plots where swayback horses stand, standing for all of their lives, past the Tri-

County Coon Club where she sees men laid out from the night's hunting with their worn out bony dogs, Renee drives home. A hippy house is afternoon colorful—the mismatched roof shingles enough to make her laugh out loud, roll down the windows and breathe. Fake snowmen shine in brown front yards. Garland snakes through rails on lonely front porches. They pass a living manger at the Oak Grove Gas and Hotdog, donkeys and wise men, a red-faced baby in the arms of a hefty Madonna, JOY TO THE WORLD painted on butcher paper behind them. What a glorious day to be alive, Renee says it out loud, ready to wake little Lara and scream—she's that joyful this second. How odd, this moment, the woman with blacked eyes who called her honey. Hadn't the horned Lucifer spoken? She breathes chill air through the open window.

Renee turns east on 164, past the sawmill. This is timber country, you can't drive down the road without passing trucks stacked with trees. Joey's Uncle Willard drove one all his life until he swerved across the centerline on scenic Highway 7 where more head-ons happened than any road on earth. It's happy hour. Home, five minutes away, Joey's setting up their drink makings. Getting music and hors d'oeuvres ready. Renee digs in her purse with one hand. She retrieves the Old Charter, screws the top off. The sun is full bright on them now, pouring in through the windshield. Cows and calves chew the deep green grass. A white horse that Joey calls White Horse shakes its head, neighs, bright as a snowbank. She's trembling—the afternoon's going holy on her. The liquor burns, is sweet down her throat.

They're a family—Joe, Renee, Lara. He's built a chicken coop just beyond the pasture gate, a nice job with wood boxes stacked on a wall for the hens and a little door with an elevated walkway for roosts. One of his students is supposed to bring a truckful of Rhode Island Reds, layers and a rooster. The barn corral's right for a pony pen and the side pasture's set up for a few cows. There's an artesian well in the back pasture; water chestnuts grow in the clear, cold hole. They have a moondog. It's a good life to live. A farm, for Christ's sake. And Joey's a professor now. Their house has five bedrooms, a fireplace built by the crazy Simms people that's big enough for four-foot logs, a wood bin that opens to the outside. They've bought furniture. Their daughter's healthy and happy and adjusting to Arkansas. What on earth more could they want? What could be missing?

Little Lara groans, her tonsils are swollen.

At the Moreland crossroads, with its grocery and lone gas pump, Renee surveys the wide open Ozark foothills—god's country. Natural gas underfoot, a ways off sits a gas rig—fire roaring out the pipe-mouth. Lara's out for the count, her neck locked that way. She doesn't know, and can't help, who she is or where she's going. The little girl falling into her daddy's arms—what was *her* name, what call came off her father's tongue on the day she disappeared? Had she been named for her mother? And after? How would such a name sound then? No matter, Renee thinks, but that's how we all are, falling and getting caught and falling.

Going home. Renee enters the intersection, gears up 124—the last mile. To her left, Last Days Full Gospel, where a billboard announces services preached by Reverend Pastor Roy Ray Shoates. At GRANNY'S DOLLS, she turns, the good sound of gravel crunching. Dust rises and settles behind her. Renee imagines the moons of Jupiter, gracefully orbiting the spotted planet. What on earth would become of them? She summons the she-ape, a moon-faced child at each tit. Beside her, in the passenger seat, the scaly carp. It's a strange life to be living, but she's here, part and parcel of stars, scientists said. Her offspring snores softly at her back. No one is disfigured. Living is the way to go; so important in Arkansas not to be dead. Tonight she will set up the light bucket reflector on the flat spot facing north, rutted from where a garden once grew. They will tuck their daughter in bed and make love on the leather couch, the first time in a long, long time, and the limbo they've shared will thin and sigh. They will brew green tea, walk out onto the dark yard past the leafless hickories. Their daughter's tree swing will stir and the sky will lure them. No need for words, they'll lower eyes to the silver lens—one with a kind that has ever looked up and wanted and feared and been bewildered.

16

Mid-January, an unforecast rain floods the basement, so Joey climbs through the trap door into the crawl space that goes *on* and *on* dragging a utility light on an orange extension cord that plugs into a light socket above the muddy waterline. He'd hardwired the sump pump after it became clear that their realtor was a deceitful cocksucker who'd concealed the ranch house's history of flooding. Now it occurs to him he could die down here, ankle-deep, fumbling with the monkey-rigged switch while mice skitter in the dark from which the poison-stoned bug sprayer'd once dragged a hog-nose snake, little strips of silvery skin flaying off its back. "This'n won't bother you," he'd said, and Joey'd found it out front, looped in the fork of a dogwood.

November, a warm trough has sailed up from the Gulf, colliding with the first brace of genuine cold from the Rockies, deer season still, so the purple-painted fence posts glow outside in the yellow light, and a troop of blaze orange hunters had tromped across the back pasture. Joey'd seen them behind the barn, aught-sixes and shotguns and lever-action thirty-thirty's in the crooks of their arms, and just as dark fell a shot came from the wood and Joey recognized the sound of a slug hitting meat. A pile of field-dressed guts lay out there steaming. That's how it was on the cusp of the millennium, when they'd hauled off and moved back to Joey's native state. Renee imagines hunter man peeking through every window, the only neighbors a half-mile off sighting their rifles in off a fall down front porch, just like some hayseed dream of the place, 333 Barton Road, Dover, Arkansas, first right before the curve—they've bought the farm.

The pump kicks on, *omp-omping* out the basement window onto the green septic grass. It's a Tuesday, Joey's off day from ArkaTech. He's dug a trench to gather the seep, sees it glisten in the side footer where he pick-axed a hole from a flower bed straight down and patched the concrete, but not the leak. Outside, thunder, wind in the trees and the far off noise of the pileated woodpecker.

Joey knows his predicament—a kid who'd played wide receiver at Jackrabbit High'd died the same way. Should he somehow ground the little hook light and extension cord into the cold water, 110 volts will sear through his blood, and, without 220's kick, glue him to the spot, so no one would find him while he cooked through the day, not until Renee walked into one wing of the huge house, holding two-year-old Lara's hand and calling his name. "Joe?" she'd say. "Joker? Stop it." She'd search room to room to room. No Joe.

Odd. His truck was in its spot.

Eventually, she'd walk to the barn, turn the light on in the tack room where a roof rat had chewed through floorboard. She'd say his name, walk back out and circle the house, see the basement door ajar, hear the pump gurgle. Surely Lara'd be with her, holding her right hand, that sweet far-off look in her eyes—*where's Daddy?* They'd walk to the little trap door together, their footprints side by side. Renee would see him first. She'd reach without thinking—what did she know of current? The juice would pass from him into her, and that would be a surprise because she'd never felt it, that hot rippling. And little Lara'd reach to Mommy, *what wrong with Mommy?* and there they'd be, the three of them bound with no one in the world to throw the switch. What a goddamn mess.

Ankle-deep with a sump pump, Joey's just thought—*goddamn mess*—when it happens. A tiny flash sizzles and pops. He holds a breath. For some reason he pictures the brilliantly green collards he'd once planted in Carolina on top of whole fish carcasses. Through the various doors he's crawled through comes the horn blast—Gabriel?—high and loud and true, as if all the dogs on earth lift snouts in a single howl. It is surely the same warning they'd had explained to them umpteen times when they signed papers, and again by the blue book labeled EMERGENCY INSTRUCTIONS. Fourteen miles south in R'Ville, the siren signals either a meltdown at Nuclear One or a tornado warning, Joey's forgot the difference. Upstairs, in the pale blue manual are the bulleted directives for such a moment.

On all fours, Joey works himself out the crawl space door onto wet concrete and away from the valley of the shadow of death. He sees light. Let the sump pump do its work. He exits the basement with the alarm in his ears. Down Barton Road, the neighbor's Walker dogs howl in sync, so the two sounds tangle and for the rest of his life he'll hear them siren-dog mix—a mutant symbol of his life up until then.

Every number he punches is busy. Cow Jumped Over The Moon, *busy.* R'ville Middle, Room 14, *busy.* Principal Titsworth, *busy.* ArkaTech, *busy.* The big house ticks. It still smells like the Elliotts, their hair in the carpet fiber, their sloughed skin down the sink drains, their shit filling half the septic tank.

Joey opens the drawer, takes it in hand. The cover sketch is a hokey Nuclear One, computer generated. Written on the sixth-grade level, the index breaks the book into parts like "What Is An Emergency?" followed by "What Do I Do?" and "Do I Need Special Help?" "Are there deaf people in my neighborhood?" the book asks in twenty-point font, every letter bolded. "Go tell them, DO NOT PANIC!"

Joey opens the cedar armoire, switches on the stereo. Nothing but static. He keeps his cool, stays calm, does not panic. The siren and its sister-dogs shut up. Maybe it's a mistake, maybe he's breathed too many fumes in the basement. It's Tuesday. What kind of a day is Tuesday for a meltdown? That'd be a Friday night sort of thing, or Sunday morning with all the church bells clanging. But Tuesday? *Monday* would be better than Tuesday, no matter what Lynyrd Skynyrd said. Tuesday's lame.

But it is Tuesday, January 18, 2000 in Pope County, Arkansas—two days from Full Wolf Moon, no doubt about it.

Renee's in her classroom at Russellville Middle, about to unwrap a turkey on wheat, stare out at ArkaTech's shining white cupola and wonder how she got mixed up in all this. Lara's at Cow Jumped Over The Moon, where they have *hot-hot* drills to practice for this very day. Joey imagines all the people he's ever loved that have died. What would it be like to be dead and not know that your people are about to be radiated to kingdom come, their wails rising in a crescendo beyond any siren or Walker dog? Would the dead know of such a moment? Would the deep silence of eternity revive their listening?

In the great room, Moondog saws logs. Last night's storm kept her up. She's been scared of thunder since a puppy back in North Carolina when Hugo blew through Greensboro and knocked all the trees down on the college golf course. They'd burned slick-barked logs carved with names of lovers for three whole winters.

The siren again.

The front porch faces a hickory treed acre where wild turkey and whitetail traipse past the well-house with a skiff of frost on it just now, the *thump-thump* from Ajax rumbling like Aztec drumbeats. Fourteen miles south are his wife and daughter—it wasn't supposed to end this way. Not like this. Hell with it, he won't let it happen.

Back in Utah he'd taught a history workshop for the elderly and in that class was ancient Harriot Bean whose memory uncoiled like rich cloth with flashing bits of her life clinging to every strand. She'd been a twenty-year-old telephone operator in Kanab, Utah, on the morning of December 7, 1941, when the lines had gone crazy over Pearl Harbor. The USS Utah had been sunk with two of her classmates from Kanab High, Leopard ball players, goodlooking kids with their lives in front of them. That evening she'd accompanied friends to the outskirts of town where they'd fired pistols, rifles, the odd shotgun, just pointed the muzzles into the dark and fired at the dark matter beyond. The barrel mouths flamed with each shot, the repeats echoing off Nine Mile Canyon. The night of Pearl Harbor in South Utah, just before Christmas, 1941. The story'd touched Joe, the thought of all those kids in the December chill, out there on the outskirts of town near solstice, the town itself on the fringe of the still-wild west. The U.S. a country at war, soon to drop the bomb fueled by uranium mined not sixty miles away from where they stood that night. And there was young, pretty Harriot Bean, her towheaded lover fresh dead across the sea, firing *one, two, three* into a place she could not see but now knew.

For some reason Joey throws the Model 11 in the front seat, a water bottle and two cans of pork'n'beans. Gravel crunches all down the line to Barton Road where Renee'd seen a pair of roadrunners that first week, when every last minute had this glow to it, and Lara'd fed the neighbor's white-faced heifers sugar from the palm of her hand through strands of barbed wire. A Morrillton station comes in loud and clear and some light flits through the clouds, silver at the edges. Joey recalls the 60 Minutes feature on Chernobyl—how they'd had to pipe in classical music, sent it screaming out of semi-truck sized speakers twenty-four hours a day so the apocalyptic silence of the vacant city wouldn't drive the finishers shithouse crazy—pouring the endless mixer truckloads of concrete over bare reactor rods, the notes had echoed off the buildings and streets where, for some reason, a deer hung from a child's swing and slide, the breeze ruffling its fur.

The blue book instructs him to drive to Hector, home of the Warlocks, to hit the road and DO NOT TAKE PETS. Joey whistles Moondog from the great room, loads her and slams the tailgate. He's to tear out the NOTIFIED page and attach it to his front door, and go. Past the Goodnos sits the Elliott boy on the front porch with a can of beer between his legs, same sneer he wore that first day when Joey moved his family in what had been his house, a chest freezer full to the gills with meat out under the August sun for spite, his little dog hopped atop it, growling. Let the son of a bitch burn.

Persons living in Zone L are to take HWY 7 to Dover, then HWY 27 to Hector, or HWY 164 to HWY 105, then Gumlog Road through the cutoff where the white horse stood, then HWY 27 to Hector. Go straight to Hector High. Principal Waylow will meet you with a bag including toilet paper and toothbrush and assign you a spot on the gym floor. There is a heated mens and womens with running water. Joey reads the fine print of Renee's hand— *if you're reading this, Joey, I love you.*

Moondog moans in back—he's forgot her food sack, but brought both bowls and the biscuit box. For a long time him and Renee had been able to communicate without talking. At first, she'd flip him off behind his back and he'd feel it, that middle finger wavering when they'd fought over something silly like hair spray or how to pronounce *flutist*, or song lyrics she'd learned all wrong as a girl before she got a hearing aid. But lately, these last few years, of a sudden Joey'd think, we really should go to Florida for Christmas, and Renee'd say, "I've decided to go see Mom and Dad for the holidays." Or, after a spring rain lifted fire bans, the yard ape schoolkids lit tire fires on days when the redbud and jonquil perfumed the afternoon and everything should've been all right. Joey'd sit on the back porch, sip vodka tonics and invent awful acts of revenge, and Renee'd say, "It's the fathers of those kids ought to have their things cut off."

Only not today—nothing on the radar. At the four-way stop where he can head one way or the other, toward Hector or back to R'ville where his good wife and daughter are no doubt being whisked to Morrillton that very second— Morrillton, not far from the Stepwell Family Cemetery out on the Trails of Tears, Solgahatchia where his grandmother'd been married under a sweetgum tree on

Isbel Creek. A semi blows by, a logger from Highway 7 with its headlights on high beam, rolling like a bat out of hell, so the back draft sucks the Pathfinder's nose toward R'ville—maw of the meltdown.

Toward R-Ville, Joey hauls ass.

As always, Billingsly's donkeys were loose at Dead Man's Curve, where on the day he'd arrived Joey'd witnessed the bride-to-be casting a spinning rod in her wedding dress for a photo shoot. Maybe it was the foreshadowing of this very moment, Joey Harvell on the end of his days, flooring it toward Solgahatchia for the wife and daughter he so loved?

He'd hardly ever made this drive save on the occasion of funeral processions, the long line of American cars with their headlights on, a trooper in the lead. Once, Sheriff Marlan Hawkins had led them on a Harley Davidson, and the last time for Jimmy. Three times he's been driven here, and then Jimmy, which broke his heart, how endlessly messed up that Jimmy was here, that such could happen in this world. What'd happened to Jimmy had broken him down until Lara'd come along. Love had lifted his heart.

Bunker Mountain to Wesley Chapel and the old gaunt Catholic church at St. Vincent to Wonderview, where Si'd attended first grade, down the gravel road into Solgahatchia Bottom, Stepwell land. He passes hunt shacks and chicken houses to the lightning struck tree and finally the place itself with its rusted gate and bushhogged grass and big old shade oak. The summer before they'd buried Si, he'd visited this place with the old man at happy hour on a rain day. His grandfather'd had a highball on his spot at the foot of PaPa Stepwell, smoked a pipe then knocked it out on his daddy's stone. "Get in Joker. Let's get," he said and drove away.

Here now, alone.

The sun's come out against the backbone of clouds so there's a silver ridge to the south and east. Uphill, beyond the big oak, Jimmy's stone shines, the blocks have held, not too many weeds.

He shouldn't be here.

What he needs is to find his people, this second, Renee and Lara, he'd pray for them if he still prayed, a long time now from that, those days when it was all real—the Holy Ghost fire. When Grandmother Dee'd take him to a full-gospel meeting and all hell'd break loose, churchfolk dancing the herkey-jerk. Somebody'd yell *Gog rajeth in the east, Magog in the west. God damns this world to hell.* He'd felt in every cell of his body, and at night he'd pray real prayers for O.W. to get sober, for them to somehow get money for food, and maybe rent the three-bedroom brick across the street from Carly Jane, so he could see her through the second story window wriggling into short-shorts split up the sides. All those Sunday mornings, stained light staining the front of her choir robe, how Joey'd read and memorized songs in the hymnals and his favorite books of the Bible, triple X-rated Song of Solomon with its perfumed breasts and heaving body parts. Then Revelations, how those washed in the blood would climb up out of their graves to the clouds while those left behind suffered unspeakable shit.

January chill, the shiver's up his backbone. Joey grips the wheel. He'd forgot to hang the NOTIFIED sign on his door, and now the stones shine so they might be seen from the moons of Jupiter and beyond. Here, where it has ended for his blood people, one-legged Si, at the foot of PaPa Stepwell and his own mother, Ella Fryer, who'd stayed forever young. Over there's Uncle Leo, the cemetery's lone college graduate, he'd got big in tomatoes and married Naveen, Si's sister who'd once argued a man to death. Babies are buried under little lamb stones and somebody lay beneath a miniature cannon, the balls stacked in a V. Higher up the hill, Jimmy, six-feet tall and sawdust brown, those sky-eyes and shining beard.

The e-brake cricks. He gets out just as a window of sunshine pours down. The two-doored gate squalls on its hinges. He walks in to join his people. There's something he's supposed to do. Isn't there? Some important thing? Or is that Renee? His life is supposed to mean something now, isn't it? This homecoming, a healing? Whose? The conviction pours through his blood and he lets fly an honest cry. He could be dead now. Around him, on the grassy acres where brown-eyed Susan may bloom on a day when you bury your brother, there is stillness, quiet. None of the last time's ruckus. Through the piece of fence where he fought the skin and bone man leaps a big-antlered whitetail, over the barbed wire inward so the sun catches its tines.

Joey has just one split-of-a-second to think *bright wings!* before his people commence to claw themselves from their graves. In all directions, that's what happens, and he hears voices speak a language never heard, but known. Leo and Si and MaMa Stepwell join the host of relatives he's never met but knows by those features he shares with his one daughter. He knows this last thing for a reason that is not yet clear to him but will be.

Love will lift him.

They're on him now, jubilant, dancing the holy ghost dance, a wreathed and shimmering array with hands thrown into the blue piece of sky where silver-rimmed clouds just now rupture, so the first of them tread brisk air. They look on him and his world with pale angelic faces, beckoning him to *come, come, come. Brothers, sisters, lovers in Christ. Look! We shall not perish.* How they beckon him.

And then on the hilltop he witnesses his brother Jimmy resurrected, how he stands to his full height, so different in face and body from the last time, the time carved into Joey's head and heart. His white raiment shines, *radiant* and *radiant* and a thing beyond *radiant*. A horn blasts from on high, and there is singing, and this is holy. The embrace lifts him skyward where his maternal grandfather walks on two legs once more amongst the newly risen. Black folk, red and yellow and white, the fierce beauties of his childhood and the time before that, a whole troop of Cherokee with the gleam in their braids, arrayed and glimmering, the Eagle Chief on a skyward Appaloosa. The Trail of Tears has dried. Joey watches himself drag the extension cord into the basement shadow, the muddy waterline's hiss and pop.

But it is the image of wife and daughter that grips him tightest. The vision severs and he is hauled dripping from the brink, very much alive. Jolted full awake, he's just a man whose imagination caught fire for a moment in the cemetery where his people lay buried. He's had a run in with an electric wire, and lived.

To turn face from this world, shed earth-skin and walk toward a home in glory that outshines the sun? Such things cannot be. Surely.

What instructions for such?

17

The dogs are confused but happy, turned aloose just as the sun slips behind Carrion Crow Mountain, an hour-old whiff of Rusty Love pulling them into the rutty bottoms of Isbel Creek where the fall leaf rot is chill and soft beneath their pawpaws. Back at Tri-County, after the shit quit hitting the fan, Sheriff Autry'd taken eye-witness accounts from the whole bunch and Dean Shock had produced the Coon dick out of thin air, waved its shriveled length over the Harvell boy to stop the bleeding. An ambulance was summoned and Paris was made to dial up the professor's Yankee wife over to Barton Road—she taught the *touched*, which maybe explained her hard time understanding the chawed-off finger part, how her husband's digit was key to the whole incident. Did it have distinguishing characteristics? Was it true he'd broke it in the third floor toilet of Old Main during a history test on how Charlemagne had marched all Christmas day around the walls of some castle until they fell down and he crowned himself Holy Roman Emperor—some silly shit like that, the babbling professor.

Now Poon Tang, a full-blood Walker with a good nose, is hell-bent for leather, her sweet voice not a quarter-mile away, headed south and west along the creek where the Love boy, who'd ever be known from that day forward as Snapper, had run.

There'd been a ruckus.

The Hector faction, braid-beard warlocks all who still spoke the old tongue, they saw the mission as rescuing Love from his own black mojo, taking him home to Rhonda who'd soothe his sore spirit. To consume human flesh—there were worse things, the warlocks claimed—look at what the Baptists and Methodists did with all that blood and body baloney. But Alderman Waylow and Sheriff would have none of it—justice would be served. Harvell was an ArkaTech man, a professor. His grandfather Si'd been a High Coon and was a penis carrier. It was first degree assault, any way you looked at it.

Should they go armed into the woods for Love?

Would they be asked to shoot the man?

Birdshot or buck?

Should the R'Ville Courier be in on the manhunt?

What would Jesus do? Had the ancestral enemy interbred with the surviving handful of mountain meadows children, sewn its seed within their ranks?

They settled on long guns in case the stray bushy tail showed itself—number six in the chambers. Reverend Shoates offered a short prayer prescribing mercy for all involved. Point was, they had to get it back, the finger. Within a certain amount of time—Shock claimed, shaking the coon wand right in Paris's face—the finger could be reattached. If they could swing reattaching Harvell's digit at regional, then maybe the whole mess, lawsuits and legal precedent regarding assault by biting, could be thusly avoided. That was the thinking.

Paris pictures the finger down there in Love's belly, curling and pointing, the little curlicue of quick under the nail, a scar across the knuckle where a lock-blade shut on him once, Harvell claimed when pressed for distinguishing characteristics, that and breaking it in the shitter.

Dark's full on them.

The dogs choir the woody bottom, slosh across Isbel Creek one way, then meander back the other, the men's headlights zipping through the bramble—it's going to be a night. Paris wishes he'd thought to grab a pocketful of hushpuppies on the way out, a crappie filet, a mouthful of coleslaw sure would hit the spot. Back there is a fish fry feast going to waste—a damned shame. How about that pie steaming on the shelf, a scoop of that vanilla from the freezer? Damn Love, pull this shit at the Lupercalia Mardi Gras fish fry.

Biscuit Mouth chimes in, her voice a shade yelpier than Poon Tang, the two on the scent for real, the way Walkers go bat out of hell for it, run a deer to death, only something's wrong. One of the Taylor boys is down on the ground. "He taken his shoes off," Elvin, the eldest of the family of concrete finishers says. "Barefooting it."

Another hundred yards they find the stripped off shirt shining on one bank, and pants on the other, tighty-white skivies hung head-high from a tree limb.

"Boy done stripped nekid," Sheriff says.

Alderman coughs. "He'll freeze his pecker off."

"Look here," Taylor says. From the pants pocket, he's removed a baggie full of white stuff, the snort powder that's fucked up all the country kids, makes their teeth fall out. Paris once walked up on a dead elk stuffed full of dynamite near a shack where they boiled the shit up, a six-foot pile of kitchen matches with the tip ends broke off. Word was they'd cut the head off this woman informant, teased the hair all snakey and wired it up wide-eyed to guard their stash—a hillfolk Medusa. No wonder Rusty was shithouse.

"And this."

A wrinkly picture gets passed around. Second grade—Miss Belieu's home room. Little Shiloh Love's smile is tranquil under Paris's headlight. He plays through all the dead he's seen in his life—right many as grave digger, standing under a shade tree while the voices of weeping folk sing "Amazing Grace," mix with the sweet-sick smell of flowers. A sister once to the river. His own mama not so long gone. But that little girl he dug out of Illinois Bayou, word was she'd had to dig her own hole. How that must eat at the daddy, make anybody with a mind shithouse. On the back of the picture, she's written *For Daddy. I luv you.*

Paris passes it on, wishes he hadn't seen it.

A way off the dogs go quiet. And the quiet gets louder, until Paris wishes he had earplugs to block out the bone-rattling quiet. The men stand there in the dark, one by one turn headlights off, so the starry night shines through the crowns of trees. There's the dipper, its corner star ever pointing north, so slaves once followed it, Paris's read, toward free states, scattering their poison-laced hushpuppies along the way. *Here go, sweet dog. Pretty dog. Good dog. Honeybabe. Want a biscuit. Good dog want a hushpuppy? Alls you want, now, sweetie.* And those dogs would lay down and bloat and explode from the insides out and never get up again. If he was a slave, he'd damn sure run like hell, fry up a batch of killer fritters for any dog try to trail him down.

A picture of his dead daughter and pocketful of crank. Well he won't have either one of them now, and maybe that's best, Rusty Love, stripped to the nuts, under the bare bone sky.

The collar tags jingle as Poon Tang trots up, Biscuit Mouth, the rest. They've lost him. The wood thunders with quiet and the stars shine, and there's no moon, none at all. Cassiopeia's W floats by, and there's the hunter, high already, his stick raised to whop the bull's head.

And what's he up to now, *nekid* in the woods, Love?

18

If she reads one more word—just *one more word* about Roger Gene Simms—she'll spit. She'll spit. Renee's had it up to here with the whole mess, what he did to Shiloh Love, not to mention fourteen of his inbred people that Christmastime. She'll spit. She'll bygod spit. Sick to the bone with the whole crock—she can't quit stirring it.

Some monumental task, a job for the ages?

It has to do with the Love woman. Renee knows it in some part of herself she can't call by name, but has known since a girl when her father—a Navy captain whose name was up for admiral—sailed into Charleston port flying the number 1 flag, and she felt this wordless space inside where dwelt a nameless knowing—how it had felt to be three months pregnant when the baby kicked—this holy knowing and dread. Years ago, it had guided her to Joey—for better or worse—and love, and life without love, as the poet said, "isn't worth a dead dog nine days unburied." It drew her that day from Celestial Universe to a yardful of lawn ornaments where a stone Beelzebub had offered her the world in exchange for her gift. Somebody'd hit Rhonda Love in the face. Her eyes were blacked when she opened the door, and there'd been a picture of her husband, Rusty, throwing Shiloh into the frosty air, catching her fall, and the light was golden like October, maybe the autumn before she'd ridden a bus to the Dover complex with the Simms girl—and that had impressed her because Lara was asleep in the carseat, and they'd only just escaped the razorblade incident at the telescope shop, and a funeral was going on downhill, and she'd drunk whiskey, and every last thing had gone holy on her.

No accidents in this life.

Some monumental task, a job for the ages: she's been on the trail for three weeks now and has finally tracked it down, sees its trace glowing in her peripheral vision, the way stargazers turn away and thus perceive what they seek. But if she reads one more goddamned word about Roger Gene Simms and what he did she'll spit.

At the library, Renee has to fill out triplicate sheets of yellow paper, show her driver's licence and social security card and teacher's ID, and make a two-dollar-and-fifty-cent deposit against future late fees—all for a dinky temporary card—the plastic-coated one would be mailed to her home in seven to ten working days via U.S. mail, but the temp would give her all privileges except movie rentals, which required the bar code on the plastic card. Has she printed her address out legibly? Internet use is restricted to approved sites. She should be aware that there's a porn blocker in place, and should she visit porn sites she'll lose all privileges, and the plastic-coated card would be revoked, and she'd lose the two-fifty for porn usage in lieu of late fees. She should not use obscenities in the public library, nor touch or show her body parts to children. Under no circumstances were library materials allowed in the restrooms. Did she have questions?

In another week, February—a month named for cleansing. Wash her hands of the whole mess, that's what she needs after a year like this—a hundred long, hot baths lined up in a row, a bottle of wine with every one, chocolate butterflies with no southern accents. Josephine had that right, a hot tub in the bedroom with a door that locked.

Obscenities? Renee's shiny new prisoner-made licence plate is Arkansas 668DMF, and yes, she does know that DMF could stand for a half-dozen top-notch obscenities this sunny day, in the R'Ville library to study Pope County abductions, especially those of young girls named Love by long-beard practitioners of the Fundamental Latter Day Saint faith, whatever on earth that might be. She's forty years old now, a white female who's married and has a daughter and lives somewhere between Dover and Moreland so she gets to choose either but not both on the multicolored forms that follow her hither and thither. No, she's never had her library privilege revoked for porn use; yes, can you please point the way to the flipping microfiche, *sweet Jesus*.

Renee's tracked Simms across Texas, eight children in tow, one of whom was a seventeen-year-old named Sheila with whom he'd had a son named after himself. He'd lived and got in trouble in Cloud, New Mexico, where he'd crossed paths with the fundamentalist sect of the Mormon church, whose incestuous practices got him investigated up one side and down the other until he fled, only to end up not ten miles down the road from Renee's own bedroom door and the windows she feels eyes looking through on moonless nights when the dark is impenetrable and the cicada husks cackle in a bone-cold breeze.

Roger Gene Simms, a retired Army master sargent, had built on a compound he shared with some fifteen family members—his offspring and wives—on the Long Pool side of Dover, way out in the sticks, so the kids had to walk the woods every morning to a gate that opened onto a gravel stretch of Gumlog road to catch the bus toward R'Ville middle. It'd all happened before Christmas, gifts wrapped under the tree—the detectives had worked the murders backwards from the last three in R'Ville, the finalé being a beauty queen secretary who'd turned down the geezer's advances at a surveying company where he'd clerked for one month, to a 7-11—his next job—where he'd shot the attendant. Officers climbed the tin fence into the Dover compound, found a body in the trunk of every car, and a whole shitload in the cesspool he'd had the kids dig for an outdoor latrine. Each had been strangled in a water barrel and thrown in the hole, all except Shiloh Love who'd been a mistake—she had not been invited to the Simms's Christmas, little sneak, she'd ridden the bus over with one of the Simms girls, a classmate in Ms. Isom's second grade at R'Ville Elementary. Somehow, her body'd made it just down the road to Illinois Bayou, where it lay until the day Renee and Lara arrived to see the silver gurney roadside, the vomiting men bent over in the snake-smelling heat. The extended family'd arrived last; seems Simms had drunk beer and watched T.V. with the head-shot bodies still sitting at the dining table, the Christmas lights blinking.

There was more—a book was in the works. But the kicker was Shiloh Love, how some way she'd made it to the Dover compound where she spent her last hours in that house of horrors—Christmas party from hell. And her daddy, Rusty, had he given her permission for the sleepover? Had he hugged her before school that Friday morning, winter solstice, shortest day of the year? Had Mama Rhonda packed a Cinderella backpack, carefully wrapped the Simms girl a gift that would never be opened? Had she sent Mexican wedding cookies for the party, the powdered sugar dusting the countertops ever-after?

The *Courier* photo from the day after Christmas freezes Renee, the sweet face with her father's cold black hair and mother's hazel eyes twinkling.

Shiloh Love Missing, the headline said, *Reward.*

Joey'll shit about the FLDS part.

When they'd first moved to Utah from green North Carolina, all they'd known was that there were mountains, and that it snowed, and that there was a temple founded by folk who'd escaped Missouri, and that they called it Zion, heaven on Earth, that everyone had nineteen wives and certain among them were rumored to be born with the tails of pigs. The real place ever seemed like the backdrop to a movie Western, the towering, snow-covered Wasatch with its sawblade teeth, and the line 'round the valley at the base of the mountains, like a bathtub ring from a dirty bather—ancient Lake Bonneville, when the cold green Sea of Cortez stretched inland, and natives harpooned whales from skinny boats if legend be true. Who knew about the Mountain Meadows thing—even Josephine was shocked to hear of the Fancher Party's demise, the white flag flown near the spring well, the Arkansans dying of thirst, the promise of safe passage from the mouth of Mormons, the laying down of arms and then, in the early afternoon with the burning thought of water, every last one of them head-shot, stripped, one-hundred-forty some thrown into a ditch—the single largest massacre of manifest destiny, perpetrated by white— dressed as Indian—upon white.

Today is Children Read To A Service Dog Day at the Pope County Library. She can see them from where she sits, a whole line of kids snaking up to a smug-looking yellow lab which nods its head when it's time to switch readers. Renee hears their voices, how they roll the vowels in their mouths, stumble over hard words. There's a window and outside the window are leafless trees whose limbs are dark against the blue sky. Life sneaks up on you. Her dad had warned her not to be a teacher. Marry a dentist and go on cruises. Life is short—living well is the best revenge. Isn't that what Mom always said? Revenge for what?

The dog nods its head and another child steps before it for reading. This one's got a black Bible in her hands. Renee recognizes Beatitudes from her childhood. She was a Job's Daughter. The blond dog nods, and there's another child before it, the book open between them, *Are You My Mother?*

Simms had made the girl dig her own hole. Christmastime. A stocking with Shiloh written in glitter glue hanging on the fake mantle in the Love's house trailer. In between the one for Mom and the one for Dad.

Just like home.

19

Three weeks after New Year's 2000, on St. Agnes Eve—coldest of winter nights—while the maidens of Pope County walk gownless into the unplowed fields sprinkling fistfuls of Silver Queen corn in the name of the Virgin, having in her name baked phallic cakes and walked backwards thrice around their houses in the direction of the pole star, then climbed akimbo into new-made beds lined with mistletoe to lay and pray for a vision of their husbands-to-be—in this new millennium with all its zeroes humped back to back, Joey, Renee and young Lara lean deep into blanket-draped camp chairs and witness the total eclipse of the Full Wolf Moon. It's big as a barn in the western sky. Already, a fingernail is missing.

Far below, light shines through the drapes of the sliding doors. They've made it through Christmas and the new year. Lara's adjusting, using her Elmo potty and laughing out loud nights in bed while Joey and Renee take turns reading *Finneas The Fish.* Something's eating Renee—who knows?

A thumbnail is missing.

It's midnight, skunk-hour, and they're happy with dinner wine. The air is brisk. The Starhopper leans barrel-end towards the spectacle above, but there's no need. The moon's big as a bucket lid, going red, just the faintest hint of alpen glow.

Asleep on Renee's lap, wrapped in a mummy bag, Lara's breath rasps through swollen tonsils.

"Can she breathe through that?"

Renee pulls the bundle to her chest. "It's Thursday. We should be in bed."

"What's wrong with you? I want her to see this."

"She's asleep. What's to remember?"

"Wake her up."

Last week Renee'd gone and spent five hundred dollars on polka-dotted blouses and wispy skirts at *Mon Cheri*, R'Ville's fashion boutique that his colleague, Darquah Banchie, theorized existed primarily because of the lower middle class's innate desire to fart through silk.

"She won't remember any of this. None of it. She'll never even know we lived here."

The silence is cut by their daughter's breath, the air over her tonsils.

"I remember when I was two." He adds, "What do you do at the library?"

Headlights skitter a half-mile off where the gravel road zigs and zags into a giant Z. Lara wakes with a start, and Joey remembers the white of her face, the milky light of Renee's breast and the suckling sound of his daughter nursing on the Eve of St. Agnes, under the very moon she was birthed under on a night when women howled across the maternity ward, so the place sounded like a house of horrors.

"What? What do you remember from when you were two."

More of the moon is missing. "A tricycle. A flight of stairs. Being afraid. You have a lover at the library?"

Renee leans back in the camp chair, sighs moonfaced.

"Say."

She makes the sound that means she wants a smoke. The cold's on his face, under a tooth, working its way.

"Remember when the duck walked into the backyard and stood under the sprinkler?"

"What are you talking about."

"The duck."

"I asked you about the library."

"You should be a lawyer."

On some nights Joey dreams she's left him, wakes with a start in the big dark house, only she's there, breathing, she's never left him. And there's Lara. They are good people. What more does he want?

"Tell me, Joey. How long does it take to fall out of love?"

Out on the gravel, the vehicle's barely moving, and Joey thinks of once when he was bailing hay, swung a heavy bail up on the trailer and got sucked under and run over, so he got to drive the rest of the day, make big squares behind the bailer with dust powdering his face inside the cab. It's late. They *should* be in bed.

Joey says, "Five more minutes."

The chair creaks. "We're off."

"You're the one who bought the scope. We can build a fire."

"Why are we here?"

Eyes acclimated to the dark, Joey can see the trail from where they sit, not far from the compost he built next to the gate into the back pasture, to their house deck—the one he's walked all those nights after dinner with food scrap and the day's coffee grounds. It has a shine to it, the path home.

"Here?"

"Here."

Lara pops her head out, smiles. "*Here, here,*" she says, giggling.

"Look, sweetie," Joe says. Above them, half the moon's gone, just a skiff where it ought to be. "A dragon's gobbling it."

Gravel crunches on Barton Road. Headlights craze the woods as laser beams fired by palsy-stricken aliens might. Animal eyes redden, shine in the briars and it feels like someone hunts them, that feeling of being hunted by some clawed and toothed thing just off the periphery. A hundred yards away, just at the end of their drive where the catywhomp mailbox leans, someone kills an engine, cuts headlights. A focused beam shines into the roadside thicket and a gunshot—.22, long rifle by the sound of it—echoes off the barn.

"Son of a bitch." Joe says it and the light goes dead.

Out on the road, a car door opens, slams. Someone or thing, heavy by the sound of branches cracking, bushwhacks into the dry brush.

Lara moans, turns hazel eyes skyward. She flinched at the shot. Above them, what has ever been the moon has turned to blood, no light nor illumination nor lover's muse, just rock, a stupid hunk of stone strung up where the moon once dazzled.

"*Da, da, da, da, da,*" Lara says loud, the first words she ever spoke as a baby, then *baas* like a lamb as she's ever prone to when waked abruptly. Born under a Full Wolf Moon, all the birthing mothers shrieking in unison. "Da, da, da," she bleats.

Light from the car sweeps them over. A door thunks shut and the engine turns over three, four times, doesn't catch.

"Fuck this," Renee says.

She trails blankets and mummy bag along the dark way home, where the light is soft through the blind-covered door. Lara *baas*, says, "Da, da, da."

The eclipse is total now.

Heretofore invisible stars appear in conjunction with the moon. A fierce wedge of light rides up the ragged backside. Joey leans to the eyepiece, spins the Dobsonian mount and the flash sears his right eye. He witnesses the terminator, a ragged line between light and dark as its curve falls across cliff and crater. Earthshine ghosts the trail home.

On Barton Road, the ignition grinds and Joey thinks "give it some gas," just as she fires and throws gravel. Without thinking he's pivoted the scope, tracks the moon faces of the man and woman inside, their wide eyes and lips and the hue of their complexions. The interior light dims and the truck crunches away. Later, at a crucial moment, Joey'll understand that this was the Love couple—Ronnie and Rhonda—whose daughter was taken from them. He'll know they hurt terribly. They were poaching roadside deer with likely no idea of the full moon or eclipse or St. Agatha and the virgin cult that so worshiped her. He'll remember Lara calling out, *da, da, da*, and feel the light sweep their faces, how his little girl's voice must have pierced the winter husks of their hearts.

20

There's a moment before light reminds Edgar of when he was a boy and his daddy'd taken him down to the deer woods, Weyerhaeuser timber land where he'd walk the moonlit trail back to his tree stand, the frost slippery beneath his boots. He'd climb up into the stand and stillhunt the sunrise, sight the whitetail doe kneewalking the marshy creekbed of his dreams and it felt as if he was caught up in some ancient world where Pan himself walked with faun and nymph, and wild tusked hogs rooted in the briars. Dogs would holler across Starks Bland Road, and the first shot would sing out ricocheting off tree and sky. That's how it seems to Edgar, no food in his belly, Ash Wednesday now, the cold under his homemade filling. He's walking beneath the night sky in half-sleep, remembering how the eight point shook his viney rack, the tines slick and white near the points, the sound of it, how it woke some old part of him that needed to kill, which is exactly what he did, click the safety off his bolt-action, lay down 'til the crosshairs fell to the shoulder, pull the trigger three times fast, shaking so hard he could hardly breathe.

The buck had fallen like a feed sack.

He'd field dressed it there at the creek side, run his lockblade under the soft belly skin, reached in and pulled out the innards. Stomach stuffed with green acorn, liver, steaming heart and kidney, he dressed the sweet bread and the hot blood was good on his freezing hands. There was the smell of his kill in the frosty air, how right, how very right under gold leaf and he gave thanks to the Good Lord, Edgar did, to whoever or whatever was that'd accept him into the fold. And it was then that he knew there was something more than what you can see, a thing or way or energy, maybe, that had its grip on your lifetime, your blood and bone and brain.

God?

A pissant kid—had he found Jesus in the deer wood? Was it like Tina's mama believed, the dead rise up walking, thunder and lightning, heaven, hell, worms crawling and the damnation in between. Shit-fire.

Let the dead bury the dead: who was it said that? *Jesus? Holy Ghost?* Was Holy Ghost even a historical person? Edgar'd grown up Pentecost, hop around the pulpit with a fistful of rattlesnakes, the copperheads scraping around in a cardboard box that Reverend Roy Dale'd shit-kick every now and again when he needed a *rat-tat-tat* for emphasis, the spittle flying sideways out his mouth, goggle-eyed, put the pucker in your soul's soul—those Sunday mornings. He of course didn't have a lot of say about being Pentecostal, no more than being red-on-the-head like a donkey's dick, nor a grave digger, which just kind of fell in his lap, him being good with a shovel and all, though that's a skill gone MIA these days, with the big work all done by backhoes in about ten minutes for a six foot hole. Sometimes a family will be dead-set on digging the grave with their own hands, Hector warlocks with the coon dicks swinging, though that's rare, but not altogether unheard of, some could still wield the spade.

Ronnie Love dug the hole for his little girl Shiloh, wouldn't let anyone watch him or be around, or say kiss my ass or I'm sorry for your pain or nothing. There'd been a nondenominational service in R'Ville and they'd hauled the little casket out in the country where the Loves were still put down in a family plot surrounded on four sides by a wrought-iron fence with rusty curlicues all covered with blackberry briar and twisty vines. Edgar'd ridden in the truck with Alderman Waylow who'd kept his air on high even after they hit gravel and a gaggle of wild turkeys strutted across like they knew the high and low of things, stupid birds. And there'd been shirtless Ronnie Love, digging. The top of his head bobbing in the hole at first, then nothing. A shovel full of red hardpack burst up every other minute, the curved blade like a smile on fire. When it was all done, after they'd sung "Amazing Grace" and "To God be the Glory" and the whole party'd driven off in a shroud of dust, Ronnie'd covered it up, hammered the mound hard until its dark dirt would collapse no further. Later there'd be a stone.

Now, night nearly gone, the new day will come—there'll be breakfast and coffee and a nippy nap after noon. This world, it'll shake itself off and be new.

It was Jesus said it: let the dead bury the dead.

They find Love just before sunup.

Biscuit Mouth and Poon Tang stand at the foot of a sweetgum too tired to tree or bark or wag tails even, they just stand there looking up. Sheriff Autry circles the viney trunk with his headlight cranked up to high, though he pushed the blink mode by accident so its a flash-flash that finally gets Ronnie in the face, like somebody's taken his picture at a birthday party before cake and ice cream. His eyes shine in the fork of an oak, a good tree, a place where one would nail a tree stand and still hunt on opening day, R'Ville schools out and fresh meat for supper. Sure enough, he's stripped to the nippers, hugging the mossy bark when the headlight strikes his face, and the dogs sing out. They find him in the fork of a sweetgum, no food nor water, nothing save the gold wedding band on his left hand, and the finger length of foreign flesh in his gullet. He's shivering, crying, Love, like a full-grown baby man there in the mossy limbs with his life full on him. He talks to them, Love does, for the first time he talks about what happened, the heft of guilt and sorrow.

He cries.

Says his daughter's name a time or two, voice falling then rising.

The sun comes up then and there and the Hector faction has their way, conjures up some kind of mojo, so they've got him down and wrapped in a blanket, shoes on his bare feet, speaking the old words into his ear, witch talk, the snake tongue Grandma Stang called it.

Edgar gets close as he dares. He sees the eyes. The warlocks have him. Yes, they will take care of him, get him home to Rhonda, get some food in his belly. This last thing strikes a chord with Edgar.

He turns his face to Love. "Did you, uh, *go* yet?"

Love looks him in the eye.

"What?"

"*Go.*"

Edgar holds two fingers up for number two, thinks better of it and snaps them back. He sees the instant of recognition in Rusty's face, the guilty nod. In his eyes is the look of a man whose woke up after drinking himself Cooter Brown, whose gone and done things that'll turn your pee blue and worse—Edgar's been there himself—then woke up and can't remember a thing save the fringes of the deed, the stink of his own shit, his face painted purple oncet.

Alderman Waylow repeats the question. "Man," he says. "Did you shit yet?"

"I ain't. Here," Love says, offers up the thing itself.

21

The lawn ornaments have not moved, which half-surprises Renee, as they seemed to have life of their own last time she visited the Loves. Spring's on them though, thick Bermuda curling through the toes of the perky-titted mermaids and mermen, up entangling the legs of dwarves and bullfrog alike, even to the beard of the goat-eyed Beelzebub, whose gaze turns upon the stark white image of a girl caught in the act of leaping, knees drawn to her chest as if launched from a tree swing into the current of Isbel Creek in summer. Behind the leaping girl is another in the same likeness, only she's leveled a long-gun on a target just above Renee's head, man-high, and behind her another, grown in stature to a full woman, wielding a two-edged sword, and behind her, another, this one with a man's severed head clasped in her right hand, the eyes cast blue in this one, frozen in sky-blue agony in the severed head of a man whose name was no doubt Gene Simms, and all those of his ilk who'd ever come before and would, no doubt, come after, all violently slain on the battlefield that was Love's own backyard, the very earth where once the father broke the girl Shiloh's fall with his own hands and now formed the concrete fury his daughter would never muster. As if the sight might turn her very heart to stone, Renee whirls around and sees the world descending green down to the foot of the Ozarks, the first blooms of redbud already shining on the limbs of far-off trees so the beauty of this place strikes her to the core. She feels herself dying to herself, transformed into one of the fierce-willed beauties. Surely the moment is at hand—with her now the army of Shilohs, armed and armored from girl to woman, the guardians of all who have ever been desecrated, grown in stature, they rise up as far as Renee can see into the wooded hills, an army of Shilohs tromp from the stone world through new-green grass, sweeping Renee into their great host. Some of them are singing words in otherworldy voices, a song of love and hope and terrible vengeance. Renee is one of the Shilohs now, Lara beside her, Josephine and Floradee, a slate-eyed woman she knows is an Incan princess and the head-shot

Fancher girl waving the a white flag. The first of the men join in, marching toward the day of reckoning, toward a light manifest between flesh and stone, daughter, mother, father, their voices twine through the hollows where the four-legged, the creeping and winged lift, shake themselves off at first light, make ready to join the force of Love on this earth.

The Shiloh army rises—fierce and trembling for the battle long foreseen—and the hateful of this earth flee.

Such is the dream she wakes from, the sweet song's foreign words still on her lips, reaching for Lara's hand amongst the stone Shilohs, the army of them, the wisps of battle twisting up through the hickories, heartbeat thumping in her throat. Outside, snow is falling, big silver-dollar size flakes, so the barn's disappeared, the yard and trees, total whiteout.

Beelzebub, the old serpent, he is there, how he beseeches her. He's going to talk some sense into her uppity ass. Who was she to walk with the stone girls against one of his own? A cold day in hell, he'll make it snow fire.

Who did she think she was?

Just how much of this path was she willing to walk?

Say, woman? What hath thee to say?

The colors swirl and blend, and there's the sound of many mountains and thunder and the sound Lara made at birth, the sound of her own mother telling her it would be okay, it will be okay, it will be okay, sweetie, don't worry. And her father's voice and her brother's—*alethea, alethea, alethea,* and then Joey, whose voice had come to her from a thousand miles hence, so the dreams merge and are gone. She wakes in the dark, forty years old and it is snowing. She knows, Renee does, for maybe the first time in her life, why she's here, why she's been born a human being on this earth. The snow whirls, ten-thousand fell Shilohs, dance, leap, the shock-faced heads held by the hair before them, the trace of their black and white countenances ever on her mind's periphery.

Joey's in the kitchen scrambling eggs, a cast iron skillet of slab bacon going on the back burner. There's the good aroma of coffee and a nip in the air. He's lit a fire in the fireplace, odd for the morning, but right.

"I can make biscuits," he says, hugs her, his flannel robe an odd comfort. The fire burns in a hearth of flat stones quarried from land behind their back pasture, back in a grove of cedar where wild flowers bloom, deer and wild turkey walk, and copperheads lick the air with black tongues. The original owner—the Zimmerman man who'd built the great room from plans he'd drawn himself—had hired a stone mason to lay these stones. Ash fell into a compartment underneath, and Joey'd found the bones of a fox squirrel in there—how did he know it was a fox squirrel? Firelit, the room is all different, a place worthy of bearskin rugs and cognac, a place to make love on a morning when big snowflakes fall over Arkansas, when school's already been cancelled and there's a whole lot of wine in the cupboard.

"I just had a dream."

Stairs fall from the kitchen to the great room.

Joey studies her. "So should I do biscuits?"

"I want you to listen to me." The vanity in the bedroom shows her all she needs to know about what he sees.

"Fine, toast?"

"Joey."

Today was Friday, the 28th of January 2000, the beginning of what's big in her life, in *their* lives. A sunrise snow has come to the Ozarks, six fresh inches glistening on the big deck so it's like waking up somewhere you wanted to be after dreaming, and there's a fire and the smell of bacon, and school's been cancelled, and Peck Titsworth can jump in the goddamn lake. The snow's fallen on the grave of Jimmy Harvell over in Solgahatchia; it has blackened the windows at R'Ville Middle where her line of sight falls down Main Street to Nuclear One; the silver dollar flakes have come to rest where Shiloh Love lay, white and cold on her stone.

They sit on the leather couch before the fire, the blower gusts a warm thrum. Renee pulls the Indian blanket over his legs—an old boyfriend had bought it for her once, a guilt-gift for cheating.

"The snow makes me think of Utah. I want to ski."

"Me, too," Joey says. "What was your dream?"

Renee tells him.

She tells him the story of Shiloh Love, how she'd ridden a school bus to the Simms house on the last day of class before Christmas break two years ago. She tells him about the Pooh Bear gift wrap and the homemade card for the party, about the Mexican wedding cookies her mama'd baked and the Cinderella backpack. And the rest. The telling takes time. The fire burns down. Late January sunshine pours down on the half-foot of new fallen snow, rare in the natural state. Magical—great good luck, the hillfolk claimed, and the custom among Joey's people was to run barefoot around the house in winter's first snow. That's what they do, the Stepwells. When she's finished, they sit in silence. The fire's dying.

"I met her, the Love woman. She was our waitress at the Holiday Inn when you were taking forever to come."

"It was forever for me, too."

"Not as long of forever as it was for us." Story told, the smell of bacon's working on her. "It's where I got your fish. From her house."

"What's that got to do with your dream?"

"Everything."

"How? Look at that."

Outside, where the gravel road is supposed to be, the man they've named Killer jogs by, barefoot, mirrored sunglasses like balls of fire. Joey's out the sliding glass before she can speak, the wind blowing his robe open to bare balls and ass. Off the deck he leaps beneath the snowblown trees, jumping and falling and jumping, pitching fistfulls of powdery white into the air, shaking his head, making the I love you sign and beckoning her to come. Join me, he lips.

And so she does, the crazy Stepwells dancing barefoot in the snow. She's one of them now, and it's not so bad, is it? The snow burns her bare feet, and she feels it on her face, like no-seeums on the Outer Banks, the lightest touch. Together under the tall hickory where Lara's Pooh kite lodged on a windy afternoon in October when she wore her little moo-cow outfit for Halloween and cried because she loved her Pooh kite, and she couldn't understand how something could be gone but still there. They'd driven clear to Dover for trick or treating, over the very bayou where the little girl had lain, and knocked on strangers' doors on streets they didn't know the names for—anyone at all answering those doors. Still, she'd let Joey walk her up onto the front porches with their skeletons and witches, hay bales and cornstalks. He'd trained her to say "trick or treat" but Lara always froze when the doors swung —her first All Hallows in Arkansas, it hits her now, the Pooh kite waving up on a limb, how it is to love a child with every bit of your heart, how it must have killed Josephine to lose Jimmy.

"Here," Joey says, and the flannel is soft against her face. "Can I have this snow dance."

"*Oui Monsieur.*" She takes his hand. "*Un coeur en hiver.*"

Numb-footed, the two embrace, and there on the piece of earth at the foot of ancient mountains, their footprints merging in the half-foot of powder until the deck light flashes and there behind the shining pane of double door is their daughter's face, the ecstatic moment when she sees the first snow she'll remember in her lifetime. The oft-recounted vision: her mother and father hold each other, dance barefoot in the snow under the Pooh kite tree. So will she, one day, and the ones who'll come after, barefoot, they'll snow dance under the tree of life.

Joey comes from a long line of people that pull other people out of ditches. That is, when the snow flies and Arkansawyers begin to fishtail and spin, go into conniptions with the first skiff of black ice, when the schools have let out early because it's snowing a hundred miles away in Fort Smith, and all the Piggly Wigglys and Price Choppers are swamped to the gills with folk buying chili makings, the bravest and most desperate risking Carrion Crow Mountain to I-40 for Blackwell bourbon and schnapps for Alpines, when all the tow trucks in Pope County are en route to carwrecks, Joey zips his brother's coveralls on, laces on Utah Sorels and throws a logging chain into the Pathfinder.

"Come on," he says. "We need stuff for chili. And snow cream."

The power's been off all morning, which strikes Renee odd as Nuclear One is cranking it out to the south. They've burned their way through the wood bin that opens outside and romped and sledded and built a snowman family replete with a white dog named Moon. Renee busted her ass on cross country skis right in front of the Elliott boy. He'd stared at her like she was an alien woman crash-landed on the road, then made a sound like a road runner—his call for the inside hillbillies to step out and get a load of this.

So there was really nothing, really nothing to do after snow dancing but go pull people out of ditches and buy stuff for chili and snow cream—*snow cream?*—the first thought out of these people's heads the moment they saw a flake—do we have vanilla and dig out the chili beans. Is any of uncle's deer meat left in the freezer. We need a can of beer, don't matter what kind. The sun comes out just as they roll up the driveway. A silver wing of snow wallops them, and the pileated woodpecker flaps from a tree limb, its crown blood-brilliant.

In her carseat, Lara's asleep already—snow girl. And Joey's got the windows rolled down looking for ditched cars, listening to a station out of Conway, the Reverend Jody Love.

Love?

So the first time the Harvells ever walk into Dover Grocery and Supply is on the morning of the Great Snowfall of 2000, eight inches officially measured by Edgar T. Paris of the Tri-County Coon Club, when everyone not in a ditch has made a run on ground beef and ranch style beans, including Rhonda Love, who materializes beside Renee in produce, which is mostly just onions and iceburg lettuce, turnips, the stray collard and withered pepper.

"Fish woman," she says, smiles. Her black eye's gone. She's pretty.

Renee says, "Hi. We're here for chili."

The Love woman laughs. "Everyone is," she says. "How'd he like it?"

There's wrinkly bells, jalapenos.

"He?"

"Your anniversary. Your fish man?"

Ten pounds of unbleached flour and a can of baking powder are in her cart, Velveeta and RoTel, a fryer and a pound of salt. The smell of bread baking splices with the vision of the girl falling into her father's arms.

"I've been thinking about you."

Rhonda Love laughs a second time and there is this look in her eye Renee's seen before, but she doesn't know where, or why.

"What on earth for?"

Since moving to R'Ville she's not made one friend, not one, save maybe the black lady at Cow Jumped Over The Moon.

Renee lies.

"It's about the Holiday Inn. You were our breakfast waitress there when we first moved last summer."

"Yeah?"

Renee leans close. "Is it true," she asks, "that there's a nightclub there on weekends? That serves drinks?"

Joey and Lara wheel their way over, him in that silly blaze orange hunting beanie she's forbidden him to wear in public. What the hell, it's snow day. Lara's got this big cookie with green frosting and a red heart. The sun turns her hazel eyes gold.

"This is Rhonda," Renee says. "My husband, Joey."

"You're a cutey," she says to Lara. "Nice to meet you."

"She made your fish—the one in our lawn."

Lara holds her cookie out to the Love woman, just like that. She glances at Renee, just for a second, then, to Lara's delight, takes the tiniest bite.

"It's a great fish. I love that fish," Joe says.

Rhonda says, "Thank you so much, cutie pie." And then to Joey, "Was Rusty made it. Bet was, nobody'd ever want it. Like most the rest of that stuff."

"Tell him I like it. It's a good luck fish."

Two horses appear through the glass storefront, saddled with bridle bits reflecting the fierce sunshine that pours down over all of snowy Arkansas now. They toss heads, nip each other. The riders come walking in wearing earmuffs and spurs. The oddest thing.

"I will."

On the way to checkout, Renee and Joey are offered a membership to the R'Ville Social Saturday Club, two-for-one specials from 5-7, barbecue on the first Saturday of the month, childcare on premises, free for Techies. A dress up Mardi Gras this year. Totally private, against the law.

"*Techies?*"

Renee watches the Love woman pay. It had been a shock to her the first time she saw food stamps come out of a wallet or purse, the way a person avoided your eyes and how their hands moved faster, like dealing cards in a game already over, throwing out a five for Marlboro Lights.

Rhonda looks Renee in the eye, counting stamps without looking. "You are ArkaTech people? A lady dame?"

Renee fights the urge to throw in a twenty, intuits the shame in doing so the moment she unsnaps her pocket book. Maybe Rhonda sees it coming, maybe not.

Spurs clink from canned goods.

"Joey," Renee says. "He's history."

Outside, the brisk air is good to breathe, and the sky above the parking lot is the sweetest of blues. Her daughter's little tracks curve this way and that beside the big Sorel prints. Joey's chair had sent her an invitation to be a lady dame, to join the assembly Homecoming Weekend at the country club for champagne brunch. *Dame*—it sounded like a dog.

Rhonda says, "My car's over there."

Her cart, weighted with the big sack of Martha White's flour and potatoes has left a thin pair of wheel tracks clear back to the door.

"Good seeing you," she says.

The horses are tied to a rail outside the front door. They've both turned toward the women, bright eyes shining.

"I'm no *dame*," Renee calls to her. "Not in a million years."

"Me neither," the Love woman says.

"Good."

"Yeah. Good," she says, waves bye.

On the way home they pull an old man from a culvert, the spinning tires wheezing on the hardpacked snow. The old man gives it gas while Joey and Renee put their shoulders to the nose. Out, the old man offers Joe a ten, which he waves off just like all the Stepwells before him.

22

After snow, spring comes fast.

Joey's office is a windowless room in Witherspoon Hall that smells like farts masked over by Eureka Springs candles and he can't see but knows that the world outside's gone haywire—violet and lavender and redbud scenting the air and lob-lobed daffodil, what Joey's mama calls jonquil because the name's pretty, bob in tombstone straight lines from the famous phallic ArkaTech cupola to Once More For Glory Field, a shimmering dogwood at strategic moments, the whole shebang presided over by Nuclear One's signature mushroom in the blue, blue sky. Dean Shock's office is a weight at the end of the hall, Joey can feel the heft of the coon penis in his bones, in there under glass. A door down, Darquah Banchie holds court with a bevy of blonde coeds, the prettiest one of which, Banchie has assured him—she's lead pianist at First Methodist whose Easter recital will feature her accompanying him to "Up From The Ground He Arose—has a butterfly tattooed on the right cheek of her ass, a monarch. Banchie's famous for books on the Negro Jesus and Abraham and Moses of the King James Bible, which has made him none too popular with Chair Dunlap, but hell with her. Joe likes Banchie—a man who can belt it out, Joey hears the deep bass bellow though the wall, the white girls giggling.

His specialty, Ass. Professor Harvell's, what he wrote his dissertation on and used as evidence of scholarship to land the gig at ArkaTech, and therefore be enabled to return to his native state clothed in the gown of academia, is the long-time enmity between Southerners and Mormons. But Joey's hammerheads wanted nothing to do with Mormons nor the fact that they themselves were living products of a defeated nation, nor that there were reasons why they walked around with names like *Shiloh* and *Tumcumsa* and *Hector*, they'd have none of it.

Today, before a World Civ class of a hundred, Dr. Joey Harvell asked that they all stand in the first minute, stretch their bodies and thus their minds to a CD of opera arias, especially the lilting passage from *Madam Butterfly*. Joey belted it out of the killer sound system built into the mammoth classroom. And all the Shilohs and Tucumsas and Hectors, Titsworths and even the shitnose Shoates boy, they'd rolled their eyes like nobody's business.

Finally, today, Monday after the great snow of the new millennium, the powder all melted and spring crazy in their blood, he'd had enough. Not an hour ago.

"What?" Joey'd said, standing before them rolling out a neck crick. A guy named Presley mimed vomiting, stuck a dirt-nailed finger down his throat and gagged. The Casteen girl with the butterfly on her butt that had made Joey think of *Madam Butterfly* to begin with stopped cooing into the Shoates boy's ear who she'd no doubt fucked silly, and an obese girl with a red braid snorted back laughter. Joey cut the aria. "You don't like this?" he asked.

"It sucks dick," the Presley boy said.

Today they were to cover Equiano—the African slave who'd become an English squire—who'd bred little black squire children and written rhymed couplets. Escape was possible. Even from Pope County. Hope was not lost. They would not fuck this up.

"Brother man," he said, "how about we listen to some of *your* music?"

Pregnant silence, the kind one hears in church when the offering plates are passed the week before payday. The red-braid girl had tears in her eyes. She'd split her pants out—Joey'd heard them go. Both the Casteen girl's hands were under the table, no telling what she did to the Shoates kid under there.

"No problemo, sir," Presley said.

He'd marched up in greasy jeans and delivered a CD right to his professor's hands. The Shoates boy—son of Reverend Roy Dale who was rumored to have a floozy and nip now and again—gave Joey a look, shook his head side to side. Beside him, Tina Casteen's smile was electric, like she'd walked barefoot through a bed of Tupelo clover and it had felt *so* good.

Joey'd slid it into the player, the Kid Rock CD. "Everybody stand back up," he'd said, pushed play.

Staccato, of a sudden, before he could turn the thing off, the words *nigger,*
cocksucker, motherfucker, bitch, blonde little pussy-snatch and *shove it up yo big ass*
ho had poured over them—the clean bass and tremolo reverberating.

Now, in his windowless office, Banchie's deep bass booming from a door
down where the girls giggle, Joey tacks a photo to his door, just under the Dr.
Joey Harvell Ass. Professor plaque. Renee'd taken it in D.C. the year they met,
when she'd studied at the Corcoran and photographed street people. A plate
glass window has GOING OUT OF BUSINESS SALE writ on it. Three black
kids drum five-gallon buckets in front of the window, their faces thrown back,
catching light.

"This's for you," Raylene, the office secretary says, lays a linen envelope on
Joey's desk. In calligraphic blue-black ink, his name with Witherspoon 114
looped perfectly underneath. TRI-COUNTY COON CLUB is embossed on
upper-left, the back side wax-sealed, stamped with a horned symbol that strikes
at Joey's heart, so his first thought is to throw the thing in the trash.

He slits the invitation open and reads. On the way to Shock's office he thinks
on his maternal grandfather. How the last time he'd seen him Joey'd hauled a
weight set and bench to the old man's trailer, set it up right under the boat
shed. He'd loaded the bar lopsided, trying to show off for Si and Jewel, show
them what a strong man he'd grown into, how he could pump iron. Only he'd
loaded the bar too heavy on one side so it flipped off the bench and bashed him
in the face.

"I heard teeth break," Si'd said.

His two front teeth were chipped for five years. And even now, driving the
deep curve toward Dover and happy hour home and family, he can feel the seam
where they'd been epoxied with his tongue. The bond was never perfect. That
Dean Shock knew his grandfather and had written out his full name in flowing
black cursive, a jolt.

The door'd been wide open. The light was on. A whole slew of diplomas
piled on the wall, their gold frames glittering. A big-ass glass covered desk was
spick and span, save an ArkaTech envelope with *Joey Harvell* writ in pencil on
its face.

Out in the Pathfinder, a bundle of white sage from a Utah sundance refused the cigarette lighter's red eye, so Joey crinkled a leaf, sifted it into the envelope's contents, the shriveled length of flesh and sinew that hillfolk wield as a sort of wand to wave under the Full Harvest Moon when a circle had been gathered under a persimmon tree on the night of first frost. He'd tasted hard liquor for the first time on such a night while Grandpa Si spoke a curse in the old tongue against O.W. How the red-faced warlock had bit off the words, snapped his fist open and spit on the dark digit he kept wrapped in red cloth ripped from Mom Dee's dress on the day he'd cut his leg off, a hank of the makeshift tourniquet she'd tied around the stump that kept him from bleeding to death on the way to St. Mary's where a lawnful of Danville Littlejohns sat gathered on blankets, the news of his bloody accident hard on them.

They'd all be nearly a hundred now, the 1949 Littlejohns, men who'd fought Hitler and bygod won, returned to Arkansas believing the world was better because of them, Joey's mother's father chief amongst them, about to sweep the Dixie League Pennant and have true momentum to propel their lives forward. He's inherited the team photograph Mom Dee'd once ripped in half, right down the noseline of her ex-husband, a sure enough sign that she still loved him, Joey's gleaned that much about love through the years. It hangs on his study wall in the big house where he does his daily work, pouring over the incidents between his kind and theirs.

Joe'd found the letter to Hallie, Dee's older sister, written when his grandpa was thirty-two. Private M.W. Stepwell, it said in the upper left corner which was ripped through so the address is hard to make out, though Joey picked out Plat 660, and San Diego, California. Marine Corps Base, June 28, 11 a.m. 1944. The letter was addressed to Mrs. Hallie Carter, Danville, Arkansas and hand written on United States Marine Corps stationary, neatly, in cursive, U.S. Marines, June 27, 1944:

Dearest Hallie,

Hope you are o.k. I'm doing fine still miss my darlings so bad I think I can hardly stand it at times. Marines can't dish out anything that hurts any think like as bad as having to be away from them. I love them so much, and realize now I've let them down in so many different ways. If I can just ever get a chance to make it up to them. I get two long letters from Dee every day. She's the sweetest thing ever was. She has never failed in any way as a wife. I know this isn't of interest to you, but she's all my mind runs on when I'm out in the field. It's hell without her. Guess I deserve it.

Jean will be ok. Navy sure is making a man out of him. He's tops. Like to run across the little rascal some time.

There's a rumor that platoons in boot camp now are to hit the Philippines, I really don't think we'll get there in time. Enjoyed the letter, write often.

Love, W.S.

Josephine had kept the Littlejohn photograph on her dresser for as long as Joey'd been alive, and only given it to him as an heirloom gift that first week back, after she'd broken her collar bone falling off the great room steps trying to take a picture of the cathedral ceiling. She'd turned him over to her father at an early age, and trusted him fully, something Joey doubts will ever happen between him and his Lara—he'll be too old, won't he? He can't help but wonder about the last of the Littlejohns, and what they'd have to say about their time, the last tenuous cracked and splitting ligament to that perished time and place, and the departed souls who shared it.

Their names are written on back in Dee's willfully plain cursive with its tiny loops and scrawls—thirteen of them including the coaches, some looking straight into the camera while others, Weldon included, gaze at some unseen subject in the field beyond the concrete dugout. One, the big chested man standing center, smiles, he the tallest and beside Joey's grandfather, wide grin showing good white teeth, about to belly-laugh, looks like. And then, to his right as Joey sees it, Marion Weldon—Si he was called—who'd paid him five dollars once for tilling half his Lake Ouachita garden, a man who, like Joey, could suffer no boss, and when Joey glances quickly and then away, he sees his daughter there in his place—the same muscular shoulders, the athlete's body.

He'd been a carrier, Marion Weldon Stepwell, who Shock referred to as a High Coon in the letter inviting him to speak at the Mardi Gras Lupercalia Fish

Fry Supper at Tri-County Coon Club on Seven March Two Thousand at Six in the Evening—*you will find something more fitting as a formal invitee to our circle on my desk this very day.*

Coon penis.

Now he, Joseph Marion Harvell, as the blood kin who have come before and will ever come after, is carrier. Sometimes you'll do some crazy things. Run barefoot in the snow for a warm heart. String moccasins from tree limbs to tease rain from passing clouds on a summer day so dry even the witchdoctors quit riding each other. Show your buttocks to the crooknecks to make them flourish. Cut hair from your private parts and sew it between the halves of an apple, feed it to the horse that's foundered. March snow's better than chickenshit. Arkansas was, and remains to a degree, a frontier state, and the Ozark hill country has not, to this day, been penetrated by any major highway or railroad. It was said that practitioners of backwoods witchcraft were common as Methodists, and sometimes one and the same. No dew in the morning, rain by nightfall. Deep in the hills, the old ways, rattlesnake and bone, a hank of hair from a loved one cached in the family Bible, four leaf clovers and the ears of seven rabbits, a braid from the mane of a buried horse, prayers said by moonlight, wrapped in owl's wing laced with blue sage, fabric from your grandmother's fake silk robe tied into a red willow hoop, say it, the old word. The scarecrow's blue shirt flounces in the dry corn—his hickory arms turning the crow, the boy's face dipped into the blood of a first kill, his shirttails cut off if he misses. It has been said that the Ozark hillfolk are the most superstitious on earth, even the educated ones, even the ones whose rank would seem to supercede such thought, in their secret of secret places, wrapped in the delicate pink cloth of the lover's seven-day worn underwear, a wand for the ages.

Tomorrow's payday, day after that, Groundhog. There's a back way home, across I-40 Old Number 7 runs north, skirting Lake Dardanelle through the pine and pinoak thickets—a road which could be driven clear to Boone County with its hokey Dogpatch U.S.A. where they blow snow on a fifty-hard hill and rent skis by the hour to the after church crowd up from Little Rock or down from Clay County on the Missouri line. War Eagle's up that way, and the Buffalo

River—wild and scenic land with its canoe wrapped boulders. Born in Arizona to a father he'd never meet and knew next to nothing about, save he'd been a dope smuggler and his brother was a dwarf who'd been in movies, and his great grandmother was Katy Tremain whose father'd been the famous gunslinging sheriff of Tombstone, and that his mama'd left him for reasons unclear to Joey except that the man was a liar, could lie up one side and down the other—that was Joe's history, who he was.

Renee and Lara are home by now, surely. They've made the quest for booze at Blackwell, and it's a Monday, homemade pizza night, Italian sausage and black olives, easy on the mushrooms. There'll be happy hour on the big deck and Joey'll pee on the patch of dead grass toward the barn. Maybe the woodpecker will swoop through the hickories, its red crown blazing, jackhammer bark and tree meat for beetlebugs. As the crow flies west, Subiaco with its Benedictine monastery where they made good wine and the famous poet Frank Stanford who'd shot himself was buried in the cloister. Further, Scranton, where Mom Dee grew up in the Great Depression with nine brothers and sisters—Hallie, Arthur, Edna, Mildred, Mary and Gladys, born on winter solstice 1916 with the second sight so she would dream the future or about something going on in the present a long way off like when Joey's house caught fire while they were off in California and O.W. was home alone and a hot ember fell through the ceiling and burned a hole into the heart-side of his chest and he would have died right there with the ceiling about to collapse, only Gladys was dreaming it like a movie in her head and had called him that second, willing him from out of bed. O.W. got up, answered her phone call, and in that way made it out in his underwear, found the hide-out key under the Pontiac's bumper, and drove off to Uncle Earl's house for help.

After Gladys was Virgil who'd died young, and then Dee—the eighth, who was followed by Hoyt, named after Jessie James's last alias, who'd discovered that the whole bunch of them were second cousins to the Youngers. A son was named Cole, another Frank. Hoyt was a Green Beret. He'd killed men and told the stories. He was called Hoyt for some reason, and hated Joey's grandfather with a passion. He'd been a basketball referee in Danville when Weldon and Dee met, and called the suitor out three games in a row for fouls, and she'd married him for his letter jacket, and moved to Danville where they bought a house, started a floral shop named Eternally Yours, and Weldon played for the Littlejohns—a semi-pro Dixie League team.

The photo has secrets to tell—eleven vets who'd returned from war with Hitler and his concentration camps with their ovens and gas showers and six million dead—who returned and wanted to play baseball and did for a while. They were photographed together in 1949, when Marion Weldon Stepwell was thirty-one, handsome and stern-faced, the last picture taken of him standing on two legs.

Before Joey can make the garage, Lara's galloped her stick horse out the front door and is barreling down the stairs. The afternoon sun is good and her eyes light up so the future seems fair and golden before them.

23

Love asks for a cigarette and Elvin Taylor rolls a skinny in a flash. Lights it with the butane Harley lighter Edgar's jealous of, the chopper red and shiny on the flip lid that creaks just a little before the light gets Ronnie's eyes, his nose and chin. It's Hector blend, the tobacco. Edgar sniffs mullein and red willow bark, a hint of cherry—Borkim's Riff maybe. New worm's on them, a fingernail of silvery white floating above the tree's wavy canopy, faint and sweet with the smoke rising, the white horns punctuated by Jupiter below with its four moons aligned and ringed Saturn above, the triangle marking the year's first major conjunction. Edgar remembers from the new-stiff Farmer's Almanac Tina Casteen'd stuck in his stocking Christmas night, her long shaven legs high-yellow in the firelight as she tiptoed over the hardwood of TriCounty's great room to the hearth, and then came back to where Edgar feigned sleep, slipped under the flannel sheet and put her head on his pillow so he could smell her shampoo and the night seemed a garden of earthly delights. *Damn.* Time to plant tomato seed, peppers and Big Boys, butternut, hot-damp seed starter soil clumped in his fists, why'd he have to go and think of Tina? Her hair? Before daylight even, out here in the goddamn wood she comes to him, and he can feel her in his bones, the way air sounded over her teeth when she breathed and how the fine hair on her belly stood up when she lay out naked afternoons by the well house, her toenails glinting in the sunshine. How they'd fish a bream bed until shadows came, rig a trotline with bluegill, run the mother in the moonlight. He'd smell her hair and the skunky water and the forty pound flathead would whomp the aluminum boat bed and she'd laugh that laugh of hers, so he'd wish that she was his, that she'd give up on ArkaTech and love him like she ought to. And all this while Love smokes his rolly, daylight coming. *Damn her.*

Sheriff Autry's radioed in so cars are waiting at the highway which they make in time to see the school bus go by, a shitload of house-apes that go wide-eyed when they see the lot of them come traipsing out of the thicket. Ash Wednesday, Edna Goodno has a smoky cross fingerpainted on her forehead, goggle-eyed in the driver's seat at the sight of them—was it even season? what's Ronnie-boy doing yonder in that blanket—Edna raises her brows so the cross shows, flies on by. Deputy loads Poon Tang and Biscuit Mouth, has to lift the latter's ass, poor tired dogs. Love's next, they don't have the heart to cuff him. He's put his pants back on, shirt and one Redwing boot, who knows what got the other. He's led to Sheriff's patrol car, set behind the metal screen. The whole lot of them cram into the three cars, so Edgar has to sit on Alderman Waylow's lap, and he doesn't like that a bit. The radio monkey-chatters.

Sheriff picks up the mic—clicks the talk button. "This is 32," he says. "Over. Love's in custody. Out."

Edgar spots a Slim Jim on the dashboard. Bacon and eggs sure would hit the spot. Some buttery biscuits and redeye.

"Where to?" Deputy asks.

Autry's beside Love, one big black boot over his knee.

"Coon Club," he says. "Chop chop."

It's not a morning Edgar could have ever seen coming, how it all bleeds together, the fish fry and Lupercalia Coon Speech, Dr. Joey Harvell come walking in wearing a black suit coat, carrying that guitar case with the D-28 inside, leaned it aside the fireplace, the wood knot burst, and next thing you know Ronnie Love done and bit off Professor's finger, the right index, the one he'd press against the thumb to hold a Fender thin pick. Long-legged Tina's ghost had witched him under the horned new moon—she was like that, sneak up behind your back, stick her tongue in your ear.

Deputy says, "Should I turn the siren on?"

"Lights," Sheriff says. "Get us there."

Beside him, Ronnie Love's eyes flutter shut. Fucker's asleep, taking a nippy-nap. Paris eyes the Slim Jim, the 8th of February fully dawned now, rolling down 105 toward Oak Grove and Tri-County, his warm bed where Tina'd once hid a perfumed love letter—and the other thing—under his pillow on Christmas night not three months ago. He'd lit it afire, the letter, but saved the other. Beneath him, Waylow groans.

Somebody's cleaned the kitchen, scrubbed all the pots and plates and silver, wrapped the leftovers in sheaves of the Hector Spector—neat little rolls of crappie and catfish fillet, hushpuppy and squirrel back inside the double-door refrigerator. No sign of blood on the big table, nor evidence of any ruckus whatsoever, she's all sweet and clean. The mystery laborer has left no note, nor as much as a footprint. The whiskey's all accounted for. Nobody's messed with the bacon nor fucked with the butter. The money box is good. It's as if last night just didn't happen, Paris thinks then gets sight of himself in the glass. Look it—damn sure did.

Sheriff Autry's tromped Ronnie into the great room where Deputy rekindles the fire and the sun shines in the eastern window straight onto the black guitar case that still leans against the wall where the Harvell boy left it. Paris sees the light play over the *M* insignia on the case cover, the sunlit curlicue, and he can feel that guitar in there, the rosewood neck, the sweet spruce box top, how the fretted mother-of-pearl squeaks with a bar chord, the tremolo on a hammered D. *That* guitar could get his goat if he let it. Best leave it alone, no good in coveting, though Doc Harvell surely wouldn't begrudge him having a look, just to make sure it's okay, the heat didn't get to it. What would a little picking hurt?

Paris makes a pot of coffee while Love is interrogated in the great room, Sheriff's deep voice going over the thing that happened again and again, Ronnie nodding, saying something now and again, Deputy taking notes while the fire pops and hisses in the hearth, the odd sideways glow on their faces. They take their coffee black. Love's hand shakes when he takes his.

"I'm sorry about all this, Edgar," he says.

Paris's old man had been a long haul trucker, drive to California and back in six days, could sleep with his eyes wide open and you'd never know it, and he drove that way too. Once, on a Fordyce deer hunt, Edgar'd spotted a wild hog while they were driving Starks Bland Road looking for deer to spotlight. They'd been up since 4 a.m. that morning and it was late, a November night, frost coming. His old man'd hit the brakes so they both slammed open their doors, stepped out on the gravel and shouldered guns. The old man was shooting an ought-six and Edgar'd thrown up a twelve loaded with slugs. He'd shot first, Edgar had, and the hog collapsed roadside—300 pounds if it weighed an ounce. They grunted under the thing's lard ass for an hour and finally the old man'd hauled out his tire jack and together they'd jacked Snorky's ass up 'til he fell into the trunk of the Pontiac where his mama'd hid some wrapped Christmas presents already, and an unwrapped bird book, the fowl so real they seemed about to flap off the page. The razorback's tusks scraped across the word *Audubon* and snout blood ran down the cover.

Why he's thinking of that, how they'd hung the thing in the barn and just like the idiots they were had tried to skin the thick-hided beast the way you do a spike buck, skin come crackling off like a soft glove, knife in one hand, hide in the other. The hog skin was four inches thick and they ruined two buck knives and an Uncle Henry skinner under the bare bulbed light, so the whole scene of them with gore to the elbows, compounded by going on two days without sleep. It had stuck with him, how things got otherworldly. That's how it was right now, like knife-skinning a dragon-hided hog in the November barn without sleep.

"I know it ain't right," Rusty says. "What I done."

Edgar looks down at the man and sees that he's *there* again.

Rusty Love has come home.

24

Straight up happy hour on Fat Tuesday, Renee hauls Lara out of her carseat at the R'Ville Holiday Inn where the pool's full of brilliant blue water now that its dead of winter and nobody can swim. The lot is filled with Chevrolets and Fords and Pontiacs galore, Towncars and Caddys and Jimmy's—no goddamn foreign wheels here for the Mardi Gras All You Can Eat Gumbo Supper with drinks available for members of the Dame Club and their guests. Two queens in beads and purple feathers sashay in the front door, their eyes covered in sequined masks, which strikes Renee odd here in plain-Jane R'Ville where the Methodists are just Baptists who can read. When Joey'd lived with her at 12th and N Street in D.C., she'd taken him to a club called The Rogue where men went in the womens and women went in the mens and Joey'd opted to pee in a plastic cup under the table during the drag show. There'd been Trios pizza and Mama Aisha's where the old whiskered matron made Joey sit beside her and listen to the Armenian folk tale of bears before she'd serve them baba ganoush. Their third floor apartment had overlooked Dupont Circle where queers and transvestites and dealers crisscrossed lives and a flashing police car seemed always to scream by on the late-late nights when they'd listen to Billie Holliday and pretend to be grownups in a sane world, and then Joey's brother died, and then she'd got pregnant and had an abortion without telling—so Joey went ballistic and everything changed.

The Love woman will be here.

Renee'd called from work, had got the front desk woman with a lisp who'd said that yes, Rhonda L. would surely be on shift that night, filling in for Millie whose House of Tap had burst a pipe that very day and flooded with a ton of *poo-poo*, ten dollars at the door, all the gumbo she could eat, was she a dame?

Inside the hotel, what was once the breakfast hall has transformed into a dimlit French Quarter, where a husky black man wearing a snake around his neck leans behind the hostess stand.

"Are you twenty-one?" he asks in the sweetest voice with a hint of African chocolate in it. "I'll need to see your license."

Renee cracks open her purse. Zydeco music oozes from the dark from whence she can smell the sassafras filet powder from stews built of gulf crab and roux, boudin sausage and *fumé blanc* so her stomach growls right then and there. Lara's picked up a southern accent already, refusing to use her elmo potty—*No* she screams, rolling the *O* sideways. *Auchoo, Auchoo,* she says to the pepper shaker, sweet, strange girl. Weren't they all?

"Ms. Harvell," Darquah Banchie says, "you are lovelier than your husband deserves. Shall we escort missie to childcare?"

The man's teeth are immaculate. "How do you know me. My husband?"

Lara's hand is sweaty. It's hot in here.

A voodoo priest walks by passing out Mardi Gras beads—yellow, gold, red and white, Lara strings a slew around her neck so they clack together the instant Rhonda Love appears in a cocktail dress and heels, a little tray of drinks in mason jars balanced on her right hand.

"But we are colleagues. Why he goes and spends his life arguing with Mormons when he has you? *Why* is the question."

"Hi," Rhonda says. "You came."

"I did. How do I get to be a member?"

"Here," Banchie says, "I'll dame you." He takes Lara's hand in his huge black one and smiles. "Do you trust me to take the girl?"

"No. I guess," Renee says. "Should I?"

"She'll be fine," Rhonda says. "I'll get you a table—this way."

Her daughter, dwarfed by the black man, disappears down the hall. A drum thumps somewhere, so she thinks of Ajax, out there in the wood where they live now. This looks nothing in the least like the Holiday Inn she remembers from summer, when she was dizzied by the heat and the thought of inhabiting a place where grown women said *tee-tee*.

Rhonda takes her to a two-top with a red cloth thrown over it. "I'm almost on break," she says, flipping her beads. "I'll kill the next one says show me your tits."

Over there's the shining window she looked out of on the morning that this was a breakfast hall, when she and Lara had gorged on mile high biscuits with sausage gravy and wild muscadine, her first days in Arkansas where people were named Peck and every last voice grated her ears and she'd asked the waitress—Rhonda Love—if she had children: one little girl, *Shiloh, gone but not forgotten*, the stone says. Now the window's covered in heavy drapes, some kind of Arky blue law that said it's against the law for people who're not drinking to have to look upon people who are—or was that Utah's wacky Mormons? Two kinds of people, Joey said, those that want a drink and those who don't want them to have one.

Darquah Banchie takes the seat opposite Renee. It's a little after happy hour, Tuesday, and it's still light outside which makes the dark inside even darker. Historically, according to Dr. History of the Cow Pasture Harvell, this day marked the last date it was safe to eat meat dressed from winter, cream, cheese, wine, beer and stumphole whiskey—it all had to go today in one shitkicking *kabang* before the big fast tomorrow 'til Lammas and the first of the summer wine. Fat Tuesday, that's how it felt—fat.

"Would you prefer a beverage, Ms. Harvell?" The voice rolls over her as molasses might, though she didn't really know what molasses was to tell the truth. But it sounds good, the word, the long vowel and and all those *s's*.

"My daughter's all right?"

"Little sweets is fine. There's a whole slew of them in there. The music department's here *en masse*."

The zydeco switches to fiddle—a *reel*, Renee thinks that's what it's called. "So you're in history? Dr. Banchie?"

"Darquah."

"I'm sorry. Dr. Banchie."

She'd once dated a black man, had brought him home from U. of Maryland for Thanksgiving dinner, so the Cap glowered over football and her date had carved the bird with an electric knife. Cath had dropped by with her girlfriend of the month. Whew.

"Yes. I will for sure have a drink. Wine, house red. Whatever. Where are you from, Dr. Banchie?"

"Darquah," he says. That voice. And then, "Where do you think I'm from."

Her old boyfriend's name had been Elijah, who was an English major and whose favorite word in the language had been *rejoice*, so that was pretty much much his response to everything anybody said. Turkey's ready. *Rejoice.* I have to go potty. *Rejoice.* I'll have more of that dressing. *Rejoice.* You carve well, son. Work with a knife a lot? *Rejoice.*

"Smackover. You're from Smackover."

The teeth catch what little light's here and magnify it by a power of ten, but that's a cliché, isn't it, about black folk, that they have white teeth. Is she racist? Of course she isn't, no way, Jose.

"Nairobi. Do you know where that's at? Of course you do." Banchie points the length of a cinnamon index finger toward the ceiling. "You from up there, right?"

Renee laughs out loud. "Up there?"

"North."

"What's north to some is south to others."

"Well said."

"Wine," Renee said. "Is there a bar here? How do they get away with it?"

"Kenya. I was born in the Great Rift Valley. Where our species first breathed air. I learned to walk on the Serengeti Plain."

Here was a voice that would issue from an African Moses, someone to follow through the split Red Sea, Pharaoh's army drowning behind. Africa. Renee'd once received a letter from a boy in Africa that smelled like flowers.

Rhonda Love carries the tray on the fingertips of her right hand, sashaying between the two-tops where sit horned men in feathered masks with the ladies in boas and low-cut silk blouses. Polyester, probably. Spiders make silk—what was polyester? Renee catches her eye, waves. She holds up two fingers, mouths red wine.

"Virginia," she says. "I was born in Virginia."

"Virginia," Banchie says, breaking the word into three melodious syllables. "Virginia is for lovers. That's what the license plates say."

Rhonda nods, holds a finger up. Just one sec, she mouths.

"Norfolk. Pronounced *Girls from Norfolk neither drink nor fuck.*"

"A wonderful mnemonic." Banchie smiles. "And likely not true. How do you like this place, Renee. How does Joey like it here."

Renee's gained twelve pounds on the dot as of this morning on the digital scale in the bathroom that won't give a goddamn inch beside Lara's Elmo potty. "What is your specialty, Dr. Banchie. I mean what do you teach."

"Morons, mostly. The profoundly inarticulate."

Renee laughs out loud—she snorts, on the split second verge of laughing sickness, it happens with Joe all the time. Once at Snowbird, when they'd plowed through steins of Oktoberfest stout and all the St. Paulie's girls were drunk and bouncing and flouncing on this outdoor trampoline, for no apparent reason other than the fact that it was fall and snow would fly soon, the sickness had come on her so hard that beer squirted out both nostrils and her and Joe lay down under a juniper gulping air and laughing, like when they'd painted a closet with Kilz primer and got so high while 35,000 Utah Utes walked past their house to the stadium, and they lay out in the grass, a spectacle for the red-dressed fake Indians. She could lose it any second.

"Rejoice," Renee says. "Here's the wine."

In another life, in another place and time, when she was twenty-two and tall and weighed a hundred and forty, she'd hitchhiked across Europe to Amsterdam and met a Dutch boy there who was a truck driver, only he worked for a company whose sole purpose was to transfer art. One day in winter she found herself at the mouth of a stream that sluiced through the lowland of her ancestors to the sea with its breathtaking silver wings V-ing forever to the west, and her sweet Dutch boy had geared the truck down, drove right onto the golden grass and said that he wanted to show her something. Then, beneath a cloudless Netherlands sky, he'd led her to the trailer door, flung it open on its tracks, and there with the full sun shining on it was a painting of her, a nude on the beach, dancing naked with arms out flung, a face that was not quite her, but was. Then he'd asked her to marry him that second, the moment etched in the waxy world of what might have been. By spring, she'd met Joey. They'd fallen in love in a flurry of blurry springtime in Arkansas where she'd flown into Fayetteville on an Easter Sunday and spent spring break with him and his derelict friends there, and they'd cooked a whole hog in a pit and Joey'd reunited Wayne Coomers and the Original Sins at the Ice House, and taken her to a creek not unlike the one where her Dutch boy proposed, and by May they were living in D.C., an apartment at 12 and N overlooking Paradise Carwash where all the embassy drivers lined up each morning and the transvestites and queers would scream at the dealers and she was pregnant. That life belonged to a time that was receding the way galaxies recede toward the universe's edge. When her Dutch love's ship made port in Annapolis, she was gone already. He'd slipped out her life forever, and that was that.

Renee's Cabernet is jug wine—Gallo, Franzia box at best, but she toasts Darquah Banchie and Rhonda Love, and the three of them drink deep as drumbeat turns to fiddle and then again to zydeco. A few couples dance, and Renee has a turn on the floor with the African man, his shaven face smelling of licorice and—she was right—chocolate. By Best Costume of the Night Contest, she's sufficiently plowed to actually applaud the snockered Voodoo Priest who shakes his chicken claw at the lot of them, speaking unintelligible curses, mumbo-jumbo on a March night. She half wished Joey was here, but he's off delivering his Southern Conflicts Involving Mormons talk at some hunt club in the boondocks that was named Coon-something. What on earth was a *coon club*, I mean was it a bunch of Davy Crockett wannabees running around in coonskin caps? The thought strikes her funny-bone, and by force of will she keeps wine from shooting out her nostrils. Rhonda Love is off the clock now. Banchie's left them for two queens on the far side of the room, where shadows are cut by flickering candlelight. "Want to go outside?" the Love woman asks. "I'm dying for a smoke."

The thought of little Lara in childcare snaps through her head, the fact that she's wine-buzzed and will be driving the backwoods country ass roads home where there's no street light and a loose Brahman bull flipped a short bus full of kids last month.

"I should check on my daughter."

For an instant the Love woman freezes, goes rigid. Then she's nodding, the slight smile—a country girl, raw-boned with music in her voice, the queenly authority of her vowels—the heartbreak city limits they've shared without even knowing, not knowing this second, some monumental task, a job for the ages, Renee feels it in her blood, in her bones, in the place where they dissected the teeny square of flesh from the breast on her heart side for biopsy. Maybe it's something like how Josephine feels when someone mentions Jimmy, her blue-eyed boy who she'd had to see in a casket, know the violence he'd passed through, and how she'd collapsed, just fell down and knocked her head on a square of Italian tile and wanted to crawl in some hole and die and go on dying every moment of her life until she had her son back—that's what she'd said, what she'd told Renee, the tear in her eye swiped away, a little heat there under the embarrassment.

"Sure you should," Rhonda says. "I'll be on the pool deck. You want a coffee?"

"Yeah," Renee says, trudges up the hall to daycare, where she finds her Lara wrapped in a calico quilt on the lap of the same old black woman who greets them each morning at Cow Jumped Over The Moon, a plate with a biscuit and sausage gravy for little missy. Little Missy, she calls her this second, rocking, beneath cataracts, the bluest eyes shimmering.

With no moon the dark is navigable by touch. The aluminum gate creaks ever so slightly and she feels the roughness of washed aggregate beneath her shoes, sees starlight on the pool's watery face. She makes her way to where Rhonda reclines in a chaise lounge, two cups of steaming coffee on the table beside, the curl of smoke rising from her right hand where a ring flashes then disappears.

"You've been following me," she says, offers the pack to Renee.

"Not really."

"I know what you want. It's okay."

Renee lights up, breathes in the smoke so it singes the back of her throat and she can feel it expand in her lungs. She'd once smoked a pack a day, and this instant, the rush of nicotine in her blood, she knew she could again, smoke like that.

"My fish lady," Rhonda says. "You swam to me."

"It's just that. When I met you I didn't know."

The stars are brighter in the pool than in the sky—odd, how the water focuses the light into a shiverless pinpoint, and she could make out Cassiopeia's delicate W, Orion about to club the bull's red eye, Sirius—the star man.

"You didn't know about Shiloh. My girl."

"I'm sorry."

The woman blows the most perfect smoke ring that rises, pierces it with her right index finger, and they can't know that this is the moment of truth for her husband, their husbands, how they've been hurled together in this story that is the story of Love, how it is lost, how it is found.

"Everybody's sorry. Sorry, sorry, *sorry*. Why people are so goddamned sorry I can smell 'em a mile a way being sorry."

The coffee's cooled enough to sip, imitation cream. Carnation, maybe.

"What else is there to be?"

"She liked bread. Shiloh. I learned to bake bread when she was a baby. The whole trailer'd smell like it. And once, after she'd learned to crawl. This kick-ass thunderstorm rolled through and the sirens went off, and I was afraid the meltdown had come and the world was over. I was at the screen door and turned around. The leaves had done that turn backward thing. And I was afraid. And I turned around and there she was on the floor with the cabinet door open. She'd got out the big tub of flour and dumped it over her head. And there she was on the floor looking straight at me with this half-grin like Rusty. Thunder ka-booming outside and those sirens wailing. That sulfur lightning smell and bread baking. Rusty was still on at the plant then, and it was payday, even. I took a picture. And that's how I picture her. What I carry in here." Rhonda tapped the butt of her cigarette to her heart. "Ain't nobody gonna take that picture away."

The smell of bread baking, the little girl's picture, falling into her father's arms. Renee has not forgotten, nor the time when Lara'd done the same, only it was a bowl of spaghetti on a snowstorm night, when the plowblades threw sparks down their street and the faces of the elderly looked down from the retirement high-rise across the way.

"I've been here before," Renee says. "It was so hot."

"My husband is fucked. This has killed him. He's dead."

Renee says, "It was so fucking hot. Unbelievable. And there was no water in the pool. I'd forgot wine. Who's ever heard of a place with no wine?"

At Tri-County Coon Club, Joey Harvell has just launched into the words and gestures that would cost him flesh. Paris hears the wood knot burst in the old hearth, and Rusty Love hears another thing, the lilt of a girl's voice when she says *I love you* and there's not a hint of deceit in those words, and the realization comes that such unconditional love is the only thing on earth that matters, everything else can go jump in the lake.

Above them the sky ticks, quasars and pulsars and white dwarfs and black holes, Cassiopeia, or was it Andromeda. The cigarette is good, and the coffee.

"No water, no wine, the blue blazes of summer. You tell me. What kind of place is that?"

"You tell me," Rhonda says.

The moonless night lay down around them, around them on the pool's perimeter the draped windows behind which the rooms' inhabitants doze on pillow-top mattresses—queens and kings—aglow with *Happy Days* or *Dukes of Hazard* reruns, the radio waves rippling out through time and space, following the trail through space and time blazed from the century's beginning, *Amos and Andy*, *The Grand Ole Opry*, where Hank Williams is walking the floor over you, and now the doorsteps of the Twin Towers and the Shock and Awe that will follow, here at this moment, the clear water shining.

"I'm sorry you lost your baby."

"Honey?" The Love woman stands. Her cigarette shines in one and then is gone. "Here," she says, reaches a hand down to Renee. "Me too."

Renee is surprised by the woman's strength.

"Fish woman."

Her white cocktail blouse flutters to the deck, her skirt, the rest. There is no one watching them on this earth, no one to see Renee follow suit, strip off the layers until their skins are white beneath the moonless sky, the draped windows glowing, the cold water a shock that waked her to the core. No one witnesses the naked women walk into the water on Mardi Gras night of the infant century, the infant millennium, the clean slate of a thousand years before them. No one sees their giddy play save a wayward maid who bows her head and smiles, crazy white women.

25

The ER wait room is full of idiots. There's house apes and shit kickers and barefoot trailer trash, wrinkled old men in flannel robes whose tobacco-stained teeth have long ago fallen out of tobacco-stained gums, one of whom plays peek-a-boo with an idiot ArkaTech coed who props *The Book of Human Development* on knob knees while pretending the old man isn't there, nor the idiot janitors mopping idiot floors upon which walk the grandmaster idiots of all time and space, driven in from the bloated idiot river where they've accidently hooked a number ten Aberdeen through their left cornea while angling for the whiskered catfish, most idiotic beast of all.

"Your insurance card, hon?"

Behind a sheet of plexiglass, a woman he's never seen but somehow recognizes is asking him for his insurance card, the one issued by ArkaTech with a $20 copay and *Generic Drugs When Possible* notation. It's in his wallet this second, tucked above a photo of Lara bending to pick a red tulip.

His right hand throbs like a son-of-a-bitch, though somebody in the ambulance gave him something—he can feel the loop de loop thrum through his veins.

Joey lifts his right hand, the blood-soaked Ace bandage dripping. "I can't reach it. Will you?"

The woman he's never seen but somehow knows walks around the plexiglass wall. "Officer," she says.

An idiot security guard cranes his neck from a *Courier* at the entrance, and a whole troop of devil worshippers stump their way out of X-ray. Somebody pats his ass, right side then left. "Ain't nothing down there," the guard says. "You have a ID?"

There's the hospital smell, the crappie fillet roiling around in his belly, the aroma of gangrene and ancestral vomit, the piss and feces of the ages sweltering through the root rock of this place. He's come here to die. That's it.

"Can somebody call my wife?"

The woman says, "Who are you?" She types something into her computer, fingers click-clacking away.

"That thing on?"

"Yeah."

"Type my name."

"Don't know your name."

"I'm goddamn bleeding."

"Why that's the oddest name I ever heard."

Behind them, the security guard's put down his newspaper, has that look on his face cops get when they sniff for whatever it is you're trying to hide from them when they've pulled you over, black beauties in your guitar case, an open tall boy shoved under the driver's seat. A buzzer goes off.

"Listen," Joey says.

The woman says, "You ain't got nothing down there. Officer DeWitt?"

Another face appears beside the woman that he has heretofore never seen but knows nonetheless, a boy who'd once walked into his class with a python around his neck, who'd claimed that his daddy kept his glass eye in a water bottle beside the bed when asked to comment on Soviet espionage during the cold war.

"Hi, Doc Harvell," he says. "That thing with the music was way cool."

"You know him?" the woman asks what must be her son.

The boy nods at its mother, says "Professor Harvell. What happened to you? Our butcher one time stuck his hand in a meat grinder."

"Well why didn't you say so, hon?"

She click-clacks away on the computer and Joey tastes the whang of his own vomit, pictures how the ambulance has retraced the route of his grandfather Marion Weldon Stepwell, all those years back, when he'd cut his leg off with a buck saw. A hundred or more stood waiting on the lawn of this very hospital when the ambulance wailed up, half the Littlejohn baseball team. They'd got him to the hospital before he bled to death. From the ether-induced netherworld, Joey witnessed his mother and grandmother moving blanket to blanket, accepting the sympathies of kith and kin. He's lived long enough, Joey, to know something of sudden change, that sucker-punch life throws.

Later, a voice hollered from the stone balcony, "He'll live!"

Somebody said, "Praise God."

Before Christmas he was hooked on morphine. That, and phantom charley horses got him flown to Boston for a six-week rehabilitation with specialists. The rehab facility overlooked Boston Bay, so the old man could no doubt hear the foghorns and whistles of vessels departing and returning from sea. A prosthesis was fitted to join just above the knee lost to gangrene. Joey sees the old man sitting in a room overlooking the white-capped harbor, in winter. He'd learned to walk again out on the catwalk, maybe, turned a corner into a stiff wind and knew himself for who he'd ever after be.

Joey's wheeled down mustard-yellow halls. A nurse takes his blood pressure in a room with a sheet-covered gurney and sink, a rack with *Good Housekeeping* and *Outdoor Life*, a golf magazine and *King James Bible,* red-letter edition.

"Can you tell me why you're here to see us today?"

Her smile radiates.

Since it happened, Joey's bled steadily—not heavy, but steady. The blood has a smell about it. His, it strikes a chord.

He holds up the injured hand while she pumps the bulb for his pressure on the other arm. "My hand," Joey says. The image of what happened swoops down on him.

"You hurt your hand?" She unwraps his left arm, sticks a thermometer in his ear.

Joe says, "Yeah."

"Can I have a look?"

"Sure."

She unwraps the Ace Bandage that somebody'd ferreted back at the Coon Club, when he'd swallowed a handful of Tylenol with a shot of Old Crow Whiskey, and Dentist Brucker'd let him huff on the tank of nitrous oxide he kept with him at all times, so the pain lay down.

"*Ouch*," the nurse says. "*Ouch, ouch, ouch*."

"Sorry," Joey says.

Outside the closed door, somebody says, "Your wife and kid are here," the snake boy from World Civilization.

"I think we'll need a doctor for this."

"I guess so. Yes."

"Should I bring them in?" the disembodied voice asks.

"Not right yet," nurse says. The Ace bandage curls around her wrist, and Joey sees the time on her watch, how late it is, how what's happened would sound to Renee. To Lara.

She says, "I don't know how to ask you this."

"What?"

"Do you have it?"

"Do I have what?"

She turns red, or maybe she was that way already. He tastes the whang again and his stomach rolls over audibly. It's embarrassing.

"You say tell 'em to wait a while?"

She caresses the hand, runs her fingertips across his palm. There's a soft sound in her throat, soothing.

"The *finger*," she says. "Were you able to keep it?"

She holds her right hand up in front of Joey's face, points an index finger of one hand to the knuckle of the other. "Sometimes they can reattach digits."

He takes his hand from her, holds it in front of his face, swivels the wrist so the knuckles of three bloody fingers wrinkle before him. Severed at the joint, cleanly, he feels the missing finger just like it's still there. He'd split it open on the peckerwood's head at the cemetery, sliced it once with a lockblade in the Fordyce deer woods, broke it in a bathroom door at Old Main during a history test, and he can sense it there now, the missing part hurts.

"Daddy," he hears his one daughter say. "See my daddy," she shrieks.

Behind the closed door, seen through the phantom finger that points to her, the anguish he'd seen on Rusty Love's face. Who would think such a thing possible?

"*Daddy*," she screams again. Through the walls of time, the kick-thudding heart, he thinks of his mother. He sees her fully.

In that last second before he hits the floor, he's seeing his mother, Josephine, the sound she'd made when she saw Jimmy.

He's retraced the blood trail of his grandfather, fifty-six years before, and now lay in the ether of a room not so far removed from the other, the morphine drip of time, how the severed lines tangle, the wife and daughter waiting for the wife and daughter waiting. They've bought the farm, the failed house of dreams he'll call it, twenty-five miles as the crow flies from Barton Road to Lanty and the family cemetery where Jimmy's state champion football photo smiles from a granite stone, the block-encircled plot where Joey'd left a burning sage bundle, how it whirled up through the shade oak when Joey left him there, afraid he'd start a fire, burn the bridge between him and his people for good and ever. The photograph's secrets, he sees his mother—his daughter—stare at him from either side, him the bridge swinging back and forth, back and forth. *Daddy*, she'd called.

Outside on the empty lawn all the phantom Littlejohns pray for his survival. The wife and daughter and being cared for—rest now, sleep. Everything's going to be alright.

He'll live.

Joey summons Jack Wilson, the last living Littlejohn: What was it like, after the war, to come home and play baseball? Tell me about Danville then? Did you know my family—Weldon—who they called Si, Josephine, Earl? The Stepwells, what were they like as a family? Do you remember my grandfather's accident—how it happened and what happened after? What was he like? Do you recall any stories about him? How is it to look back now, as the last living one? Is there anything you'd like to say or have known that you haven't told? My mother, Josephine, has kept that photo on her dresser for her whole life nearly, and it's been up for a while in my own home office, where I work. I'm in history. I've studied it a lot. You're beside Mama's daddy. Your expressions couldn't be more different. He's brooding, intense. You're clearly happy, looking straight at the photographer.

Why?

How has that joy sustained you in life?

What are the others looking at?

What does he see?

He hears birdsong. Birdsong erupts the hour before light with Si in the trailer kitchen, the radio tuned to the National Weather Service, forecast for the Ohio Valley—high pressure, the threat of thunderstorms for the deep south with hot and humid conditions for the heartland.

And there Joey is with his maternal grandfather, fresh-shaven, cooking in the kitchen before light, birdsong through open windows.

They were a family there in Danville and spring blew in and the flower petals caught the hill breeze and floated by outside when they walked out of the Methodist Church into bright sunshine, when they prayed over Sunday dinner. They walked together to their nice home, past the floral shop named Eternally Yours after the inscription on their wedding service. They walked together and they were a family and there was love and hope and brightness in their days.

O.W. and Josephine, married and divorced the three times and in-between the brawls, the split heads at bowling alley parking lots, the kicked down doors of his upbringing, had that been what this was all about, this homecoming to right the ancestral fall, to make the history fit?

On Si's side Joey is related to the Poteets, the strand of family that reaches up into the Ozarks toward Harrison. In 1857, a company of one-hundred and twenty Arkansawyers, men, women, children including Harlow and Marion Poteet, were led by Civil War captains John T. Baker and Alexander Fancher across the vast frontier with some forty wagons. Well-dressed respectable people, they were quiet, orderly and genteel, some would say, with three fine carriages in the mix pulled by splendid oxen, one of these bearing strange markings, a stag's head emblazoned on its frame. They were, truth be told, one of the fairest caravans to ever venture upon the plains of Manifest Destiny. They did not know what they struggled toward, could not perceive the sovereign country Brigham Young had proclaimed Deseret, with its odd laws and religion, the doctrine of blood atonement practiced by its Danites who believed themselves the lost tribe of Israel and called their land Zion. They could not have known of the avenging angel, Porter Rockwell, Brigham's personal assassin who Mark Twain met and wrote about in *Roughing It*. They'd heard tell, the Fancher party, of polygamy, how the men would marry younger and younger wives, upwards of fifteen, twenty even, until the girl-wives of the household could have been, and were at times, granddaughters to their sister wives. They'd not heard the story, likely, of Joseph Smith, how these very Mormons were routed from Missouri, nor Parley Pratt, member of the LDS church's Quorum of the Twelve, how he'd chased his nineteenth wife clear to Texarkana, only to be shot down on the front porch of her Arkansas lover, nor that the news had got back to Salt Lake, and the would-be prophet Young had drawn a line around his faux country encircling parts of what would become Idaho, Wyoming, Colorado, Utah, Arizona, New Mexico, and Nevada, much of this Spanish territory where they'd squatted then claimed. They would never have heard of Mountain Meadows where they'd be allowed to walk into treachery with nine hundred head of cattle, horses, mules and oxen, one fine stallion valued at $2000 and a great sum of money to start up in the new land—a great moving rain of wealth, these Arkansas gentiles.

They were doomed.

When they were refused all goods at Salt Lake and headed south through the passes, a letter in Brigham's hand followed, commanding that the train be destroyed, that not one old enough to tell the tale be allowed to survive. The Mormons, in the name of their god, dressed as Indians and killed them all. Stripped them and left them for the wolves. Their bleached skulls are displayed in plain sight at Brigham Young University. Joey has touched one, run the tip of the finger into the bullet hole where an infant's brain exploded.

MaMa Stepwell's father's sister was Grandma Poteet.

The sister of Marion, a name that would pass to her own son, and then grandson, she didn't want to go to California and had stayed put in her native state. Grandma Poteet smoked a pipe and lived up in the hills, a cabin she tended herself, grew her own food, took squirrel and deer, wild turkey and rabbit with a long gun. She knew the ways of trout and deep river flathead on the Fourche le Favre, all of the ways Joey's grandfather Si had loved and took to his own heart, even the proclivity to take a sip though he never tried his hand at the still she was famous for through that neck of the Ozarks, but he got the rest in full-measure, and passed it on to Joey whole hog. And it was said that the only time Marion Weldon Stepwell ever wept was when he got news that Grandma Poteet had died, how he broke down when he heard that news. For it was Grandma Poteet's flare that had passed through the line into Josephine herself and now Lara, that Stepwell tendency toward the grand, that desire to leap out under the good Utah sun into a snowbank and bygod dance barefoot—the stinging bite of cold nothing against the joy of this life, of being young and finding yourself surrounded by unspeakable beauty, and then the false white flag, the ancestral cold at the spring where they'd been promised, sworn to, after the forty days in the desert, that if they lay down their weapons, they could drink their fill of the clean cold water and go free.

A lie.

For Joey, it was personal.

The words from his mouth, delivered at the storied table of the Tri-County Coon Club, where his grandfather Si had been High Coon, carrier of the penis, sworn enemy of the betrayer, the black and blue hurt he sought to undo was very real to his heart, so that even the man who'd bit off his finger in rage had his sympathy, or, if not that, his weapons and intellect, blood and bone should the day or reckoning ever come, and the great wrong done at New Harmony be made right.

So help him God.

"Joey?" His wife is talking, Renee, her sweet voice, another. His girl.

The light is fierce, the shock of it.

"You'll get some mobility back," a masked man is saying. "But not all."

26

He'd burned all of Tina Casteen's perfumed love letters, the ones with the curlicues and little stars dotting the I's, the purple ink on lavender paper from whence her voice would come to him by candlelight, drip red wax on each page and print her lips, the little creases, the scar from the horse that reared, say she couldn't get him out of her head, that they were together this second, right bygod now, and guess where *this* piece of page has just touched, and *this*, and *this*. Edgar knew well enough. The smell tortured him. He retrieves the one thing of hers he hasn't burned, wrapped in red cloth from his sock drawer, why he had to take it out tonight after everything is beyond all. She'd left it under his pillow on Christmas— naughty elf come sneaking around the Coon Club. The gauzy fabric is nothing in his hands, a scrap of pink with yellow trim where it once rode her high above her shaven thigh, the faintest color in front, the ghost-sweet scent. She'd worn it that last night in the deserted hunt shack, the hearth spark-full of woodfire. He'd barbecued venison over charcoal, roasted butternut squash laced with brown sugar and cinnamon sprinkled with cracked walnuts. She'd baked him a German chocolate cake, lit three candles on it, said "Guess why there's three, Edgar."

He couldn't guess. Why were there three?

"What do you want in this world?"

"You," Edgar'd said.

And they left the cake burn on the table. She walked him to the room he sits in now, taken the undergarment down to a knee and kicked it sailing with a foot so he witnessed the thing's airy flight.

Why three? Hell. Hell, hell, hell.

He hooks a finger through either leg hole, pulls 'til the elastic snaps. It's dark in their room, where caretakers of this place have ever lived with free room and board in exchange for tending the garden, keeping the ticks down at the dog pens, mending the roof, cooking breakfasts after night hunts, other things. It was enough for Edgar. Why not? For one thing, he had no boss. Not even High Coon Shock talked down to him. He'd been promised his own coon penis, and in time he, too, would be a carrier, an elder statesman. Beat the fuck out of working down at the reactor, all those straw bosses staring down your throat, the time clocks and coffee breaks and bologna sandwiches in paper sacks. The carpooling with eight ladies wearing ten shades of perfume, chitter chatter about little Shelby's first football game. Not even able to go to the shitter without signing out. Not to mention the evil always about to hit the fan behind the big doors, the lockdowns and sirens and emergency instructions.

Hell with all that.

It was good here at the Coon Club, and there always was somebody or other to be buried to boot. He once dug sixteen graves in a day. Beat that with a stick. Game was everywhere. Walk out back, better than a grocery store—take your pick. Fox and grey squirrel, boil the fuckers with a pot of dumplings, a little salt and pepper. Peck Titsworth trapped an opossum that Edgar's got going in a cage out back just now. Feed him table scraps to clean out his belly. Likely as not crawled out of a cow carcass before hitting Titsworth's garage for a side of dogfood. But clean out its belly and the thing'll cook, make the best chili in the world.

But it wasn't good enough for Miss Tina Casteen. Nope, not good enough. Like she'd come from better. The Casteens were shithouse—you can bet on that. They ran with Roaches and Thermans over on Cherokee land on the Oklahoma side. All the bingo casinos had long ago banned them, and the gas stations all had Polaroids of them duct-taped to the registers, so many of the Casteen boys had pumped two dollars quick then screeched off and hit a dirt road. Fish net makers, the only job he'd ever seen any of them do—dipnets, castnets, seines? What kind make nets for a living?

The daddy, Reno, he was the worst. Just as soon take a buggy whip to you as look at you. Edgar'd seen the old man whip Tina's brother with a logging chain—*a logging chain*. And oncet, the peckerwood had made him and little brother drag two dogs up on Crow Mountain and shoot them, left them lay for the buzzards. He kept a pistol in his boot. Tina'd showed him a pair of the old man's boots with a hole the size of a quarter through his sole, pistol likely to go off anytime.

They'd once seined up an alligator gar out of the Fourche le Favre, a six-footer with jacksaw jaws, drove it home and put it in their pond. Son of a bitch swam around snap-snapping. He'd scared the girls shitless, made them wade in the water with it just for meanness, then dared Edgar to feed it a chicken leg.

Reno was not right in the head. Who with half a brain would go knock on *that* man's door, long-legged Casteen daughter or no?

Not Edgar. Nope. No way.

He folds the panties into a square, puts them under a pair of tube socks in his second drawer. What did three candles mean? Hell with it. A logging truck plows by out on 105. Through the window, Jupiter and Saturn make a tight conjunction under the new moon. Tina'd like that, she loved anything had to do with the sky. She says they've got this telescope at ArkaTech can see a tick on a horse pecker a million miles away, that they have star-parties some nights, and she's met a boy who claimed he could see Jesus and all the dead people ever lived out there in neverland through the telescope. Smartass college kids, Edgar's buried more than one of them, forever driving they daddy's cars through cinder block walls.

At least the Love boy'd come clean. They'd found professor's finger wrapped in a red bandana. Sherifff had it driven on ice to St. Mary's where they've likely as not sewn it back on good as new. He'd best find something better to do with that finger, like maybe press a Fender thin between it and thumb, flatpick the C-intro to "Walls of Time."

The thought of the guitar, the Martin D-28 Dr. Harvell had brought with him to the Lupercalia Mardi Gras Fish Fry Feast and Inspirational Speaking by an Honorable Member of the Community at Large Presided Over by the High Coon Carrier, it sneaks up on him the way Tina does, long and lean, her parts shining, that sweet woody-smell and the neck fretted in sixteen perfect dimensions. Only the guitar would do what he told it, sweetly.

Edgar'd held such an instrument once. When he as sixteen, full-grown as he'd ever be, he ran track one fine springtime for the running Warlocks, the Hector team who'd somehow managed to hire Buzzard Andrew from Hot Springs, who'd roomed at the Olympic Trials with Bruce Jenner, and who'd started this semi-famous band called the Zonks that drove all around Arkansas in 1968, playing a music called rockabilly with their long hair hanging down and that hooter smoke trailing their band van, along with the ton of *poon-tang* that followed wherever they went. They'd opened for Ronnie Hawk and the Hawks. Jerry Lee and Conway Twitty. Sun had approached them. And this very Buzzard Andrews, the Warlocks had somehow hired him to be head track coach when Edgar was in the eleventh grade, and why not go out, he'd always been the fastest white boy in his class, Paris. He made the team, anchored the 440 and 880 relays, ran the 100, 200 and long jump, cracked 51 in the quarter, but never made a decent hurdler, the Buzzard's specialty.

Out of the blue, Coach'd invited him to a weekend jam. Andrew lived out on the other side of Long Pool, and there wasn't a bridge, so you had to hop in a canoe on one side and paddle over to the other, tie off to a cuttystump and hit the footpath uphill to the geodesic dome the old Zonkster had built himself.

When he knocked, Miss Spence—the prettiest woman in the whole Warlock school district—answered with a stoned smile, blonde hair hanging to her hips, so Edgar was embarrassed. She wore cutoffs and a tie halter, nipples on high beam. Edgar'd thought he'd die that second, having crossed over Long Pool River to face such a woman out of the blue. He smiled, he remembers smiling, and it was before his teeth went on him. So maybe her eyes had gone easy on him, the boy he was twenty-some summers ago.

Miss Spence smiled back. "Help you?"

Help me right. He felt the flush on his face. He could smell the woman, there. She taught math—all those numbers. "Yes ma'am," he said. "Coach said for me to come."

Then he heard it. The sound came to him and lifted his heart, it soothed him from the inside out and he thought he would swoon right there in front of Miss Spence.

"Edgar?" Coach called from where the music was. "Get on in here."

He followed the barefoot woman into this sky-lit room where Coach sat on a stool surrounded by a half-dozen longhaired hippies, some of them picking mandolins and there was a banjo player and a dobro and it turned out that this was a band of wood-folk who'd already got famous as Black Oak Arkansas, though he didn't know it then, but the sound they made, that sweet, sad melody, it got into his blood. That first riff, it never left him.

"Sit here, boy."

Edgar sat on the stool beside Coach. The sunlight fell down on the guitar in his lap, and just as that shining registered on Edgar's sixteen-year-old consciousness, the Buzzard and these long-haired hippies launched into a composition flat-picked in the key of G. Buzz picked the melody and this blind old hippy named Doc made his guitar sound like the world come undone, clean picking the run through the G to the C, then opened his mouth and sang about how the good lord would send down his angels, and haul her on up to the sky, so he could one day join her there. Then the old man ran a lightning run down the frets that was true as anything Edgar'd ever heard in his life.

Coach took a turn on lead. The mandolin player went crazy, and then the dobro guy. They did "Old Joe Clark" and "Wildwood Flower" and "Foggy Mountain Breakdown," and one of the hippies sang a song called "Paradise" about a son calling out to its daddy to take him home to paradise and the daddy saying it's too late so Edgar wept and that weeping felt good like it was meant for him to cross the river and be in that place, with Miss Spence's nipples showing through her halter, Coach and the hippies and Black Oak Arkansas, the blind guitar player who went into "Tennessee Stud."

With all his heart, Edgar wished to ride a Tennessee stud through the Arkansas mud, but even more so he wished to play that guitar in the blind man's lap. With all his soul he desired to make sound with the box in the blurry hands of the man named Doc.

"Son," the blind man said. "This here's my son who I love." He put his hand on the knee of the seeing man beside him. "Show him how, Merle."

This Merle, he lifted the gitfiddle out of his daddy's lap and sat it right down in Edgar's. The rosewood neck was slick and warm and there was the oil from the old man's hands.

"Introduce him to Ellie," Doc said.

Merle made the fingers on Edgar's left hand into the E, told him to strum with his right, which he did. The resulting sound—Edgar's first chord and the only one, he was dead certain of this, he'd ever need—came from the guitar's mouth and held sweet in the spring air of his 16th year all of everything he'd ever hoped for in this life, coloring the spectrum of his thoughts for good and ever.

Doc and Merle, they're with the angels now, and Coach lives in Dallas where his band plays every night in bars and honkeytonks and roadhouse saloons. But Edgar never forgot the feel of Doc Watson's D-28, how he'd been introduced to Ellie and Amelia and Beatrice, when sound split him open to reveal the self he'd been blind to his whole sorry life, when light poured down through the geodesic dome and it was as if a hand, a thought, a thing spoken of in the good book called *grace,* had bent down and sung into his ear that he was a good man, that his life would be a good life, that there would be music and that he would eat and drink and make merry all the days of his life—*Amen.*

Tina had to come and fuck everything up.

Wasn't good enough for her, Edgar's guitar playing. They'd pawned his Martin for a weekend at Heber Springs in a hotel with squeaky springs and a water faucet in the bathroom that leaked a stain the color of a skunk's ass. He'd pawned his second and last D-28 after a trip to Oaklawn, when Tina'd got tipsy and Edgar'd had to drive, sit behind the wheel in heavy traffic so he tailgated a Pontiac and had to pay on the spot to keep the owner from reporting the damage to Mr. Reno Casteen, who'd bygod get an earful about his daughter's drunken boyfriend. Guitar gone, Tina'd kissed him at a railroad crossing as a freight roared by, the lights flashing and the little bells dinging, and it had been all right for a while but not now.

He imagines the look on the face of the fellow who walked into that pawnshop and saw a 1967 D-28, how his heart must have lept like a fawn to find and so steal Edgar's instrument. Dadgummit.

Damn her to hell.

27

For their spring breaks, Cap flies them down to Melbourne, where they rent a car and drive across the causeway to Melbourne Beach, with its little baitshop and barbecue shack, the Indian River on one side and the vast green Atlantic on the other, where after greeting Cap and Meg and agreeing on shrimp and fillets for dinner, opening suitcases right there on the made bed in the guest room, Joey takes down the surfrods in the garage, fills a cooler with ice and Coronas, and the three of them drive the two blocks up to Third Ave beach, set up an umbrella and cast the baited rods out into the breakers. They wade chest deep into the chill salty water to pee before taking their daylong places on beach towels, cracking two frosty cervesas and thanking God in heaven that they've made it out of Arkansas alive.

A blue heron stands one-legged at their backs, facing open sea, regal as a dinosaur. There'd been rough air when they flew over the Gulf. The plane had had to climb out of convection, banking hard one way and then the other before swooping straight up, so that somebody's silver water bottle clinked the length of the fuselage, and a man behind them had cursed vehemently. Lara'd got an earache, but all that's behind them. Low tide, the cloudless day rolls endlessly— the beer is cold. Renee'd grown up Navy—South Carolina, Hawaii, Rhode Island, New Hampshire and, when she was Lara's age, Monterey, California, home of Navy War College, whatever on earth that could be, with its jagged cliffs and redwoods and Big Sur. She and Joey have made the drive straight up this coast all the way to Carolina, with its Outer Banks and Calico Jack Ferry, Cape Lookout where they made love on a sand dune in golden October, and later that night fireworks went off on the mainland, and there was no sound save waves breaking and the swish of seaoats in the wind.

The last year is a dream.

One of the surfrods goes off, *bam, bam, bam,* then straightens and is still. Joey never lifts his head. He's a man who's had his finger bit off by another man, who he is now. Wrapped in a metal splint, the thing's mostly useless, but the pain has left off, so he's off the pills now, thank god.

Back in Utah their house has gone vacant. The nurse who'd rented has bailed, and there's been this big-ass storm, so the sidewalks have not been shoveled and a week's worth of tickets arrived at Barton Road with a note from the wacko parking lady rubber-banded to a doggy biscuit: *Tell Moondog hello,* it said. A note from the moon. Joey'd once watched the woman French kiss the dog through the chainlink gate.

It's not too hot, not really. Lara's conked on a beach towel, turning pink. She thinks of the house where their daughter learned to walk, where they'd bathed her in the kitchen sink, and the Winnie the Pooh mobile had tinked in the night, how the urge to breastfeed had come on her, and how it felt to feed a hungry baby in whose blood was all you'd ever loved.

An osprey sails by. They should have brought the bucket and little pink shovel her mother'd bought at the Episcopal thrift store. Two-year-old Lara, her love, and beyond her the ocean curves toward Canaveral, a colorful parasail takes mighty leaps.

This isn't home either. The locals here in Melbourne Beach all know each other, many in the biblical sense, one big Peyton Place, with her brother Rock and wife Bet smack in the middle. Surfers, they've bought on Sixth Avenue and are remodeling. She's Christian, Bet, and had once argued a distant uncle to death at a family reunion. Imagine, arguing a man to death. What a skill. No, this wasn't home either, nowhere was, really. Rootless, there was always the farm in Plainfield, New Jersey, with its barnful of seven-toed cats, the ancestral Rockerson stead where her Grandmother Anna'd baked buttermilk biscuits and smelled like vanilla.

Seich, the oscillation of waves, a word Kath'd used to describe the ocean on a night in France when fire burned sparks into the night sky. Before her, *seich.* What a beautiful word. If she could be a word, she'd be *seich.*

A dream.

Joey moans. Maybe he's refilled the prescription and keeps it stashed. Who'd blame him. The beach curls north toward the Kennedy Space Center where they'd toured with Mom and Dad, and Joey'd seen a black snake crawl out from under an exact replica of Apollo 13. A three footer, the serpent had winded under the control module and Joey'd said *goddamn*.

Way-way out, a ship silvers on the horizon. From here you can see the Earth's curve. Pops had taught her how to dead reckon with her fists, but no need for that here. You could *see* the Earth curve. She lay on her back facing east, the green-cold Atlantic. Out there in the vast blueness, a ship sails north along the continental shelf, blue water, river highway, the current is powerful, stronger than forty Mississippies, her father claims.

Once they'd lain on this same beach during a jellyfish infestation. Miles of fuchsia blobs dotting the path where waves had broken, lacy, delicate, the sting was horrific if you believed what the surfers said. Rocky carried a corked beer bottle full of his own piss at all times on the beach, sworn remedy for the vicious wheal. Right in his little Igloo beside the other Coronas, Joey'd once taken a swig of it by accident.

Sea turtles swim aground here, slivers of an ancient birthing site, they swim halfway around the earth and crawl aground here by the scores each night, dig holes with their strong rear legs and lay eggs in the cool beneath the dunes.

Ponce de Leon was said to have landed at this very spot, Third Ave Beach, was seeking the fountain of youth.

Useless, this.

No matter what thoughts she summons to occupy her mind, none suffice. She simply can't not think about the Loves—the woman, little Shiloh, and now the man, the poor sucked-up hull of a man.

Just like that a shadow slides through the breakers and the shorebirds go apeshit. Lara is up and running, dashing toward the wave that rips her off her feet. As if he has eyes in the back of his head, Joey's up sprinting, carries her back in his arms, giggling little girl. The bandaged hand drips.

"The saltwater feels good," he says. "Let's go in."

And that's what they do. The three of them go in, Lara in Joey's big arms, the cleansing waves erasing the miles, the rough air they've flown through, riding up the swells and falling to rise again.

Joey pulls a sixteen-inch pompano out of the dirty surf on the day of the full moon, and they grill it on Pops's grill which they have to repossess from Rocky's backyard where all the other stuff he's stolen from his father's garage resides. Tuesday turns to Thursday turns to Saturday, days on the ocean beyond the Third Ave Beach landing with its worn stairs and platform overlooking the startlingly peaceful ocean ever breaking, rising and falling and rising, a spring tide on equinox, the late afternoon happy hours on the pool deck with real bygod hors d'hourvres, Mom wading in the pool with her red hair just so, the light in her eyes, Lara kicking the Sandy shark in circles around the kidney-shaped pool with blue tile turtles swimming to and fro in threes, the fish in foil drenched with lemon and butter wafting over them, fish that had swam on whatever day it was, the clam bake and strawberry pie, barbecue sandwiches from the Georgia Pig, the good feel of clean sheets and open windows, the oleander blooming, scenting the air and the sound of the ocean breaking two blocks away, the afternoon storms and drenched towels hanging on the line above the yard gnome with its red hat and little statue of St. Francis of Assisi, the long breakfasts with jazz issuing from the big front room with its hearth never used save a paper log on Christmas and the family photograph of them together, her hair punked out in 1983, the year she'd written that first fateful letter, licked the stamp and touched her tongue to the gluey seal, sent it to Joey Harvell in Fayetteville, Arkansas—a day she'll never undo now.

On Sunday they go to church—St. Sebastian by the Sea where Pops leads the opening prayer. Beach light through stained glass flitters on the floor, her standing in it with a hymnal opened between her two hands. Joey looks on. Lara colors a zebra she's sketched on the Call to Worship. She grew up in churches like this, Renee, the Wednesday night oyster and ham dinners with all the wine you could drink that her father'd buy at the commissary where the enlistees at the front gate would go into conniptions when they drove in, falling over themselves while saluting and flashing secret handsigns to Commodore Rockerson, the Captain, and now, assistant parish priest, her father, leading the congregation in a prayer that begins *Our Father.*

Later, they will miss their flight. Joey will leave his keys in the guest bedroom drawer, and not think about it until loading. Mom and Dad will pick them up from the airport and they'll stay another night and not care one whit. The light pinkens at her feet, beside her mother, she looks at her mother's hands, the blue veins and slight tremor, a West Virginia beauty once whose eyes still dazzle when the sun hits them, who dabs Boodles Gin on the insides of her wrists, her elbows, whose piano has been silent this trip, her mother who she loves. As if she knows what Renee's thinking, Meg takes her right hand, just for a second, they are in church, their voices intertwine, the prayer said.

They will miss their flight home to the place that has never felt like home. Renee feels the Elliotts there, the carved wooden podium in the front room which they had used as a prayer room, a Baptist reading of the word, no wine dare touch those lips, more alcoholics per square mile than anywhere on the blue planet, with its sea lapping three blocks over from St. Sebastian by the Sea, where she holds her mother's hand, reaches down for Lara who looks up, smiles with her mother's eyes, so the three of them are linked there beneath the stained glass, her father's prayer nearly done now, pouring over them, *Bless those who are overseas. Bless the mentally ill and the destitute. Bless the ones who go away, and those of us who stay.*

They take Holy Communion for the first time all together.

Kneeling before the priest who'll one day say words over the lost loves of her life, Renee accepts the Host, takes the bitter wine between her lips. What has she ever believed? God? Certainly not the Baptist kind with all its damnation and guilt. Grace? Grace was good. She could abide grace. Heaven? Certainly not hell. That happened on earth plenty to the max—the hell with hell. She'd been a Job's daughter once. She's never prayed, has she? Away from the dinner table or *now I lay me down to sleep,* has she ever in her life said a prayer? asked for forgiveness? made words meant for the ear of a maker?

"Is this girl redeemed?" the priest asks. "Is she yet a member of the flock?"

On knees beside her, Lara opens her mouth.

"Yes," Pops says. He looks her in the eye.

The priest nods, lifts it from the white cloth. "Take this and eat, daughter in Christ, for it is my body."

Her daughter accepts. Renee sees, *transubstantiation*—that instant, the body of Christ?

"Take this and drink, for it is my blood."

Stained light pours over their feet, over the floor where they stand. Out in the dunes the sea turtles lay eggs under the moon, then swim the signless route back into open ocean where their mothers and their mothers before them have swum through time.

The flight they miss will land in Little Rock without them: their luggage will whirl round the conveyor belts and strangers will reach for the name tags where their names are written in blue cursive.

The photograph of the father catching his daughter from the fall-lit sky, the colorful Ozarks lit up by good sunshine, slashes by, how it was when Lara was a baby, and it was her first summertime so school was out, and they'd sit in the baby pool in the backyard under the June sky, Lara in her flappy cap, making the bird sounds and splashing, and they'd see Joey coming, walking up the street from his summer workshop—the look on his face. The golden summer of his life, so he said, walking home from work and seeing them in the backyard by the garden, his little family.

Behind her, her mother takes communion, her father. They walk through prisms and retake their seats, and there is singing of Psalms before the final prayer. The big double-doors are opened so blue sky and ocean stretch down the strand of island clear to Sebastian Inlet where the Indian River pours into the sea, and mothers with their children walk the length of the long pier and wave goodbye to lovers and fathers as they float by the jetty toward the Gulf Stream.

Down the stairs they will one day walk again, in sorrow instead of joy, the family walks into the bright blue day. Sunday dinner is waiting—the feast is at hand, champagne brunch, mimosas sweet with fresh-squeezed o.j.

And if all this is not enough, as if to punctuate the moment in time for what it is, when they turn the corner toward home on Ocean View and catch sight of surf, windows down for the sweet salt air, a wedding is taking place on their beach. The groom has just lifted the bridal veil, the barefoot guests applauding as they kiss.

Nothing has changed when they get home, nothing at all. The fenceposts are all still stained purple, the idiot woods blooming, and Ajax thump-thumps from the heart of darkness. The saltwater has been good for Joey, he's got some movement and the finger has color now. Lara's tanned in the seven days away. Her hair has lightened. The tire swing Pops and Joey tied up over Thanksgiving makes the tree top shimmy with each push. It's Sunday, and wasn't there some poet said something about the light on a Sunday afternoon having the heft of a cathedral organ about it or something like that? Their unpacked suitcases sit inside the den's sliding glass which opens haltingly, needs cleaning and a good dose of soap. The house smells like woodsmoke. The drive from Adams Field in Little Rock to R'Ville was two hours plus some. Renee'd slept in the back seat, Lara conked out in her carseat. Joey'd hit Price Chopper for brats and beans, but it was Sunday, and the great state of Arkansas will not sell liquor of any sort on the Sabbath, a thought they hadn't prepared for before leaving, so they will suffer the day sober—not even a glassful of cooking sherry in the house.

On the bar in the kitchen right this second, a letter from Rhonda Love addressed to Miss Renee Harvell, the loops of the l's too tight, and the s's and e's squashed, the penmanship of restraint. Joey'd recoiled from the letter, pointed at the return address and said, "What's she writing you for?"

"You met her in Dover. On the snow day."

Joey was still in his beach flip-flops and river shorts, a hell of a thing to wear while flying. "Her husband's a psychopath. I could still file suit."

Renee let the letter lay unopened. He was right. What had happened was beyond rational thought, they hadn't even really discussed it because a man biting another man's finger off was not something you talked about in Florida, on the beach, drinking cervesas. It defied words. Pops said that they ought to have Ronnie Love rabies tested, that's the first thing they do on ship, like a dog, or a skunk.

Lara squealed to be pushed. There she was, legs through the tire, kicking, honey-blonde twirls flipping down her back.

"They lost their daughter," Renee said.

"I *know* that."

From the tire swing, Lara yelps *Daddy*. Some monumental job for the ages.

"What kind of shape do you think you'd be in?" Here it is—on the tip of her tongue.

"Remember when I was pregnant the first time? After Jimmy?"

"Don't," Joey said.

"Why did you bring us here? Why did you?"

"We're not staying."

Lara howls both their names from the tree swing.

"I couldn't tell you. And I shouldn't have had to. It wasn't our time. You didn't even have a job. Your brother'd just been killed."

"Leave Jimmy be."

"A baby wasn't going to bring him out of the grave."

Joey had a line that she'd crossed before, once on the afternoon in DC, when she'd claimed to have had a job interview, and then a miscarriage, and Joey hadn't bought it. He'd figured it out, her elaborate lie. They'd fought, violently. At the hospital, she'd told. Officers were sent. Joey pretended he couldn't speak English.

"I'm sorry," he said.

And he left her there at the kitchen bar with the unopened letter from Rhonda Love, with the Sunday sun shining in with the heft of forty cathedral tunes, the saddest light she's ever seen.

Forgive us as we forgive those who trespass against us, her father'd said.

She looks up just as Lara reaches the pinnacle of the swing's arc, her legs kicked high in front of her, that look on her face that is part Joey, part Renee, the two of them bound incarnate.

That night she answers Rhonda's letter. She rolls a sheet of paper into the Smith-Corona her parents had bought her as a graduation gift, that she wrote her first comp paper on at the University of Maryland. It is the machine she typed Joey back and forth on all those years and it turned out he had one just like it that Grandmother Floradee'd bought him, so their letters were identical 12 point elites, with one inch margins and endstops. They'd written for most of five years, had become each other's most trusted confidants—at least that's how it seemed. And the thrill of walking out to the mailbox, out on the street, inside duplex hallways that smelled of coffee grounds and cabbage, one in the mouth of a cement turtle, the excitement at first sight of your cursive name, postponing opening half-a-day sometimes just for the kick of it, and then slitting the envelope open and taking in the words, again, and then again. What she'd give to receive a letter in the mail from the Joey she'd never met. Of course he'd lied about finishing college, other things. But like he said, was it really a lie if you meant to do what you said? The Smith Corona sits on the desk in the front den with its cute little fireplace and dents in the carpet where the Elliotts had kept a wooden alter with a big-ass King James Bible on it, opened to the verse of the day, First Corinthians 1:25 on the day'd they'd done the walk-through: *but God hath chosen the foolish things of the world to confound the wise.*

The typewriter hums, speckled in whiteout and the burn mark where she'd once laid a cigarette and forgot about it. The TV's going in the great room, Joey and Lara in there watching. *Dragon Tales* turns into *Winnie the Pooh and Tigger Too.* The lamplight is heavy.

The Elliotts are in here with her. She can smell them. She feels old.

She tells Rhonda about the beach in France, when she was twenty-one with fresh stamps on her passport, and had hitchhiked to the beaches and danced naked on a night when stars shone down on the Atlantic and she'd known in her heart of hearts that she was meant to do some great business of the heart, some monumental thing, a task for the ages rocketed her way, and she believed that she knew what it was now.

She tells the Love woman about the lump in her breast and the voice on her answering machine, about the crazy lights that hovered over their property, and how Lara'd said, "Mommy, will you die?" She tells Rhonda about the night fire burned through all the phone lines, about the flooded basement and Joey punching out the hillbilly at his family cemetery. Utah and the Kennedy plane and the palpable heat, how the cicadas made her crazy—she says all this, and how she's feared an unknown man, hunter man she called him, and sometimes Joey walked through the house with a loaded gun, checking behind doors.

Is *he* hunter man?

Has it been him all along?

She tells Rhonda about the total eclipse and the car headlights that shone crazy through the treetops, how on the first day the dog had assaulted them and the meat was rotting and Lara'd spat a tick the size of a white marble out of her mouth. She composes a line about the highway where the ambulance had been, the silver gurney and the white sheet with the small body beneath it, how the grown men wept openly. She tells Rhonda Love that there is no need to apologize, that Joey will be fine, and that holding a grudge never did anyone on this earth any good at all. What had happened to the Loves was beyond belief. She makes the invitation for dinner, the date and time, and seals the letter shut, licks the stamp and walks the gravel drive in the dark to the mailbox, lifts the silly red flag.

28

Breaking bread with the Loves—it's too goddamn much. Joey grades a multiple choice test, scores Elmo Hicks a 47/100 and red Magic Markers a four-inch F on the last page, one it hurts like hell to make, and fights the urge to add obscenities. The view from the barn loft is out the doorless east-facing opening to his backyard, three acres shaded by hickory that's burst out in new-gold leaf. Two days after the Full Egg Moon, cross-legged with Jimmy's twelve-gauge loaded with number one buckshot, Joey can smell the good aroma of horse and flydope and saddle leather from the tack room beneath him, phantom now, as the horses are long gone some years now since old man Zimmerman, who'd likely built this barn, had sold. Doesn't matter, it reminds him of when he was twelve and Uncle'd bought him a big Welch pony named Blaze, and he'd taught the horse to lay down on command, hold its breath and play dead. He'd set it up before an unsuspecting relative who'd be dazed on banana pudding, walk them out the path to the pasture beside the cemetery, and say "Oh, God, my horse." The relative would look at the horse, then at Joey, then back at the horse. It was not a thing anybody expected, after banana pudding on a Sunday in Lonoke. Then Joey'd say, "*Heal, Blaze*," and the clever horse would jump up and whinny, paw the dirt and shake his head.

The skunk has whelped under the air-conditioning pad beside the house. Joey has, for some time, studied the little fucker's ways, knows the path it walks every afternoon from the wood to the pasture to the air-conditioning pad just outside their bedroom window, where it sometimes let fly a plume of unspeakable stink just for spite.

20 April, Dean Georgina Dunlap has no doubt read his resignation letter as assistant professor of history, tenure track, with salary of $34,000 a year and full dental and health, a TIAA-CREF account and windowless office on

a hallway where one colleague discerns the future with a raccoon penis, next door to Banchie who everyone calls Black Jesus, and another wields a full-size battle sword, intent on cutting President Black-Brown's off for fucking with his retirement. Joey looks out over his failed house of dreams. The skunk has it coming, how can you sell a house with a goddamn skunk living under it?

Joey pours himself another Bartel vodka and Price Chopper diet tonic, squeezes the plastic lime bulb and adds ice from the little cooler. The next paper on the stack belongs to Elvis Shoates, who sits at a table way back with his hand up the Casteen girl's skirt like no one can see them. The boy'd invented the most brilliant cheat sheet Joey's ever seen, attached it to a rubber band up under his arm pit, so when Joey'd look out at his huge classroom, Elvis would meet his eye, the Casteen girl blushing beside him, turn loose of the cheat sheet so the thing would jump up his shirt sleeve, just like that. After three or four times, Joey called the boy out in the hall, said, "Let me see it."

"See what?"

"Let me see it."

"What?"

"Listen," Joey'd said. "I'm going to give you one chance and that's it. Give it to me now or you're out of the class. School, maybe. Same goes for her."

"Tina's got no truck with this."

"Give it to me or you both fried."

Through the door window, they could see a whole slew copying off each other, checking their books and consulting Joey's desk for whatever might be there. Shoates reached up his sleeve and pulled out the elaborate sheath of cardboard upon which was scribed the totality of World Literature II: The Enlightenment Through the Present, Equiano through *The Unbearable Lightness of Being*, with a nod at De Bois' concept of *otherness,* what Shoates showed him was nothing short of brilliant.

Joey's stomach sank. He'd done the same thing once, though not as well.

"Somewhere along the line," he'd said, that professor voice he'd never get used to coming out of his mouth, "Someone has caused you not to believe in yourself. Who was it?" In the class, they've ferreted out his master copy.

"Don't know," Elvis said. "They cheating in there."

"It was your daddy, wasn't it. All that guilt and sorrow shit."

The boy looked down at his shoes.

"Do you know," Joey said. "Do you know that you studied twice as much, *ten times* as much to make this as anybody in there?"

"Nope," Shoates said.

"Well you have. Get you another exam off my desk and quit not believing in yourself. Tell your girl in there she's on her own too. Your daddy know you're diddling her?"

Joey rifles through the multiple choices, holds Shoats's paper up against his template, marks a B at the bottom, then adds a plus. The Casteen girl's paper is identical, little cheat.

The skunk's halfway across the yard when he looks up.

Without thought, he lifts his brother's gun so the forestock is cold against his cheek, slips his half-dead finger through the trigger guard, and fires three times fast.

Boom, boom, boom comes the echo from the woods across Barton.

The casings *thwack* the barn wall through which pour slits of light that lay out across the hay strewn floor like the answer to a question he's forgotten asking.

Smoke leaks from the barrel mouth. His shoulder throbs from the gun butt's kick, three-inch magnums, a long time since he's killed a living thing.

Joey Harvell climbs down the aluminum ladder he's leaned into the hayloft of his barn, careful to avoid the flimsy power line run from the house. The still-hot gun rides the crook of his arm, cradled by the hand where the finger feels as if it belongs to a man who life has just that second pivoted so he now inhabits a world that is neither here nor there—he'll point with it no more. From the garage he retrieves the wheelbarrow and a sharp-point shovel. He buries her thirty yards behind the barn; soft dirt, someone's dug here before.

The moon throws his shadow west. West on the thin trail his own feet have made, going south across the big wide open yard under hickories with their silvery coats of moss glistening, up the slight bank where the terrace flattens so

Joey feels ruts from garden furrows cut years before when this bank bore tomato and crookneck, hibiscus flowered okra and purple hull pea, where he built a compost pile their first month here, and he'd bought the five horse power tiller at an estate sale, a riding mower that could double as a tractor, and dreamed himself a gentleman farmer, staking six foot Big Boys in hundred yard rows. Good Friday tomorrow, Mama's driving up with O.W., followed by the whole lot for Easter Sunday. The pasture gate creaks on its aluminum hinges and the tack house where he keeps the riding mower is darker than the rest just beyond. The night has spring in its blood, you can smell it down deep. This is the sort of Arkansas night he remembers when they'd drive to Morrillton and MaMa Stepwell's, who'd throw a homemade quilt down on the dewy grass in the yard where his grandfather'd come of age, not far from the banties clucking in the barn, and he'd lay looking at the stars with a cousin, and it seemed like life stopped there with the band of the Milky Way curving away, the gauzy star light, whippoorwill, the aroma of the land itself, the wild earth blooming before the summer heat. In the morning there'd be sausage fried in cast-iron, fresh eggs and buttermilk, and they'd eat on the front porch that overlooked Morrillton and Conway County where his mother's people were born and died, the very site where now sits a church, a house of God, built upon the same foundation that PaPa Stepwell'd poured, the concrete finished with his own hand.

Joey dumps the day's compost on the heap of coffee grounds and potato peels, shrimp shells, the mold-laden food scrap from winter—no rats yet, they've been lucky. Over his shoulder, on the neighbor's land, he can see cow shadows, and the hulking metal frame of the saddle maker's new out building. Ajax thumps in the deep, dark wood. He can see Lara, little sweet Lara back through the sliding glass on the couch with Renee, the TV glow on their faces. They've listed the house. With the same peckerhead who'd helped them find the flood-prone place to begin with, the asking price 10 K higher now.

And it's Easter time now, and his people are coming for the Easter Egg hunt, dressing their kids up in white pants like he'd once worn to First Baptist, where the Styrofoam boulder rolled of its own accord from the hokey stage tomb, and the congregation burst into song, shouting *up from the ground he arose!* Lonoke First Baptist, with its choir loft and baptismal font, where Joey himself had once gone under, where the blown up photo of Jimmy in his football jacket had sat on a tripod aside the silver casket where Joey'd place a last letter into the heart side pocket of a coat that had once been his.

He'd taught Jimmy the shortcut home, the cutoff from 319 from Vilonia. Had not Brother Dell Cain and Abled the Jesus out of him at the funeral. Maybe *this* had been to make *that* right—who knows, who can tell?

Why does anyone think they can go home?

His daughter laughs, points at something on the screen. There's the moonlight and the silver compost bucket, and the gate and the shadows. The gun's kick is in his right shoulder, radiating down his arm to the sewn-on finger. He can move it some.

Enough to pull a trigger.

He's killed the mother skunk, laid her in the soft earth. Easter—first Sunday after the full moon after Vernal Equinox—a very real day, pagan to the core, eggs and rabbits and children with baskets looking through the forks of trees, under daffodil and honeysuckle vine. Renee's bought Lara her first Easter dress, a frilly white number with a matching bonnet. A photograph will be taken of her sitting on Joey's lap, long before his beard turns grey, before the braces and homecoming dance and learning to drive a stick, a photograph of father and daughter that will become a family heirloom.

Ronnie Love no doubt saw his daughter dressed in an Easter dress. Birth, death, resurrection—the cruelest month. And now it's Easter and his people are coming to the house that is for sale, the Century 21 sign planted two feet deep out front.

Emergency Instructions, where they have made a home, a place to leave when sirens howl. Below, the sliding door opens.

"Joey?" Renee says.

Lara yells, "Da?"

His moon shadow waves its five-fingered hand at the voices from the lit up deck on the house he'd thought to claim but had not. He'd thought he could waltz home like his shit didn't stink. He was who he was forever, Joey Harvell, only *now* those two in the house, they were his story *now*.

"*Here*," Joey says. "I'm right *here*."

Sunrise Good Friday is clean and clear, a thing of wonder seen from the front porch along which purple iris has bloomed, a lilac bush—delirious showoff—and a whole bobbing string of King Alfred daffies simply shimmering. The redbud is full on now and, as if on cue, a dogwood has opened its nail-scarred hands to welcome Mama and O.W., and the ones who will come after. Renee has found the CD of opera arias, so Madam Butterfly howls from the great room, and it strikes Joey like a two-by-four to the head that he's left his guitar at Tri-County Coon Club, the D-28 he bought in 1998, the year Lara was born, so that one day the instrument will be hers, and she could say that they were born on the same day, her and the Martin. Surely he's mistaken, surely. Nobody'd forget a guitar like that.

April 21, Friday before Easter, payday, Joey rides the lawn tractor in a huge square around the perimeter of his property, lands that sit astraddle the Moreland Gas Field, 35.22.28 north and 9300.75 west, to be exact. Where he's peed off the back deck, little dead circles, and he mows over the place where the shot skunk had lain. Renee and Lara have driven to R'Ville for groceries, and then the endless trip south on I-40 to Blackwell Liquor Barn for wine and vodka, bourbon this time. O.W.'s bringing the FrostLand ham the company he drives for sends him home with at Easter and Thanksgiving, and Josephine's promised to make an ambrosia salad, because it's what Renee loves, and she's hulled the walnuts herself. Dee's dyed eggs. There'll be scalloped potatoes and they'll devil the dyed eggs after the hunt, hillbilly hoedown food, with lots of chocolate rabbits and jellybeans, baskets filled with fake grass and the candy you think's solid chocolate until you bite into the marshmallow filling and gag, leftover candy corn from Halloween and a snootful of bourbon in the coffee, pairs of white rabbits' ears for Lara and Traceleen's Dougie-Doug, fresh cut flowers in every vase.

Where the basement sump pump sprouts from a side window the grass is thick and green and Joey has to slow down, raise and lower the blade. Over the septic tank, too, slow-mo, the tractor's refuse bin heavy to bursting. He can smell it, the cut grass. The mowings from his childhood to here, from Southwest City outside Little Rock, where he'd gone door-to-door through Windermere, asking five dollars a lawn and had made a hundred dollars on one weekend in May, so O.W.'d bought him his own mower, the same one he'd pushed around the three acres on Highway 38 in Lonoke, when he was thirteen and Mama'd gone to St. Vincent's where she'd had a heart attack and Traceleen'd been born blue. The lawn in Utah where plums and pears and apples fell, so Moon would eat them and have a shit-fit when they slept at night, eat all the potted plants in the whole house, then vomit up the mix on the living room rug. How he'd mowed squares in spring time in a light snow, so the wheels made the maze lines he'd walked into the earth, and the neighbor lady's pussy willow bloomed profusely. She'd gashed her forehead with scissors one afternoon, tying to trim the blooms in a blowing snow, Dorothy English, God is good.

There'd been a yard in Greensboro with an oak growing in it that was twelve feet around, and a backhoe'd taken it down for the apartment complex from whence came drunken coeds to piss in Joey's garden, so some nights he'd sit out in the dark with a chainsaw, fire the fucker up when they squatted over his butternuts. The house in Fayetteville had forty trees and a guest house—they'd rented from a dean who'd gone on sabbatical and got the full discount for raking the leaves. They'd made a mountain of fall foliage, dragged big sheetsful into a pile they'd run at, take flying leaps into, and Renee'd disappear with the October sun shining where her gold hair had been. He'd mowed the hell out of Si's tilted yard in Mt. Ida, the cutting blade catching hunks of quartz crystal, throw them glittering out the little grassy chute. Hell, truth be told, he'd mowed his way up one side and down the other of the natural state, had once hit a king snake so the cut-in-half pieces swam away from each other, had hit a turtle once and seen its insides, had known a boy who'd cut his toes off while mowing barefoot, and he'd once thrown a rock that broke a sliding glass window, and then the picture frame where hung a lady's picture of a cow she'd grown up with on her daddy's farm in DeWitt—a framed picture of a cow he'd slung a rock through. It was all about mowing, being an Arkansawyer, all those orange-dressed dark men on the freeway in chains, swinging their sling blades into the heat of day. In his heart he'd always known he'd end up one of them, in chains.

He kills the engine on the gravel road, surveys his house and property, how the sun shines over it all, so the place seems magical—a five acre farm at the foot of the Ozarks, two barns and a corral, cedar in the back pasture. The place looks good, damn good. And he'd be damned to go to hell if he wouldn't buy it all over again, such is his desire for the place—the *idea* of the place. The front door opens and out steps Lara—she's tried on her Easter dress and holds both hands out to him, lifts her chin so the sun gets in her eyes, and the redbud and jonquil and iris coalesce in the moment. A hundred yards off, on the seat of the lawn tractor, Joey sees one fierce beauty joined by another, Renee barefoot in chiffon, she lifts her arms, hands flickering upward, so that the two of them stand there in the sunshine on the front porch of the failed house of dreams. And at that moment, right exactly then, a burst of opera pours through the open front door. Renee says something to Lara and the two of them bow deep, grasp each other's hands, and rise, so that Joey applauds them. He claps his two hands together hard, each jolt searing from his right hand to his heart, he applauds with all his might for this space and time, for springtime in Arkansas, for a whorl of color and love and meaning that flowers before his face—the whole thing making sense for the first time in his life, even the sorry well house between them on fire with daffodil, the mortar and brick goldened, the driveway before him the road home.

The Harvell's white Lincoln, the first new car Josephine Stepwell Harvell has owned in her life, bought with the insurance money from Jimmy's car wreck thirteen years earlier, the leather seats balmed soft and easy on the chrome, a tasteful vehicle, rolls slowly up the dust of Barton Road, pauses by the mailbox, then comes crunching up the drive, O.W. behind the wheel, his big truck driving hands shining behind the tinted windshield. Joey'd seen the western states from the passenger seat of his Kenworth, Highway 80, the very way they'd travel when they went west again, when the house had sold and they'd packed their lives in a Hertz/Penske and set out from North Carolina for the hotel in St. Louis with a swimming pool and free breakfast, the trailer lights flashing, the hiss of air brakes, looking for home, always looking for home. He won't let her roll her window down—O.W. She's window down kind of people, just like her daddy, just like him. Joey senses her thought, how she wants to wave and say *I love you*, and there's sadness in her, she knows already. The dusty car comes to a halt, the moment at hand.

Joey opens his mama's door, leans in and hugs her, the one half of his bloodline he's ever known, a sister almost, they'd almost died in childbirth forty years before, taken each other to the brink on Christmas Day at Pima County Regional in Tucson, Arizona, where the snow shone on Mt. Lemon, strange through the saguaro, and a troop of carolers had leaned into Delivery singing *silent night, holy night,* and the doctor'd walk out and say the baby won't make it, and then he'd walk out and say the mama won't make it—Joey's blood father Buddy Washer in a Nogales jail for smuggling weed in the belly of a Santa suit.

She's crying, already, Mama.

He helps her from the car, lupus swollen knees the size of cantaloupes. Her smell is White Shoulders and tobacco and the scent of her skin Joey will one day breathe while walking through his daughter's room on a night when wind and rain blows the blinds down. They've been down the road, Joey and Mama, and O.W. for a lot of it.

His mother's 5'2". Joey puts his left arm around her, sees O.W.'s blue eyes. He's worn a suit. O.W. in a suit.

"Don't hurt your hand. How is it, sweetie?"

"Fine, Mama."

"You haven't planted."

Imagine your mother's voice, hear it say that you are special, that you can do anything in the world you want, that nothing ever can or will stop you, so that the words get ahold of you and you believe, and somehow that gives you a leg up and you make a 70 yard run against Baxuite Pirates, and all that energy whirls through you so you're in college before you know even though not one of your people's ever done that, and then you've won a research prize for that Mountain Meadows paper, and then there's graduate school, and a Ph.D., and you entirely believe you can go anywhere and do anything you want, and you do.

"That's right, Mama."

She nods, and its the sad smile in the photograph from eleventh grade in Central High, when Mom Dee and Si had just divorced, the restraining order on him, and Mama'd smiled that sad smile and decided to leave Arkansas forever, run off with that good looking Air Force man Buddy Washer whose every third word was a lie.

Renee and Lara come, Moondog leaping down the porch steps. O.W.'s flattop is short and tight—he looks like a prize fighter, that scar down his left check Josephine had clawed into him on the night when Joey'd lay in bed, Jimmy in the bunk below, listening to them fight, her yelling for him to go get help.

"Happy Good Friday," Renee says, reaches in and hugs her mother-in-law. "We're so happy you've come."

Lara bobs in, disappears in Josephine's folds.

"I always wondered why they call it Good Friday," Mama says, looks Joey straight in the eye, "the day they killed Jesus. Seems like it should be *bad* Friday."

That grand old Stepwell talent of making the world catch its breath with a sentence manifests, and far off Ajax thumps from the wood, as if to agree with Josephine's proclamation for good.

"Mama? Joey says.

"What, Joker."

"I've missed you."

She says, "I know sweetie. Not like you will."

"What's that mean?"

From the other side, O.W.'s presence radiates.

For about as long as Joey can remember, from the dark ether of his deepest recollections, from as far back, even, as those memories researchers claim we have of the womb and the very air our mothers breathed before we quickened, from the blood message of their birth moment until now, here, not twenty miles as the crow flies from where their flesh and blood people lay buried, they have shared the language of the heart.

Mama lets the question hang, and together they make their way to the house on the unplanted land they will soon abandon: You would have planted, if you were staying. *That hurts, Joe. The day you leave, I'll die.*

Easter comes—Easter goes. The ham gets baked, the hidden eggs found and deviled. There is a moment on the big back deck when O.W. puts on Lara's rabbit ears, and hops like a bunny, so they all laugh real hard, and the laughter is real. Photographs are taken that will one day be revisited—silly O.W., Joey in shorts and a flannel shirt for the holiday, Renee with the light in her hazel eyes and sadness in her smile, Josephine with Lara on her lap, grandmother and granddaughter, the big yawing barn behind them. They've made it to the millennium, here they are, living proof of a journey and labor instructed by chance and haste and some unnameable force that was constant always, but also love.

A time will come when the girl in the photo will show the photo to her own girl—*that is your great-grandmother,* or *there is where I first tasted snow,* or *see the tire swing in the tree, that is where I lost my Pooh kite,* or notice for the very first time the hidden thing, the fresh dug dirt beyond the barbed wire, how bright the spring flowers, how her great-grandmother Floradee Stepwell wanders among the hickories, gathering moss she'll form into three Earths on pedestals she will gift them at Christmastime, so that they will remember and have a part of the home they once made.

29

The Loves—Rhonda and Ronnie—ring the front doorbell at straight-up six o'clock, and Joey answers, just like he said he would, Lara at his side. Two years old, she's a hugger, reaches both arms up to Ronnie just like she's known him every day of her life. Mother's Day weekend, Renee's selected chicken dijon and steamed broccoli, a neutral meal, an entre toward peace and reconciliation and making the best of who you are and what you've got. Her grades are due Monday, and the first of the showings are later in the week, before Joey flies off to Utah to ready the house they'd held off selling, leased instead to a nurse whose goth daughter's turned the basement into a mock dungeon, if the realtor's capable of saying one true word. Still, there's one last thing. Renee feels it in her bones.

Rhonda'd accepted her invitation straight away, even though it was terribly embarrassing, how her husband had assaulted Joey at the Coon Club, the deed that would inspire a hundred inside jokes, though it was not funny in the least, not at all. Now, in the long shadowy hallway between the front door and the bright kitchen, its bar laid out with hors d'oeuvres and cabernet, beer in the cooler, a bottle of Wild Turkey—truce whiskey, Joey's calling it—this seems like the dumbest, stupidest, lame-brain idea anybody's ever had in all time, inviting the Loves for dinner on Mother's Day eve. She sees Shiloh in the man's face—how he looks the moment Lara reaches up to hug him.

Moon's waiting in the foyer, sniffs Ronnie Love's pantleg, wags her tail.

Joey holds a hand out to shake, the right one with its angry-red scar—she can see it from where she stands, sauteeing garlic in butter, the sweet-bitter smell rising.

"Welcome," he says. "Come on in."

Rhonda enters, aglow.

"I love your barn," she says. "I've always wanted a barn like that."

"Thanks," Joe says. "It's got electric."

The two men shake. So that much is done.

Joey ushers them into the kitchen, the one room the Elliotts had remodeled. The cabinets are Home Depot, green on green, but it's bright, light recessed in every nook and cranny. Rhonda hands Renee a wooden bowl, inside of which is the *garden sass,* what country folk call the first cutting of backyard greens, she explains. The two women hug awkwardly, the big bowl between them.

Lara toddles back to her cartoon in the great room. *Dragon Tales,* the show features a two-headed dragon having a conversation with itself.

The May light outside is like honey, too soon for the brutal heat.

Ronnie looks at his boots. Joey has a pair on just like them. Renee's wearing thong sandals. Rhonda, she slipped hers off at the front door. Barefoot like Lara, her toenails are painted pink.

Out of nowhere, the doorbell rings again. The Elliotts had rigged it so the hall light blinked with each ding-dong.

Renee says. "Wine?"

"Thank you," Rhonda says. "I think of you every time I see that pool."

Joey gets the door.

"Or beer. We have beer." The air's on. The house feels huge and dark hidden places she's never expected until this second. "And iced tea."

Ronnie says, "I'm sorry."

It's nobody, if that's possible. Maybe there's a short. Joey walks back in the kitchen, pours three fingers of truce whiskey in a rocks glass, offers it to Ronnie.

He holds up his own glass, says, "Cheers."

Renee pours cabernet for Rhonda, doctors her own. "Hold your horses." Standing at the table the four of them clink glasses and that second the doorbell rings again.

It's the Elliott kid.

He's messed up, red-eyed and trembling, standing just outside the storm door that was once his own. His four-wheeler idles in the drive, a rifle, or is it a shotgun? in the gunrack bolted to the handlebars.

"Come for my dog," he says. "We're leaving tomorrow."

They gather at the door that adjoins what was once the Elliott's prayer room, a thick black Bible opened on a wooden pulpit during their walk-through inspection.

"Your *dog*?" Joey says it through the screen.

"Bandit?" the boy says. He's been crying. You can see it in his eyes, how his chin quivers beneath a thin goatee.

There's something in the kid's voice, the Elliott boy's. Renee feels for him, having to live a quarter mile from the house he'd come of age in, where his sister was married, and they'd celebrated Thanksgivings and Christmasses. Where Joey'd lassoed his dog and driven it to the Dover pound.

"It's been gone a long time," Joe says. "We thought you took it."

He moves from one foot to the other, skinny, hair the color of dishwater. "That you in there Ronnie?"

Joey's clicks the little button that locks the door.

"Reckernized your ride."

Renee steps to the door. The world is blooming behind the boy's back, blue windows of sky beyond the new-leafed hickories. She wants to welcome him into her home, to break bread and say she's sorry, and talk about what they've lost and what they've found.

"Listen man. Got anything on you?"

Ronnie's voice is behind her left shoulder. "You know I given it up."

The Elliott boy looks hurt. He blows his nose in a bandana, dog whistles. In the foyer Moondog growls.

"Bandit," he yells. "*Bandit*."

Joey says. "I'm sorry. We're 'bout to have supper."

Renee sees him through the storm door, a kid, really, not yet twenty, he has a mother, a father, off in Missouri now. They've taken his home. Why he chose to stay this close, who can say?

"You hurt him," the boy says. "You killed him."

"No we didn't," Renee says, the lie reddening her face. "It ran away."

The boy sobs, jumps off the front porch. He straddles the four-wheeler and revs it hard, jumps the ditch out onto Barton and howls off down the dirt track toward Ajax. Later, they hear the gun go off in the wood, five times hard and fast.

Rhonda and Ronnie had fallen in love in springtime, he'd drive her up to

Blytheville, across the Arkansas river to the Memphis side, where they'd once stayed a glorious weekend at The Peabody, and they'd walked Beale Street listening to blues tumble from bar rooms where people danced all night. Rhonda's cut her hair so it flips back over the nape of her neck, strawberry blonde. Lara squeals *auchoo, auchoo,* her word for black pepper. She's taken to Rhonda's garden sass which she *achoos* the hell out of. Ronnie tries to hide it when he looks at her.

Renee serves out seconds over white rice. Save room for pie. I left it in the car as a surprise, Rhonda says, the smell of it on her, in her hair. They slosh wine in glasses and drink, graze through the dijon and garlic bread, broccoli dusted with bits of brown garlic.

The stereo plays in the great room, alternating between Merle Haggard and the aria from Madam Butterfly—odd, and somehow right. Rhonda's pie is perfect after chicken. There's vanilla ice cream which taste good drizzled with bourbon.

Rhonda gathers plates, lines them up her left forearm, waitress style.

"Don't," Renee says. "I want to show you something."

She takes a plate from Rhonda's hand, slides it into the sink. "Men have dish duty," she says on the way out.

They walk through the dark garage, out the back door into the yard with its little path shining under the hickory trees. Ajax thumps in the woods, an odd heartbeat her mother'd called the inner-sanctum, maybe so, why not? Mother's day weekend, all those years with Daddy off at sea, when Mom would drink Boodles martinis at happy hour, pearl onions skewered with little red swords, and they'd pretend whatever Navy housing they'd found themselves in was home.

Renee traces the path to the fence. Above them, the experimental planes hover and moan, unearthly light flitting through the trees. Here, where she'd once embraced husband and daughter on a night when she knew in her bones that she was dying, when Lara'd asked, "Mommy? Will you die?" and the thought went through her like a spear. *Don't see me. I'm not here*, she'd said, the words a dear friend had uttered on a beach in France, when they were young and beautiful and drunk, road-weary souls who'd stripped under the Summer Triangle. Boys had watched them dance, their eyes gleaming from the fine sand. Her life's pivot. And now? Each of them on the cusp of something new, her and Rhonda.

"Happy Mother's day," Renee says. "I wanted to give you this. For luck."

Inside the sealed shut bag, each grain shimmers. Light from another world, it is luminous in Rhonda's hand, the long silvery fingers she'll pass on to the child she already carries, who'll one day lay wild flowers at the feet of the lost sister, and mend her mother's heart.

"I want a baby. Isn't that silly?"

"*No.*"

"What is this?"

"Sand. From France. I was in love there. It reminded me of you. I didn't know where my life was going. That I'd ever be here right now. Talking to you. About sand."

"And *love.*"

Renee says, "It's not much."

Without warning, the barn lights up. It blazes, strips of light furl through the cedar plank walls. Up there, their husbands stand just inside the thrown open loft door, backlit by floodlight. Between them, Lara holds tight to either hand. From up there, they no doubt see the flaming pipemouths that flare across Pope County. The night unfolds before their faces. Given time, they'd witness daybreak in the east before the earth where the women stood saw light, hear voices call out from bodies they could not yet see.

30

Summertime—Paris lays the place to sleep, everyone gone home now, everyone but him, the woods alight and alive, they in his blood, the treeful peckerwoods, he takes the Martin out of its case, a fine sweet-smelling thing, brings it to his chest, shapes three fingers into the low E and makes sound. Second week of June, the heat not on them yet, the sweet spot of morning when the king snakes shed skin, the fences all white-flowery with blackberry bloom, the well full to the brim of sweet water, and now the sun-gold room glorious with that chord from Edgar's heart, the sound his soul would make, shout it, sing out on a June morning at the edge of the wood in Pope County in sight of the ancient Ozarks on the flood plain of the Arkansas, flowed down from the Rocky Mountains across Nebraska, the Ogallala to Oklahoma and the river valley here. Edgar strums the six strings again, hammers with the index finger on the E, then slides her into the straight A, the first two strains of "Amazing Grace," the song he once played for his great grandma so she'd be proud of him and love him and know his secret soul, only she'd burst into fall down tears when she heard those first two chords, cried out just like he'd put a knife through her back. It pained Edgar so, how he must have manifest the god-awfulest EA progression of all time to make that sweet childlike lady cry, and it wasn't 'til years later that he understood, when he himself cried out at the identical sound when it tore through him standing at the mouth of his mother's grave, and he got it. How the generations of them had stood all those sad songful afternoons at the yawning holes where lay who they'd loved, and who they loved again, and who they loved again, the price of growing old among the sons and daughters of man on this mortal earth.

Amazing grace how sweet the sound that saved a wretch like me.

Today's the day he'll return the Martin to the Harvell boy who's hellbent on putting Pope County, Arkansas and the whole lot of them in his rearview mirror. Boy's giving Edgar a Japanese yammer-hammer, the kind with nylon strings, giving it to him outright for helping load the Harvell's earthly possessions into a Hertz/Penske, the guitar and softshell case, two sets of strings and a capo, little ziplock full of Fender thins—maybe he'll just follow the boy west, why the hell not? A good many of his kith and kin had made that long walking, the ancestral turn of the back on the land of the Razorback for the blue sage plain and meadow west, and some's blood had spilled on that great walking if the story be believed. Nothing without risk in this world save dying.

The B7 is the kilter point, the pivot to another sphere, the counterspin to the EA's work on the heart, that little moment of chaos against which the real world plays. It all makes sense to Edgar now, he knows what's coming, how a man now struggles across the grassy lawn, the dewdrops dripping from his shoes, a heavy heart comes this way.

No matter.

His fingers stretch across the second and third frets, the strings digging into his fingertips though the action is light, the mother of pearl, hardly any pressure needed on this handmade thing, this neck to the sound hole. How long he can hold the chord, choiring the ceiling joist to the roof rafter before coming home, how many heartbeats, the tapping of the toe on hard wood—one, two, three.

When we've been there ten thousand years.

What next?

Something's ended.

Something's begun.

He strums the progression again, the light flitting off the far wall, onto the glass blazed face of Great Grandma Poteet whose elder sons had walked away from these hills with Captain Fancher, across Oklahoma they'd followed the Arkansas clear into the Rocky Mountains through Monarch Pass where the river got so wiry a man could piss bank to bank, if word from the surviving brother, Francis Marion Poteet, the Harvell boy's own great, great grandpappy be believed, as he alone trudged back to the river valley having witnessed all. Edgar's got that story in his bones, in his blood, has sworn the coon penis oath of revenge—why not just head on west while he's ahead, no long-legged Tina Casteen making his life hell. They's gas in his truck, Fort Smith's only a hop and a skip south, the frontier's gate, Indian country full of peckerwoods and stump hole whiskey, hooter huffing field hippies and ramrod state troopers, *Federalis*, Mexicans, all those goddamn Viet-Kong boat people farming rice on Fort Chaffee, there was a wild world out there waiting for anyone with half a hair.

The knock on the door is something Paris has dreamed and forgotten a half-dozen times, and only now remembers, the sweet notes hanging still in the dead spot near the roof beam. Three knocks, resolute on the woodframe. Thirty seconds of silence, then three more—*boom, boom, boom.*

Paris knows, though he doesn't know how or why he knows, that when he answers the door, when he opens it inward on the new-oiled hinges, another door will shut, and he is both regretful and relieved at such. He wipes the guitar's neck clean with the yellow cloth, swipes at the body and around the sound hole, lays sweet mama down in her green velvet bed, shuts the lid and snaps the silver clasps—the last time he'll ever touch a Martin, he'll never have the heart for one again. Something tells him all this, he can't know why, yet still the sound of it hovers near, its magic not entirely gone.

Framed in the screen door is Honorable Reverend Preacher Roy Dale Shoates, in a glare-blue suit, a leaf of paper in his left hand and a bottle in the right. Behind him, across the yard and highway into the vernal wood and blue sky above, the morning is cleanly in his sight and the way west lay out before him like a dream you know you're dreaming and will to keep on happening.

"How do?"

Paris unlocks the screen, takes the Ancient Age from Shoates's hand, which he sees is right trembly. He has the look of having had a good many snorts, the fifth of liquor sloshing. The man's eyes are red, his face too, his breath turns Edgar's belly, the paperwork in his left hand fluttering, a blue signature darkening the bottom.

Shoates follows him inside where Paris pours a child's portion for each of them, just a dollop, no harm in that. The two men sit at the great table, oiled and shining, amber in the morning light, a place where boys learn to walk among men. The Tri-County Coon Club, presided over by High Coon Earl Fancher Shock, who kept this place sacred and whole, who remembered the old words and spoke them when need-be, who bestowed gifts of the spirit on the willing, who took away what was not needed, who carried the Poteet penis in his own right hand.

Of course he'd be needed, Paris.

The details came slowly, in between sips and refills. Shoates breathed an anguished prayer peppered with curses so vile they'd turn your pee blue. It was his only son, Elvis. His son, Elvis. It had happened in a car. He'd never seen it coming. Not in a thousand-thousand years.

Lord God, take my crooked ass in my boy's stead.

There'd been a girl, well a woman really, hard to tell. Shoates believes Edgar can identify her, that's what he's been told.

He sees the name on the piece of paper now that lies flat again the great table in High Coon Hall. There on the table, how the *T* and *C* swerve heavily into the rest, in blue ink smeared a little, whiskey spattered, wrinkled, fist-pounded, ass-wiped.

Shoates believes Edgar can *i-dent-i-fy*, a word with four hard parts, the woman. He'll know its face.

And then there's the graves to dig, at least the one, who knows what the shithouse Casteens will choose, crazy Reno and the barefoot twins. Lay her out for the pigs and vultures, likely. Jesus. Hell with them.

Today is Wednesday, June 14, 2000—a day that will be circled in the calendars to come, the year and the millennium that will ever be remembered and forgotten, remembered and forgotten, until memory is replaced by forgetting for good, replaced by lost loves not even born yet, folk undreamt of much less wept over.

He's sorry, Shoates is, will Edgar do the digging? Here is the plot, in Solgahatchia, overlooking the lightning struck tree, Edgar knows the place doesn't he? On the north facing side, up beyond the younger Harvell boy Jimmy with his big smile and letter jacket picture somebody's turned upside down on the stone.

There will be a marker.

He can't bear this.

How can he administer such a ceremony?

How is such a thing to be done?

Edgar doesn't know.

If there was a god, somebody should ring the motherfucker's goddamn neck, put him on the mainline and ask just how on Earth a daddy is supposed to preach his own son's funeral—wasn't Heavenly Father an expert on such cock and bull?

Edgar listens and nods, listens and nods.

He knows the story by heart. There's the guitar to take back, and the digging, hard clay pack on that hillside, the Trail of Tears, where the Cherokee had walked and cried and died.

Tina, she's gone home.

With the Shoates boy.

Each of them has a swig, then another. Preacher Shoates yammers on about how it's his own damned fault, how he'd driven the boy from home, made fun of his college, shamed him for the Casteen slut. He's sorry for saying that. Edgar?

Paris could give a rat's ass.

He thinks on long-legged Tina, prettiest of the Casteen girls, how she'd lay out by the well house and take the sun, squeeze lemon in her hair and drink straight from the water hose, its little bronze eye spouting. How she'd said she loved him, and he'd believed. That there were three of them, now. Even if it was a lie, this is best, the time when you can love and be loved, so everything about the lover seems right, the way her teeth came together, how her skin smelled in the morning when she was beside him on the good flannel, how she'd pretend to be asleep when it was daylight and the dogs barked to be fed, the sound of her voice in the night—all gone now. How he'd burned her letters, and the other, folded in his drawer—all he'd ever have of her now.

Could he *identify?*

Wednesday, church tonight, potluck supper at Moreland Baptist, Edgar's welcomed, there will be a receiving line, the other boys and Kate. *I just can't do this,* Shoates says.

He's gone none too soon, the sheaf of paper with the blue marks on it that say Tina's name. Why the Shoates boy? Was he bringing her here, to see him?

Had she changed her mind, some sense come on her at last?

The shovel and bar lay in the truck bed. A little sharpshooter for tight spots, twine and stake, an eight-pound sledge and pick-ax, the carpet of fake grass to cover the dirt pile and lay around the hole for people to stand on and weep and sing "Amazing Grace" and pretend their loved ones had waked up on the other side of the light, that the lame could walk, the blind see, and the wicked be righteous through grace. The great fiery light from the other side, across the river yonder, on the other side of the long pool where there was no bridge, where the door opens to a sky-lit room and the melody is clean-picked on strings wound in starlight. Sing words in the tongues of angels for us the bewildered, blind-sided, the ambushed from behind and before, sing like angels for our sorry lot. Light pours down on our heads every day and every night and what have we done to deserve that? Not one thing.

The tools of a gravedigger, the muscle to use them, all he needs now.

31

Packing, she decides to steal her own curtains.

Part of the contract they signed and signed and signed some more with the Sinyards who'd paid cash from a retirement account and didn't even mind that Joey'd somehow overlooked a dead raccoon out by the tractor barn, says that all curtains in seller's residence must remain in place for sellee. That's the deal. Joey's flown off to Utah. He called this morning from their little podunk house below the University stadium, where they're building this giant glass chalice to house the Olympic flame in 2002 when the whole world will go Mormon in Salt Lake City. He'd hiked up on a rattlesnake in the foothills where scarlet gilia has bloomed, and said that he'd thought of her because of the gilia, not the rattlesnake. There's painting and a fence to mend—the nurse and her goth daughter have trashed the place. He'll remodel the bathroom this summer after they've moved. The grocery stores have good produce from California, and the farmer's market has fired up down on Pioneer Square. He misses them, can't wait to see them Saturday at Tucker Field in Little Rock, where they will pick up the Hertz, drive it home—*home?*—for the loading to begin.

Home?

Growing up Navy, it was Hawaii and then California and New Hampshire and Rhode Island, Bumfuck South Carolina and then Maryland—was Maryland home? She'd graduated from Friendly High, sure to God, but home? was Maryland her home?

When her father's bid for admiral was up in the air, her mother had founded the Officers' Wives Club at the base in Charleston. Their sailors were away for the holidays that year and Mom had arranged to film Christmas dinner at the Rockerson's house, give everyone a time to speak, then splice in caroling and gift opening, turkey carving, a prayer and champagne toast to the fathers and husbands they so missed. There were nights of rehearsals, martinis by the trayful so it got to be a party for everyone. They dressed to the T, and the commander's chef volunteered the holiday spread. They went whole hog. Only it somehow went wrong for twelve-year-old Renee. She'd been cross, dressed up in her Christmas dress and tights and shiny black shoes that hurt her toes—a velveteen bow tied into her hair. She'd had to write letters already, make tapes, pose for pictures. She'd had it with pretending, and when it was her turn on camera blurted out that it was all bullshit. *How can you leave us here like this? Damn you. Come home. Please come home.*

Of course they'd edited out Renee's part. She's learned that such feelings are not uncommon for those who grow up military, unrooted all the live long day, the strange quarters and new schools where there was always someone who'd snicker at the new girl, call her horsey, worse.

Her mom had pulled it off. The film went off famously, the steaming turkey and such charming children with their hair done just so.

But sometimes, like right goddamn now, unrodding the pale blue curtains she'd sewn then hung with her own hands in the bedroom that smells of her daughter as a baby, she imagines her father on that third destroyer, with a whole slew of men who missed their wives and children, who sang "Old King Wenceslas" and wished for beer. Alone in the captain's quarters, how he must have desired his pretty wife with bright lips and shining skin. It was his last post—he withdrew his name from consideration for admiral, and it was never spoken of during poolside happy hours.

She imagines him at sea, viewing and rewinding and viewing again the film in his quarters, the projector click-clacking, and the grainy image of his sulky daughter beneath a crooked bow.

Lara walks through the doorway wearing Joey's sideways smile. The good light is in her eyes. She says, "Mommy, push me."

Outside, sunshine filters through tall trees, the air is clean and fragrant. Honeysuckle is blooming on every fenceline. Home, these curtains, the warmth of the sun on them, how she folds them and refolds them in her hands.

Enough.

About the Author

Michael Gills is author of three collections of short stories, including *The House Across From the Deaf School* (Texas Review Press, fall 2016), two novels from the Go Love Quartet, and *White Indians*, a book of creative nonficiton, part two of which is forthcoming. He is Professor/Lecturer of Writing for the Honors College at the University of Utah where he lives in the Wasatch footlhills with his wife and daughter. Gills' collected papers are archived at Martha Blakeney Hodges Special Collections and University Archives, The University of North Carolina at Greensboro.